bright

Thank you!
H D Knightley

H.D.Knightley

visit the author website:
http://hdknightley.com

ISBN: 978-0-9855674-4-6 (paperback)
ISBN: 978-0-9855674-5-3 (ebook)

Over Our Heads Publishing

For Mom

old things

My great-grandmother, Alexandra Snow, was one of the last of the great astronomers. She developed the Rip-Tide Theory of Universe Expansion, the theory that some celestial bodies spin out into deep space traveling and existing alone, while others are swept along in a current of sorts, of influence on, and action and reaction to others. Her theory was popular in her day, and she was close to proving it definitively when the stars disappeared completely from view. The deep black night sky was replaced by a grey mess of brightness and lights that never went out.

Alexandra Snow's daughter, my grandmother, wanted to be an astronomer when she grew up, but the trouble was you had to see the stars to study them. People had to want to understand them, to be willing to pay for the exploration. Even with the best telescopes, the people of her time lost the desire to see. The world was too full of ambient light, so my grandmother tossed her dream away. The people of our times were used to tossing old things in favor of the new.

I could vividly remember the first time I saw the stars years ago. My father, Frederick, came into my room and said, "Estelle, here's something I want to show you before it heads to the trash." He carried what he told me was a book. It was big enough that it took up my entire lap, and he had to help it balance while I flipped through the pages. It was full of big black photos of tiny pinpoints of light.

"What is it?" I asked in a whisper because for some reason I was a little bit afraid.

"This book was your great-grandmother's. She was an astronomer named Alexandra. It's full of photos of the sky and stars and constellations—or groups of stars."

I nodded as if that explained everything, though really it explained nothing, and went back to studying each of the pictures. I couldn't read very well, but under one of the photos I made out the word, *majestic*, and under another one, the word, *mysterious*. Majestic and mysterious. Even years later I remember reading those words.

When I made it to the end of the book, Frederick said, "I forgot I even had this. I don't know why I kept it so long." He looked down and patted the cover almost affectionately. "Well, we have to make room for what's new, don't we?" Confused by the whole conversation, I nodded back. Of course we had to make room for the new. Even at the ripe old age of six I knew that.

Ever since those photos I *longed*. I longed to go back in time to before our improvements came along and see that endless black sky with infinite tiny pinpoints of light. I couldn't stop thinking about how amazing it would be to look up and see it, in person. Since that night I had become the kind of person that wanted the words *majestic* and *mysterious* to describe my sky.

I sat in my window seat six years later when Frederick came into my room and said, "See anything interesting, Estelle?"

By way of an answer, I asked, "Was your mother sad that she couldn't see the stars?"

"Not really," he replied. "She told me, 'City life has just become too bright, and there's no going back to the ages of the dark.'" He thought telling me that would be comforting, but it wasn't. It was like knowing something precious was lost and would never be found again because no one was even bothering to look. I wasn't consoled at all.

"Frederick, do you still have that book?" I secretly hoped that maybe he had tucked it away in a closet again.

"That old book, from your great-grandmother? No, it's long gone. What makes you ask about it?"

"I was just thinking about the stars and wishing I could see them. I'd like to see that book again."

Tonight's sky was a paisley sky. It meant it was Saturday night, and was supposed to look frivolous and joyous—a party sky. The designs were green and purple teardrops with the color of steel grey in-between, sprinkled with tiny flecks of gold and silver. The sky designers described it as, 'Beautiful and delightful.' I heard it said the designs were 'a great improvement over the black sky of old.' Looking out, I wasn't so sure.

"You don't like the paisley sky, Estelle? It's one of my favorites."

"It's not really that I don't like it. It bothers me that I have no choice in the matter. The patterns were picked by vote before I was born."

"I can remember the sky before the projections, Estelle. Believe me, they're an improvement. The night sky was a hazy mass of glowing air that was close, oppressively close. Stiflingly close, Estelle."

"Like that comedian said, 'We need to wear a hat to keep

the sky out of our hair.' Like that?"

"We think it's funny because it's almost true." We both looked out at the shifting decorations.

"Look Frederick, there's the Congloms' logo. The projection's loop is starting again."

"Somebody has to pay for it. It's expensive to project on the sky." He looked at me as if sizing me up. "You know, if it bothers you, you could just not look up."

"What bothers me is everybody seems to *love* the projections. Just because the sky is new and improved, they think it means it's better than before."

Frederick sighed as if dealing with me was hopelessly difficult. "You know, that's why we get rid of our old things, like books, because living in the past causes pain and regret. You can't do anything to change the past. You can only improve on your future, Estelle. Remember that."

"What if the past was better, Frederick? Is everything we do *always* an improvement?"

He chuckled. "I wondered if I should have shown you that book all those years ago. I don't know why I did." He shook his head. "The night sky is what it is, Estelle. You can't change it. You can't make the stars come back. You'll have to get used to that.

"Here's an idea, maybe you could design a pattern for the projections. Wouldn't that be great? You could have your very own design up for all the inhabitants of New City to see." As if it was decided, he said, "What I'm trying to say is don't think about it too much." Sadly, I thought about the long-lost stars just about every night.

Frederick was always like that. If he noticed a problem, he would come up with a solution. He worked for the Institute of New Improved Brands and Technologies, an arm of the

Organization of Conglomerates, as a scientist in development. He thought *everything* could be improved.

My mother, Sylvia, on the other hand, thought nothing was ever wrong. She accepted it all as absolutely perfect, which is why she was perfectly fit to work for the Organization of Conglomerates in the Office of Governmental Oversee. She helped to manage the Institute and well, *everything*. The truth was when the Office of Future Affairs picked the best jobs for Frederick and Sylvia, they were completely right. Of course, they always were.

I sat in my window seat about two weeks later, when Sylvia bustled into my room to see me staring out at a different sky. This one was a green and blue plaid.

"What on earth are you looking at?" Her tone was exasperated, a common state when she caught me at the window. She came over and peered out at the street. "There's nothing there." That was true. There wasn't a soul to be seen.

"I wasn't looking down at the street, Sylvia. I was looking up at tonight's projection."

"Oh." She peered back out, looking up this time. "I just never look up, so I forget it's there. Our towers are built so tightly together that most of the sky is blocked anyway. I don't know why they even bother with the projections. This one *is* lovely though," she said, looking again.

"I think they thought it was depressing, so they decided to cover it up." She looked at me questioningly. "I mean, I think that's why they bother with the projections," I said.

"I suppose so. Some of the other workers in the Office of Governmental Oversee said it was ugly–the way it had that red-grey glow–but I think it was an improvement over the dark. I think we can all agree on *that*." Sylvia put a tray of multicolored pills and a tumbler of water in front of me. I gulped them down and handed the tray back to her.

"You know, Frederick designed this window to be a showcase display for some of your things. We didn't expect you to sit there staring at the sky every night."

"It's my favorite place to sit," I answered. "Sylvia, are you afraid of the dark?" I climbed into my bed.

Sylvia tucked me in while I leaned back against the bank of bubblegum pink pillows. "That's a silly question. Everyone is afraid of the dark, Estelle."

"Why?"

"Because it's dark! You can't see. You don't know what's going to happen. Everything is out of your control in the dark!" Sylvia suddenly seemed to remember I was young and tempered her reply, "You know, at first we rejoiced that the night was so well lit, but the red glow was unsettling and scary—some said depressing. It felt like it was too close, like it could swallow you up." Sylvia visibly shivered, trying to turn it into a joke. "We needed to master and control the way the sky looked, to keep from being afraid. So the great minds among us, inventors from the institute, like Frederick, came up with the idea to project giant, colored lights onto the grey. Lights that move and slide across the sky. We came up with the projections, so we don't have to be afraid anymore."

"So, we aren't afraid anymore." I said it like a statement. "How come nobody goes outside at night?"

Sylvia looked at me with her exasperated expression. "You know, whether we're afraid or not is immaterial. It's all lit up out there now. There's no night to be afraid of, but no, we still don't go out at night, Estelle. It's just not done." Sylvia stood up and headed for the door. "You're certainly full of questions. When's your next appointment with your doctor?"

"Monday."

"Good, make sure you tell him you're afraid at night. He can give you something to quiet your fear. Good night, Estelle."

Two weeks later, we celebrated my twelfth birthday. Frederick put a blindfold on me and walked me up to my bedroom." Ta DA!" He flourished the blindfold off my eyes. My room had been completely transformed, like it was every year on my birthday. The new popular color was *gorgeous green*, and my decorations were all in different shades, with splashes of grey and royal blue throughout. Sylvia and Frederick walked me to the bed–the big present. It had a canopy and curtains all around.

"Check this out." Frederick pointed at the canopy's ceiling. It was covered in a tiny flickering constellation of stars.

"Oh, thank you, thank you, thank you!" I said, absolutely delighted.

Frederick said, "After our conversation the other night I wanted you to be able to see them. I looked up some images and designed an intricate projection system. Now you can have the stars twinkling down at you every night." He beamed at me, proud of his present.

Sylvia added, "It's Frederick's own idea. He presented it over at the Institute, and now one of the Congloms plans to produce them. You're definitely a trendsetter. Stars will be very hot this year. You'll have to make sure you tell your class about it at school tomorrow. Tell them you were the first. Make sure they want one." She smiled at me proudly.

I tried to smile back, but during her explanation I noticed the pillows and cushions had been taken from my window seat. Now there was a shelf across the window and a new doll and small dress forms were arranged on it in full view of the streets below. My window seat was now a display for a doll. Tears welled up in my eyes. I had really liked my window seat. Why did they do that? I had told them that it was my favorite place.

My parents showed me the special features and designs of all the new parts of my bedroom, while conveniently skipping over the missing window seat and the new doll. I guessed they didn't want any negative emotions, and would do anything to avoid a scene. Then they excused themselves, so I could spend some time enjoying my star projections.

I sat on the bed, by a large pile of my new clothes, fiddling with the remote control. I was surrounded by everything new and improved, and all I could think about was what had been taken away. I was the most ungrateful kid in the world. Frederick was right—I did live too much in the past, and it only made me sad.

I laid back and turned on the projector. It was beautiful. The stars twinkled and danced around, shooting and sliding across the canopy ceiling. Did stars really move this fast? There was so much ambient light the background was at best a murky grey color. This didn't seem as amazing and wonderful as I wanted it to be. After about an hour I turned it off and went to sleep.

In my classes the next day I detailed a list of the presents I received for my birthday. The other students and my teacher asked questions about the canopy of stars. My Current Design teacher wondered if it could also be programmed to project the decorations of the night sky outside. "That's what I would really like, to have that beautiful paisley sky projected over my bed. That would be a lot better than *just stars*."

My History of Common Concepts teacher turned to the

class and asked, "Can you believe people used to navigate by the stars? They must have been lost all the time!" He had the incredulous tone that was the dominant attitude about anything old, or used, or well, really anything. I didn't feel incredulous though. It would be great to stare up at a deep black sky and use the tiny, sparkly lights to find my way in the world.

A month later, my brother, Terran, celebrated his own birthday. During dinner, Sylvia, who must have been feeling nostalgic, said, "I'll never forget the day you came home from the nursery. Your eyes were so big. You seemed to watch everything and everybody."

"How old was I, Sylvia?" asked Terran.

"You were six months old—the normal time. You had such strength and vitality, unlike Estelle, who was born small. She spent a long time in the infant incubator, not as long as some, but a long time all the same. We thought she wouldn't survive, and I'd have to have another one." Sylvia smiled encouragingly at me.

"I've wondered if that's why she doesn't seem to be of this world, with her thoughts in the stars all the time. Her life began as a struggle, and she seems to like it that way," Frederick teased.

The next morning I woke exhausted. I hadn't been able to sleep and had gotten up in the middle of the night to go to my window. Of course my comfy cushions were gone, and the view was obstructed by that new shelf. I hated that shelf. I had moved the doll and all the clothes to the floor, perched on the edge of what used to be the seat, and leaned the upper half of my body onto the shelf. It was uncomfortable, but worth it to look out at the sky. The night's projection had been multicolored stripes that careened off the tops of the buildings. It made me feel drowsy, and my position must have been a little comfortable, because I finally fell into a fitful sleep.

When I woke up I was running late and had to put the display back together before I could even begin to get ready for school.

By the time I rushed downstairs for breakfast, I was *very* late. I swallowed my pills and grabbed my breakfast bar–a peanut-butter and banana flavor. I poured profoundly pink sprinkles all over a plate, licked the bar all over, and rolled and pressed the bar until all sides were completely covered in sugary yumminess.

"I smiled around at my family, mmmmm, delicious!"

"Seriously, Estelle, four packets of sprinkles today?" asked Sylvia.

I shrugged my shoulders. "I know! I must not be hungry."

Terran said, "I hate to tear you away from your sugar overdose but we need to leave if you want a ride."

I stuffed extra sugar packets in the pocket of my dress and grabbed my bag for school.

Terran's new car was made for beginners, with just a few buttons, so it was easy for a thirteen year old to drive. The seats were high, the doors long and glass, the better to show off the riders and their attire.

Terran was dressed in his best birthday outfit, a dark green high-collared shirt, an ankle-length coat, and long black slacks. That was why I went to all the trouble to put on my favorite dress, which had a bright lime green sweeping train, so that when we zoomed through the streets in his apple green car, we would be color-coordinated. It was supremely important to be color-coordinated.

"We might be late," said Terran.

"I know. It took me forever to get dressed because of all these layers and zippers and hooks. They're *everywhere*. Do you see how many?" I held up an arm to show a row of buckles down my side. "What was Jonathan thinking? He designs so many details and *things*, it takes hours to get ready, and *then* I have to do the matching hair style."

Terran looked at me with a smirk. "You did your hair?"

"I'll have you know, this hair design is very difficult, and not comfortable at all. It's tight and piled and pinned and sprayed and…Oh never mind." I was in a complaining mood because I was so tired. "It took forever."

"I hate to tell you, but there's a hair loose."

I gave him my best, most exaggerated, I'm-going-to-kill-you expression. He knew I *liked* to leave one little bit hanging down in the front, right beside my face. I needed it to twirl in my fingers while I pondered things. "It's just a small bit of hair. Why does it bother everyone so much?"

Terran laughed. "It doesn't bother me. I just don't know if you should go around being so expressive all the time." He had heard Sylvia complain that my hair was 'too expressive.'

"I'm not *expressing* myself, definitely not. Jonathan *totally* frowns on that." I mimicked Jonathan's voice, "'Ultimately fashion is not expressing *yourself*, but *my* talents. You must wear the designs perfectly, Estelle, or it detracts from my vision.'"

Terran and I zoomed through the streets and pulled up to the door of my wing of the school with only seconds to spare. "Have fun describing your birthday presents," I said as I stepped onto the front steps.

"Hey, Estelle, wait." He stopped, like it was important

what he was about to say.

"Yes?"

"Have fun expressing yourself," he said and laughed as he sped away toward his wing. My big brother, the comedian.

Most of my classes were stare-at-a-screen classes, so I was able to grab snippets of rest to recover from my long night. My midmorning 'discussion' class was tough, though. We hated being forced to talk to each other. It was almost painful, and our topic today was: *Components of a Good Dinner Bar Would Include What Characteristics?* Um, sprinkles? We listed off our answers while the teacher agreed in a monotone voice. It was exhausting on days when I wasn't tired, so on today it was excruciating. I was grateful for the sum up, *flavor is almost as important as color branding,* so that I could go back to working alone.

After treadmill class, I went home for the evening. I barely stayed awake through dinner and told Frederick I was too tired to do my homework. "I'll do double tomorrow."

"Are you having trouble sleeping under the stars, Estelle?" I didn't tell him I hadn't turned the stars on since that very first night.

When I got to my room, I wanted to fall on the bed and not wake until morning, but seeing my window seat, or rather lack of window seat, made me feel melancholy. I pulled out a little box that was hidden in the back of my closet. It had been given to Sylvia by her mother, but she didn't want it anymore and thought it should be thrown away. I never took it to the trash, though I promised I would.

The box was blue porcelain with a pale white dancing couple embossed on the lid. The girl was in a flounce of a dress, with petticoats and ribbons at the ankles of her high-heeled shoes. Her leg was up, and she was turned from the boy's advances. He was dressed in a suit with short trousers. He held the girl with one hand and flourished with the other.

The box looked like nothing in my world. It was elegant, yet imperfect. It had a tiny chip, and the lock was tarnished. I knew it must be worthless based on its age, but I was drawn to, totally *adored* its idiosyncrasies. I traced my finger along the figures, imagining the music they might be dancing to and what it must have been like to go to a ball.

Something about the blue porcelain box's age made me feel comfortable. I liked believing that lives that came before mine had been full of love and happiness and beauty.

I lifted the lid. Inside the box were treasures. There was a paper origami crane hanging from the tiniest string of thread. I was told my great-grandmother folded it for wedding decorations.

There was a silver thimble that was probably a few hundred years old. I researched and learned it would have been worn to protect the fingertip while hand-sewing clothes.

Lastly there was a small sprig, dried and flat, of what I thought was a flower called heather. When researching, I learned it mostly grew in a place called Scotland. I didn't know why it was in the box or who put it there.

Holding the box and handling the treasures inside made me feel better, but I could only take it out when I knew no one else would see. Everyone would think they were worthless, especially Frederick, who would complain that old things caused regret and sadness. He would want me to throw them away, definitely. Like sitting in a window seat or walking in the dark, keeping a box of old things around just wasn't *done*.

an improvement

The melancholy that descended on the night of my birthday settled in and seemed like it might stay. I had trouble eating, and no amount of sweetener made the dinner bars palatable. I couldn't sleep, or rather I could, but only with half of my body on the shelf in the window. Could you call that sleeping? I visited with my doctor and he added medicines to my pile, but they didn't help. I just sat around feeling sorry for myself and sighing.

One day a student stood up to proudly describe all her new birthday presents. Her favorite gift was a ring that glowed and projected videos on the wall. Yeah, okay, I had that ring first, mine projected farther, and I could code it with my voice. I totally won, but didn't even feel like gloating. What was wrong with me? I had the most stylish clothes and the best things, but I was still unsatisfied. I had a desire. I just didn't know what it was I wanted so badly.

I excused myself to my room right after dinner and stood with my back to the door and took stock. My canopy bed, my dressing room, and my giant closet were all perfectly designed, exactly as I wanted. That window though, I didn't like that window. The shelf obstructed my view. I had to take the doll down and put it back when I was through, which was a hassle. I knew what I needed to do. I had to dismantle the window display.

I cleared a shelf in my closet of shoes and one by one brought in the doll and her things to store away. Jonathan had designed the doll with pale blue eyes and long light blonde hair, a small, uncanny, replica of me. He had designed exquisitely detailed mini-versions of my best outfits and displayed them on the four small dress forms. The doll and I were perfectly alike in almost every way, except it didn't have the loose bit of hair in the front. That stupid doll beat me at expressing Jonathan's vision and almost looked like it was gloating about it. I felt no regrets about putting it away in my closet.

The shelf was connected to the window frame by four fasteners. Putting my weight on it, I could feel it give a little. I figured if I stood there, held onto the window frame, and shoved down with my foot, it *might* come down. I was a slight twelve year old, but if I really stomped and threw my full weight behind it, the shelf might come down, *easily*. I hit it hard. Then I hit it three times, each time harder, until there was a big crunching noise. The shelf crashed to the bench below. Done!

Ignoring the mighty noise, I leaned the shelf behind the trashcan and put all the scraps and detritus inside and looked at what I'd done. There were two massive gouges in both sides of the window frame. I'd never done something so destructive, *ever*. What would my parents say when they...

"What was that racket?" Frederick opened the door. "Are you okay?" His eyes roamed the room and stopped at the window. "Did your shelf fall? What happen..."

It might have been possible to lie and say it had fallen down, but then I would have to explain how the doll didn't get damaged. Then, I would have to explain why I had cleaned it up, and I might get the person who installed the shelf in trouble. So I went for simple and truthful, "I took the shelf down so I could sit at the window again."

Sylvia rushed up behind Frederick and looked at me with her mouth agape. Frederick looked speechless, like he didn't know what to do with me, the shelf, the window, anything. Ever since I was old enough to know better, I never did anything I wasn't supposed to do. Not like this. No one did. Everything was supposed to be orderly and totally under control, and with this one stomping action, I had become disorderly and completely out of control. My parents didn't know how to handle me. Frederick's mouth opened and closed. He started to speak and rethought, losing his nerve. After a minute or two he said, "It's time for bed," and they turned together to go downstairs.

I sat there for a few minutes getting my breath back. That was intense. I changed into my pajamas and climbed into bed and then heard a faint sound like a beat coming up the street, growing louder and louder. This was odd because no one was ever outside at night, ever. Soon the commotion was right outside my building. What was going on out there? I rushed to the window to see a procession snaking along the street below, hundreds of people, maybe more. They were wearing strangely colored, drab, ill-fitting clothes, like the peasants I had seen in historic photos. *Peasants*, right outside my windows. They were yelling, screaming and chanting. Where did they come from? Where were they going? They were marching and dancing and holding hands. Their signs were covered with pictures of animals.

I leaned on the window trying to read the signs before they went by. A woman came close to the bottom floor of my building and yelled up toward me, "Save the animals! You can't let them kill the animals. Wake up, you need to…" Her voice was faint and faraway. I could barely hear her through the glass, unless I fully concentrated, so I did.

Just then Frederick returned and said, "Come away from the window, Estelle. It's time for bed." His voice was firm, so I didn't even think to argue.

I went to bed and climbed in while the beat could still be heard in the street below.

Frederick perched on the edge of the bed and said, "I don't want to you to go to the window tonight Estelle. I want you to stay in bed, understand?"

I absolutely understood. Between my destructive act and this strangeness happening outside, I had enough of things being out of control. I wanted order and sleep. I would definitely stay away from the window.

None of the teachers the next day mentioned the strange procession. I tried to figure out who else I could ask. I didn't have any friends, no one did. We competed for everything: grades, awards, success, celebrity, notoriety. We didn't talk and didn't make friends. Add those to the long list of things that *just weren't done.*

Sylvia said, "You never want to give someone else the upper hand. In life never look to the left or right, but straight ahead, because that's where you're going. Don't let anyone distract you from that goal." Every parent coached their children in the rules of competitive life living. We all worked toward the next new thing, individually and unencumbered.

If I wanted to know more about what I'd seen last night though, I'd need to find someone to explain it to me. I cautiously approached the girl who sat next to me in my

Scientific Management class and asked her if she'd seen the parade of peasants. She looked startled that I had spoken to her, and told me she had slept right through it. That didn't seem possible, but whatever, if she had asked me, I probably would have answered the same way.

That night when Frederick came to the table, he answered, "Those are protesters, Estelle."

"What are protesters?"

"People who don't like the way the world is."

This was new. How can you not like something that just *is*? "Frederick, why did that woman yell, 'save the animals' at me? Are the animals okay?" I had seen the animals when we went to the zoo on one of our vacations.

"The animals are fine, but, I won't lie to you, many years ago we had some animals die, and some disappear, but since then we have been carefully studying and breeding and caring for them. There is not an animal on this planet that is not being carefully protected and housed somewhere."

"She seemed really upset." I still felt unsettled and didn't understand why.

"That's just because she doesn't understand the improvements we made and the new things we do every day." He patted me on the arm and sent me off to get ready for bed. Our discussion was over.

I walked slowly up the stairs deep in thought about animals and my discussion with Frederick. So deep in thought that I was completely taken by surprise when I opened my bedroom door and saw that my window had been transformed *back* into a window seat. The window frame was repaired and freshly painted. The bench below the window was covered with a plush cushion in dark forest green, and there were pillows of a deep plush purple velvet. Ah, so the new color this year would be dark purple. I fingered the silver cording along the edges and sank down into the seat and stared out the window at the leopard print sky. I guess breaking the rules worked out pretty well if no one expected it of you.

Months passed before another protest, this one soon after I turned thirteen. Sylvia was late for dinner, a rare occurrence, and when she came home she was flushed and excited. "Frederick, the protesters are at it again." She motioned to the door. The faint sound of chanting could be heard as the procession wound down the street toward our building. "They've been at the government buildings disrupting things all afternoon. They should go back to where they come from." She looked out the window and closed the blind. "It's definitely time for them to be taken off the streets. I said so today, and everyone agrees. I need to put forward an ordinance with the Congloms."

"What are they upset about this time?" asked Frederick, carelessly getting up from the table and easing to the window. He pulled the blind open, and then let it drop back quickly.

"Peace," she answered under her breath.

I left and went to my room. For my thirteenth birthday my entire room was decorated in what Jonathan called, *proudly purple,* the hottest color this year. My closet was even bigger than before, yet I still needed more room for all my new clothes. My window seat was still a window seat. Except now the pillows were round, and the fabric was purple brocade.

I could make out the edge of the protest march as it headed away down in the street below. The protesters were carrying huge peace signs, a symbol I had seen once in History of Past Cultures class. I watched intently until Frederick came in and said, "Come away from that window and come back downstairs."

"What does peace mean, Frederick?" I asked as I followed him down to the dining room.

"It means the opposite of war." He sat down at the table again.

"Are we at war?" I had heard of war as a historical event.

"No, we aren't at war with anyone. There are people who have weapons. Sometimes they're aggressive, but we're a peaceful people. To keep the peace, we have to have better weapons, new and stronger, and we have to threaten to use them. We only use them in rare events. I know it's hard to understand when you're so young, but I assure you it's an improvement over how it was hundreds of years ago."

I felt a lump rise in my throat. Tears threatened to rush down my face as I wondered who *they* were, but I let it drop.

from out west

Over the next year all was quiet again, until I turned fourteen, and the largest protest I had ever seen happened outside the gates of my school. It was like they came from nowhere, and then the street was filled with people. They chanted, "Thick air is dirty air," and, "clean air is a human right." They danced in a frenzy. It was impossible to study with all the commotion outside, so instead my mind wandered. Who were they, and where did they come from?

One of the other students, Bill, told the teacher he would outlaw protest once he was in the government. "They should go to prison. The law says they have the right speak their mind, but I don't think they should do it in the streets where everyone can see."

"Well, we hope you go into government," said our teacher, smiling warmly.

"Wait, if they go to prison, what happens to them?" I asked.

"We won't be bothered by them anymore. They disappear like everything worthless. It'd be an improvement. Everyone says so," said Bill. The students around us nodded their heads in agreement.

I decided to add this to my list of questions for that night at dinner. When I entered the room, Frederick had a forced smile on his face. "So, they surrounded your school today, Estelle?"

Terran, who was fifteen at the time, butted in, "Yep, but it disrupted my *Historical Management* class, so I was okay with it."

I ignored Terran and asked Frederick, "Where do they come from?"

He said, "Most of them are from out west, The Beyonds."

"You mean where the dirt is?" asked Terran, who loved the mysteriousness of growing things. There was an earnestness to his voice, that made me remember a vacation years ago at a small, fully paved, completely night-lit resort nestled in the woods. For one of the recreational activities, the staff brought in a low table covered in dirt and let the kids dig in it. Terran pulled up a stool and played there for hours. When the staff sent him home for dinner, they cleaned him up as best they could, but Sylvia noticed his soiled hands.

"What have you been doing?" she asked, her voice raised.

"Playing in the dirt," he answered.

"*We* don't play in the dirt," she said and imperiously swept him into the bathroom to scrub him some more.

I knew it was gross he had played in the dirt, and weird he seemed to like it. It was unsanitary, and Sylvia was only trying to protect him, to keep him safe and clean. I understood all this, but the look in his eyes was unsettling, like his heart was broken. I felt sorry for him, and even though he was older than me, wanted to protect him. I just didn't understand from *what*. I wanted to make it better. That was years ago, but I still remember the look in his eyes, and here he is talking and thinking about dirt, *still*.

Sylvia interrupted my thoughts. "Yes, Terran, *dirt*, but also all the discards and trash. I had to travel there once with an

Oversight Committee. You wouldn't believe how they scavenge and attempt to live off what they grow. It's unimaginable how they live."

"I'd really like to see that," said Terran to nobody in particular. Sylvia shot him an exasperated look, and we all sat quietly and ate our dinner bars.

The description of The Beyonds explained their attire, a brown color, reminiscent of chocolate, but dull and unappetizing. Jonathan would hate it and probably call it *putrid putty,* or something, but he was good at color names. I couldn't even find the words to describe it, much less know what to call it. Dirty colored? Everything here was so thoroughly clean. Where did our browns go? Did they rinse away in the wash?

I decided not to ask Frederick about what the protesters were chanting about. I assured myself if there was a problem with the air, he and the other scientists in Development were working to develop a solution. Maybe some filters, or perhaps new air, or maybe a dome, or I don't know, but I planned not to worry about it. That night I could hear the muffled voices of my parents talking long into the night.

For the next two years the protesters came at an ever-accelerating rate. They protested the energy reactors. When I asked Frederick, he said those were necessary for our power, and the government oversaw them, and the scientists were making them safer all the time. They protested for old growth forests and old rain forests. Frederick said we have more trees now then ever, and they were better trees, because they didn't catch on fire or have diseases anymore. He said we could go see some on vacation soon. Each time the protesters chanted Frederick had an answer for their complaints.

I had to hand it to Frederick, he never talked about throwing the protesters in jail and believed the people of New City were above that kind of brutality. The statistics were grim though, broadcast on the nightly news: 73% of all New City inhabitants believed the protesters should go to jail.

Going to jail meant a criminal never came back. Our world was *new* and *clean* and *orderly*. What would the citizens of New City do with someone in their midst who was out-of-control and unfit? Criminals didn't belong anymore, so they were disappeared. I wondered a lot about what *that* could mean.

An even bigger protest happened the night of my birthday party, the year I turned sixteen. My parents gave me new pre-programmable floral designs for my make-up printer, and a Hair Styl-a-matic that could recreate the elaborate, sweeping updos that were popular. 'Effortlessly,' the box claimed, also promising there wouldn't be a hair out of place. I considered *that* a personal challenge.

I also got a new car that had mirrored sparkles running down the middle of the roof. It glinted and shimmered in every direction. The windows made up the full height of the car, so it was almost entirely see-through. A car like this was made to attract attention, so I planned what outfit I would wear tomorrow. The purple floor-length number would be perfect, the skirt piling dramatically against the window, while my silver shoes peeked out underneath.

After the birthday dessert squares, I excused myself to go to my room and experiment with the make-up designs. "Oh good," said Sylvia, "you'll want to look your best at school tomorrow. Try the hair designer, too. See if it can get that hair to stay back."

Instead, I sat at my window seat staring up at the spirals

swirling on the sky. Wouldn't it be wonderful to be famous, and have a special decoration projected for me on my birthday? I definitely wouldn't pick this one; it made me dizzy. Which one would I pick, the striped?

My wondering was interrupted by a faint chant coming from down the street. The sound grew and grew, until it was the loudest protest of any I had heard so far. I craned my neck and pressed my forehead against the glass to see. It was large, maybe the largest ever, and it was about the condition of their water. I watched as the protesters yelled and sang and danced down in the street below. It looked like they were having fun, but they also looked angry. I couldn't figure out how those two things existed together. I pondered this while my fingers twirled my long strand of hair. My father never came to the room to check if I was watching. I guess he had become *resigned*. I watched until I fell asleep, in a kind of a trance.

The next evening, I looked at Frederick and asked, "What do they mean, clean water? Isn't our water clean?"

"Yes," he said with a weary sigh.

"So what do they want?"

"Estelle, your water is fine. We have the best filters, improved cleaning agents, and more trapping mechanisms than ever. You don't need to worry about it."

"What about their water?" I asked. I figured if I prodded enough, he'd stop being evasive.

"I don't know about their water, Estelle. Maybe they live downstream, or they aren't buying the new technologies, or planning for their future the way we are by storing and filtering. I don't know why anyone would chose to live that way, but you don't have to worry because our water is just fine." His voice was testy, like he expected more questions. He was right. I continued on.

"It doesn't seem fair that I have clean water and someone else doesn't. Can't we make sure everyone has clean water?"

Frederick ran his hand through his hair exasperated. "They have to buy the things they need for themselves, Estelle. Our whole society is based on buying things. We can't give things away, or our whole system falls apart."

"Oh," I said, searching for something more eloquent to say.

"It's time for bed," he said and closed the whole conversation down.

I slowly removed to my room. I looked around at the things I had been given for my birthday. My entire room had been decorated with shades of grey and accents of orange. I ran my finger along the ruffle over the canopy bed. Where did the last canopy go, into the trash? Where did the trash go, into that place, The Beyonds? Are there just piles there of all the things I've tossed away? I opened my closet door; there were racks of my new outfits, drawers full of the accessories, and shelves for my shoes all lined up in a row. Photos ran along the wall of the outfits, paired with the accessories and the shoes, so that every day I would perfectly represent Jonathan's vision. I wondered what it must be like to live in a place where designers didn't organize your look for you. Was it difficult to go about your day without someone telling you how to look, how to act, and how to be?

Tonight's conversation about the protests was the first time I noticed Frederick was defensive about my questions. He had seemed open to them before, or had I just not noticed? It was almost like he was trying to get me to stop asking. Why? Because he himself didn't know the answers? Why would we, the people of New City, have fresh clean water and they, the protesters, have dirty water? How is that fair?

I plopped down onto the window seat. Through the yearly redesigns my parents had let it remain. I had told them over and over that sitting at the window was my favorite thing, but it took an act of disobedience for them to listen. I had to show them how far I was willing to go. I had to fix what was wrong, for them to even *see* it was wrong. I leaned up against the window frame and looked out at the night sky. Tonight's sky was checkered, and the squares' colors changed. I watched for a few minutes. This sky was wrong, so wrong. I couldn't believe I was the only one who saw how wrong it was.

I sat there for a long time, question after question running through my mind. There were so many things I wanted to understand that I needed to ask about. I concluded that I would question *everything,* starting tomorrow. In my first class, Theories of Human Behaviors, I would ask what my teacher thought about the protesters and their right to clean water. Maybe if I asked enough questions, listened to enough answers, maybe *then* things would make sense.

As I made my way to bed, I tripped over one of my new pairs of shoes. Jonathan had designed them with heels that were higher than ever before. When Sylvia showed them to me, she said I would need to practice walking in them, and that they would probably hurt. I walked for just a few moments, and she was right, though she greatly underestimated the amount of pain. They were excruciating. Great, turning sixteen meant I would have to wear painful shoes to school.

Sylvia had said, "You'll need to look graceful and elegant, *especially* tomorrow." Because tomorrow I would be assigned to the boy that I would eventually marry. At twenty. Just four short years from now.

the kind of guy

The next morning, in my first class, I asked the teacher about the protesters, and she said, "They need to understand that they complain at the discretion of the Congloms. New City's patience is wearing thin. Their time might be better spent buying the water filter system and cleaning their *own* water, instead of complaining we haven't done it for them." This was verbatim what the Congloms' spokesperson said last night on the news, and very similar to what Frederick had said. My teacher added, "You know, Estelle, I think you should go to the Office," and she pointed toward the door.

Oh well, I was scheduled to go to the Office of Future Affairs and Behaviors anyway; I might as well be there early, right? I tried to act nonchalant, though tears welled up in my eyes. The other students gaped as I struggled to put everything into my bag and teeter out of the room on the extremely high heels.

The Office controlled everything about our young lives, from our preordained academic course selections, our reading choices, and our elective assignments; to our betrothal, our marriage, and our future family structure. They chose our partner for us, by multiple choice test. They controlled *everything* and I visited it a lot. We all did. The Office adjoined the school to make our frequent scheduled appointments convenient.

Today, though, this was an unscheduled appointment. Asking questions had gotten me in trouble, and because I was *in trouble,* the Office's job was to fix me. They didn't get much practice fixing people, because it was unusual for anyone to be *in trouble.* Rare, unless you were a kid by the name of William Loftin. He was notorious for being insolent, disrespectful, and angry. William was a year older than me and at the School for Managerial Behaviors with Terran, so we'd never met. I had heard of him though, everyone had. He yelled at teachers, at administrators, when forced from the room, the only person who I had ever heard of with anger issues. I also heard that because he was angry, William visited the Office many, many times a year.

The waiting room for the Office had chairs all along the walls facing the receptionist desk. There were twelve chairs and only ever four kids in the waiting room at once. If I planned to question everything, I should definitely ask them why they had eight extra chairs.

I sat in the farthest corner from the receptionist desk and slumped down with my feet up on another chair. This was my favorite chair and the perfect position for hair twirling and pondering. The screens all over the walls showed celebrity fashion news. I watched the shifting images as they covered the latest in hair and clothes. Come to find out, lilac was the hottest color. I would have to ask Jonathan next time I visited him.

When it was my turn, the receptionist said, "After we clear all of this unpleasantness up, just come back out here to wait for your Betrothal Appointment." Her voice sounded cool and slightly irritated.

The Inquiry Room, the first step in every appointment, was sparsely decorated and too cold. My guess was they kept it frigid, so we wouldn't dawdle or fall asleep. There were four big comfortable chairs at desks with screens. Was the chair we chose part of the test? I chose the one farthest from the door.

Once seated, my screen flashed a welcome message, "Hello, Estelle Wells, Welcome Back," and up popped a short multiple choice test about the question I had asked in class that morning and my feelings and thoughts about the issue.

Once done, I was sent back to the receptionist's lobby for a brief wait before they called me into my assigned Behavioral Counselor's room. The test had been checked, and my counselor had what I assume she thought was a compassionate smile on her face. That smile bothered me. Did they teach it in counselor school?

I also found it unsettling that she knew *everything* about me, yet I couldn't even remember her name. It was distracting that I couldn't remember. Had we been introduced at a first meeting years ago? She didn't wear a name tag. Was that another test? I was sure her name started with a J, Betty Jones? Mrs. Jefferson? This never bothered me when I was at a planned appointment, but today, when I was here *in trouble,* I found it very irritating. So irritating I had trouble keeping my voice steady. I thought I might cry.

I looked over my test results while she watched, the same smile on her face. There were three issues I needed to work on:

Issue #1: I Asked Questions. Seriously, I had plenty of questions, but I literally started asking them in public that morning. How was that already an *issue?*

Issue #2: My disheveled Appearance. That was what they

were calling my loose hair that dangled in the front. I *liked* twirling my hair while I pondered things, and frankly, there was plenty to ponder. I needed my hair loose to think all this through. Great, my finger was in my hair, right that moment. Way to prove a point, Estelle. I glanced down. I had kicked off my shoes without even noticing. My feet hurt; they couldn't blame me for that, right?

Issue #3: I Cried. Well, sure, I cried a little when sent from the room today, and yes, I felt a little cry coming on right then, and overall I had never seen anyone else cry. Fine, point made. There were two footnotes. One, a quote from Sylvia Wells that said I had cried too much as a young child, and my tantrums had been completely out of control. The other was from the doctor that oversaw my care as an infant. He said the nurses wore earplugs around my incubator, because I cried every night.

My Behavioral Counselor asked, "Do you agree with this assessment, Estelle?" Then without waiting for an answer, "As you can see, there are many things you need to address. Here's a list of recommendations for you to follow, and we'll send the results to your current doctor, so he can adjust your medication. He can definitely give you something for the questions and the crying, but it's up to you to take your appearance seriously. You need to apply yourself, Estelle." She looked down at my bare feet and smartly knocked the papers into a tight pile. Tears welled up in my eyes. I tried to brush them away, but she noticed. She clucked disapprovingly, her compassionate smile completely gone.

"Let's not be a repeat offender. You can go back to the waiting room for your scheduled Betrothal Appointment." I was sent from her office, sniffling along the way. The three other kids who were waiting watched me lurch across the room, red-nosed and swollen-eyed, the town crier.

I kicked off my shoes and rubbed my feet. So this was it. The day my future-husband would be picked. Seemed like it should be more...*special*, not this same waiting room, these same chairs. In every direction I looked, the celebrity designers discussed the latest developments in exercise shoes. I slumped down and twirled my hair. The buckles seemed excessive. What a day this was. Sylvia was right, it was a *big* day. The first of many momentous days. My future-husband was about to be chosen for me. When I turned twenty, I would marry him. I would become a mother of two children. It was all laid out, all planned. This was the first *gigantic* step.

The receptionist acted like I hadn't been there most of the morning, and smiled at me cheerily as she sent me through to the Inquiry Room *again*. The screen there said, "Hello Estelle, Welcome Back," which made me think it was being ironic. I was given a multiple choice test, the biggest by far, which I guess makes sense.

One of the questions asked this:

> When looking for a lifelong partner you value most:
> - Complacency
> - Contentment
> - Kindness
> - Obligation

Another asked this:

> When you think about your future, you look forward to:
> - Routine
> - Satisfaction
> - Association
> - Success

And on and on and on. There was no way to know what answers they were looking for, so I just went with best guesses.

After the test, I was sent *again* to my Behavioral Counselor's room (Sandra Jenkins?) Her smile was back. If she was taught how to smile that way, did she fail the lesson? I wanted to ask her, as part of my question everything plan, but couldn't build up the nerve.

She asked, "Would you like the result now or sealed in an envelope to open later at home, with your family?"

"Later is good." She took a page, folded it up, sealed it in a white envelope, and handed it to me.

"Your results will be sent to your current doctor, and your next appointment will be with him tomorrow. Have a good evening, Estelle. You're embarking on your future. It's an exciting day!" With that she stood up and showed me to the door.

On my way to my next class, I held the envelope up to the light and tried to make out what it said; nothing, nada, zip. Great, now I wished I had said yes to reading it in the office. Still, having the leering Counselor watch me read the name of my future-husband seemed too obtrusive. However, here in the hallway was as good a place as any. I ripped that envelope open.

Dear Estelle Wells,
According to your personality, aptitude, and behavioral exam, we are pleased to tell you that of the 10 types, you are a #6-reflective. As you learned in your Types of Personalities class, the #6-reflective personality matches best with a #4-attentive. Taking into consideration also your aptitude, your behavior, and your future plans (form 84.B), we have paired you with:
Jack Maranville, also of Total Immersion School of Scientific Discovery, Education Section 7

On behalf of the entire Office of Future Affairs and Behaviors and the Ministry of Medicines, we would like to congratulate you on your future relationship. May your wedding be joyous and your marriage be comfortable.

Sincerely,
Clarise Jordon, Counselor of Future Affairs, School Section 7

Jack Maranville, huh? I'd never met him. Well, no time like the present. He was in my last class of the day and would probably have received his envelope by then.

I walked into my last class of the day, Invention of Common Spaces for Selling Brands 201, and there was Jack Maranville at his seat three rows back. I sat in my usual place to his left and stole a glimpse at him. Did he know his fate yet? There was a white envelope unopened on his desk. Okay, he must be taking it home to open with his family. That's the kind of guy he is. I placed my left ear on my desk, squinted my eyes, and twirled my thinking hair while I took stock:

Hair: light brown, cut tight to head, clipped over the ears, wavy.
Skin: clear, clean
Face: light
Height: medium
Build: lean
Clothes: perfect

He must have noticed I was looking at him, because he glanced my way for a moment. I closed my eyes and pretended I was asleep. When I opened them again, he was putting his desk in order. He got out his supplies, brushed off the desktop, and took out a rag and wiped his hands. He put a pen in the corner and adjusted it just so. Then he worked. He did it all exactly as he was expected to do. It seemed fussy, but other than that I had nothing to go on.

If I squinted my eyes and stared, he looked a bit like one of the news celebrities my father watched nightly. A guy who was stuffy and prone to bombastic statements. Could Jack be like that?

I felt a tap on my desk, and my reverie was broken by my teacher's voice. "Why isn't your desk ready for class yet, Estelle?"

I jerked my head up to answer and realized that my contemplation had been so deep there was a tiny, but noticeable, puddle of drool. I quickly wiped my lips and said, "Oh, uh, sorry."

My teacher tapped beside the drool on my desk top, drawing more attention to it. "Do you have a question that pertains to the class, Estelle?"

Why yes, I did. I blurted one right off the top of my head. "Why don't our common spaces promote meaningful conversations? I'm sitting in a class with students I've never even met before, much less talked to. I don't know where they vacation..."

That was how far I got before my teacher stopped me and pointed to the door. The tears welled up in my eyes as I grabbed my things off my desk. In my embarrassment, I accidentally wiped my fateful white envelope through my mortifying puddle of drool. I went back to the Office of Future Affairs and Behaviors for the third meeting *today*. Beat that, William Loftin. This had to be a new record.

That night, I laid in bed wondering what the next day would bring. Would Jack walk up and introduce himself? Would we sit beside each other and talk, and get to know each other? Would this be a long friendship and a happy marriage? Everyone older than me was in an arranged marriage, and they were all happy, right? Of course they were. Frederick and Sylvia Wells had been married for twenty years and seemed content enough. That's definitely what I wanted, contentment. Now my marriage was planned, and the boy chosen, I could settle into that next part of my life. Everything from now on would be comfortable happiness and contentment. It had to be.

The next day in class, Jack Maranville didn't even look at me. He didn't look when I stared, even when I glared, and definitely not when I tapped my fingers on my desk and made an 'ahem' sound in my throat. I knew he had read my name in his envelope, but he pretended like I wasn't even there. Okay, well, at least I have four more years until our wedding. This, like the protests, was probably nothing to worry about.

glowing silver with an M

At my next appointment my Doctor was looking over my latest files as I came in. "Hmm," he said. He glanced inquisitively over his glasses and asked, "How are you feeling?" This was usual at these appointments. He leaned in, which made me pause for a moment. I was uncertain if there was a new answer I should give, now that I had been assigned to my husband and all.

"Fine," I said.

"Good." He seemed relieved and leaned back in his chair. "It says here you *cried*, at school?"

"Yes, yesterday."

"The day you received your Marriage assignment?" He squinted his eyes as if there was a truth he was attempting to discern. I knew from experience however, that what I answered, or even did, in these meetings was irrelevant to his diagnosis. Diagnosis came from the quiz I had taken at the Office.

"Yes, but I cried because I was asked to leave the classroom, for a question."

"That brings me to my next point," he said, taking notes. "Has your mind been wandering off task? Are you distracted by these irrelevant questions?" Oh, *my* questions were irrelevant.

"Um, sure?"

He wrote more. "Are you still spending time sitting at your window seat?" I nodded, and he finished his notes. "Okay, I've adjusted your medications. Delivery will be this evening, and the instructions for each pill will be sent to your mother, Sylvia Wells. I'll see you in two weeks, Estelle."

"Excuse me, I've been meaning to ask. Could you tell me, um, what the pills are for?"

"What are the pills for? They help you maintain normalcy. They help you get along. They make you feel better. You know what they're for, Estelle!"

"I was wondering, *individually,* what each pill does, *exactly?*"

My doctor squinted at me again. He wrote something new on his screen. "I have another appointment, Estelle. I need to cut this short."

I felt embarrassed as I headed for the door. I couldn't help wondering a little bit why he hadn't answered my questions, and why I never asked them before.

Later that night my mother brought me the medicine tray. There were so many pills I couldn't remember which ones I had been taking and which were new. There were two pills that were shades of azure blue, one with a little z on it, and one with a capital A. There was a mottled grey pill with an O, and one that was grass green with an N on it. A bright red one had no letter at all and was somewhat heart-shaped. Both a white one and a yellow one looked too big to swallow. There was a smaller pill that was a solid medium grey, with an embossed Q on it. Next, were three capsules, each with multicolored little balls inside. Okay, now that I was paying attention, there was a pale glowing silver one with an M stamped on it. That one was new. While I stirred and sorted them with my finger, my mother looked at me and tapped her foot. "I don't have all day Estelle, please take your pills and head to bed."

"What are they for, Sylvia? Like, individually?" I was certain of her response.

"They're to keep you healthy and happy, silly Estelle! Now take them and let me get back to the work I need to do." Yep, exactly what I expected.

like waking

The next day at school, we were surprised by a male voice yelling in the hallway. It was so out of the ordinary that we turned and stared at the door of the classroom. My teacher said, "Um, stay in your seats," and left.

For a brief minute when the door was opened, I heard, "You can't make me. Take your hands off me. I refuse to..." The door closed, and the voice was muffled again.

I rushed to the small window in the door. My teacher and a couple of others were struggling to lead a young man down the hall. That had to be William. No one else would ever be so defiant. He kept pulling his arms out of their grip, but they kept grabbing him tighter. As their struggle continued by the door, for a brief moment his eyes met mine. His eyes! There was so much anger. I quickly looked away, frightened, and went sheepishly back to my seat.

Minutes later my teacher returned. In a calm measured tone he said, "Estelle, for disobeying me, you'll go straight to the office." Seriously, this was getting ridiculous. It wasn't an entirely bad thing though. Maybe I would get a chance to meet William while I was there. I could ask him what happened and satisfy my curiosity. But, no, when I entered the Office waiting room I saw the back of William as he headed through to the

Inquiry Room.

"Interesting to meet you," I said to myself.

My questionnaire that day included this:

> Anger is a negative emotion. Negative emotions are:
> - Too complicated for civilized society
> - Best channeled into competition
> - A sign medications should be adjusted
> - All of the above

The questions made me wonder which of my medications kept me from experiencing anger, and should I be angry that I didn't know?

The following day I laid in bed and dreaded going to class. I didn't want to sit by Jack, my future-husband, knowing he wouldn't speak to me. I didn't want to get sent from the room for asking more questions, but all I had were more and more to ask. I didn't want to do what was expected of me. I didn't want to go to school.

I considered the effects of not going. I would definitely get in trouble. It broke the rules, and I would get sent to the Office for sure. Then again I got sent there all the time anyway, so what would it hurt? After thinking it through for a while I convinced myself it would be okay not to go to school. Then I told myself I had to go. Then I gave myself permission not to. Okay, it was decided.

Next I had to decide where to go instead, and figure out how to get my car to take me there. My car was preprogrammed with limited destinations: school, home, my doctor's office, and my designer's studio. I spent the morning locating the instruction manual, figuring out how to override the programming, and learning how to set it to self-drive.

Happily Frederick hadn't seen a reason to add the parental controls. He trusted me. Before I left, I turned off the location tracking on my phone. Would he still trust me if he couldn't locate me?

As I drove through the city, I was acutely aware that my car's see-through doors exposed me to scrutiny. I was too noticeable. A teenager out of school was an oddity. I was breaking the rules, and not hiding it very well. I needed to find a place to go, quick. Hopefully someplace interesting enough to make this trouble worthwhile.

On the edge of the city there was a sign for The Old Town History Museum. My Historical Facts class had taken a school trip there a few years ago, and it had been sort of interesting. There was, at least, plenty to see, and I didn't have many other options. Plus, it was open. I pulled into its expansive and completely empty parking lot, kicked off my high-heels, pulled on a comfortable pair of exercise shoes, and went up to the ticket booth. The guard looked bored and was nonchalant about seeing a teen-ager out of school. He sold me a ticket and waved me in with a grunt.

I pushed a red button with 'begin' on it, and a recorded tour guide's voice said, "Welcome New City visitor. You are entering a complete village that's hundreds of years old. The Historical Preservation Society moved it piece by piece from a place called California. It's been perfectly restored, down to the smallest details. An entire Conglom was created just for building replica tools, antique furniture, and historic products for the shops. Please note the exquisite details and don't forget to visit the gift shops."

"Thank you, disembodied voice," I said to no one.

I walked into the grocery store first. There were boxes and cans on the shelves and bins full of what I assumed were fruits and vegetables. I picked up a brown one with leaves poking out of the top. Another disembodied voice coming from a speaker in the corner said, "Hello visitor. This is a replica of a store that would have contained food and other supplies. You are holding a pineapple."

"Thank you for stating the obvious." I recognized it was a pineapple, but I had never seen one this close before. It was hard and tough on the outside, probably because it was just a replica. I pulled a box off the shelf, Sugar Puff breakfast cereal. I shook it, but there was nothing inside.

"Hello visitor. You are holding a box of breakfast cereal."

"Hello voice, you're annoying." I'd rather the disembodied voice explain these nonsensical food labels. Like how wet cheese and noodles could be kept inside of a box? And the brands were the same Food Congloms from here in New City. Were they the same brands from two hundred years ago, or did they just pay to sponsor the boxes?

I left the store and wandered through the town. The street was paved gray instead of the more dramatic colors of the pavements in New City. Beside the road was a tree and some grass, plastic—just like the tree outside the door to my home. How long have we been using plastic trees and bushes in landscaping? Would there have been real trees growing in this town hundreds of years ago? How would the citizens have kept everything clean?

This time, from a speaker under the tree, a disembodied voice said, "Hello visitor, this is a replica of an Oak tree." I wished there was a real human tour guide to talk to.

I passed a small house that was open in the front, so I could look into the restored rooms. Another voice said, "This was a kitchen," and listed the appliances. The only thing I recognized was the appliance for heating things. We called it a zapper, and the voice called it a microwave. I was fascinated by two dishes on the floor for dogs to eat and drink from. How odd that animals lived inside with people. Didn't they worry about disease? I wandered by a bedroom. It was so tiny compared to my own. How did they sleep on such a small bed? And where did they keep their clothes? The closet was only big enough to hold my season's shoes.

Everything was so quaint: the rooms, the billboards, the shops, the screens. I meandered for hours, fascinated at this glimpse of a simpler time. I stood for a while looking in a gardening shed full of shovels and buckets, with a pile of dirt in the corner. Could I trust Terran to keep a secret? I wished I could tell him about it tonight.

Lastly, I reached The Old Historic Library. There the voice said, "Welcome visitor. This is a library. Past cultures kept their written thoughts in books, and kept those catalogued in repositories for everyone to read." I had studied libraries in History of Archaic Technologies class. My teacher had explained that entering a library was like entering a computer full of information, only you had to locate all the answers yourself. Libraries sounded confusing and exhausting. What if you needed to know something fast? You really had to read the whole book yourself? Every book? Could you pay someone to read them for you? If I had lived back in the time of libraries, would I have been able to ask anything I wanted?

The Old Historic Library contained shelf after shelf of books. I picked one, pulled it out, and flipped it open. It was empty, except for a block of plastic that kept its width intact. Who removed the middles?

I walked up and down reading the titles: *On The Road, The Freedom Manifesto, The Power of Myth,* and *The Cosmos Explained.* Cosmos and 'explained' in the same title, I wished I could read that one.

Around a corner in the back there was a dusty door with a padlock. It looked like it had been undisturbed for many long years, but on closer inspection I realized the padlock had been recently used. I reached out, casually pulled on the lock, and it popped open easily. I stood for a second, surprised, and wondered if I should go in. I discussed it with myself. What would be in there, cleaning materials? I removed the padlock and then thought twice about it. I was in trouble for ditching school; did I really want trouble for breaking and entering? It wasn't really *breaking* though, was it?

I walked out of the library into the street outside and stood for a moment taking in the scope. The guard was walking farther down. I yelled, "Excuse me?" I walked a bit closer so he could hear, and asked, "Can I go into *any* of the rooms?"

"Sure, as long as they're not locked," he said.

Okay, that was good enough, right? I went back into the library, walked up to the door, opened the padlock, and stepped inside. The walls were covered in even more shelves, and they were in turn covered in dusty old books. Books so dusty I couldn't touch them without building up my courage first. I pulled one down and blew. A big cloud of dust wafted into the air and then seemed to settle right back where it started. I opened the cover, inside were real pages filled with words. Not tiny snippets, little quotes, and truncated paraphrases like we read in school, but full sentences, lengthy chapters, and complete stories. There were beginnings, middles, *and* conclusions.

I fell into the closest chair and read in rapture the rest of the afternoon. The first book I read was called *Little House on the Prairie*.

That week, every chance I could find, I went to the Library in the Old Time Museum and read books. I missed school, too many days of school.

One night, late in the week, my father confronted me about it. He spoke calmly and guessed this was 'just a phase' I was going through. I wasn't so sure. I wanted to read every single book on those shelves, and that would probably take a while. I didn't tell him that, though, because the library was my secret. He wanted to transfer me to the Managerial Immersion Behavioral Academy, but I assured him I would get myself under control. From then on, I didn't miss school to read in the Library. Instead I took the books and read them at home. I felt okay about this because no one else was reading them, and besides, I always brought them back.

I read *Percy Jackson and the Lightning Thief.* The following week I read *Little Women*, and then *Charlotte's Web*. Over time I read books by Mark Twain, Charles Dickens, and Jane Austen. I had read small quotes from these authors over the years, but never their full books. It was difficult to find words to describe how wonderful these stories were, almost *alive*. Under this dust and disuse, they had been waiting all these years, for *me*. I hid the borrowed books in the back of my closet, stacked under my box of treasured things, because they had become treasures, too.

I carried them back and forth under my clothes. I stayed up all night reading until I was exhausted. I barely pulled my act together in the mornings. I looked rumpled most of the time. My Behavioral Counselor found this dismaying, because my issue #2 had only gotten worse. Lots worse. I didn't care though, the whole wide world seemed different. It was like waking up.

someone I could talk to

I barely knew my brother. Our paths rarely crossed except
once a day at dinner, and then we just ate and recited a list of
what we had accomplished that day. I tuned him out most of
the time and had no real idea what his interests were. All I
knew was he was usually quiet, but when he did say something
it would probably be a funny something. He was good at
seeing the humorous side of things.

He was a year ahead of me in school and studying for a
completely different career. It was planned that I would be a
scientist like Frederick, so I studied at the Total Immersion
School for Scientific Discovery. Ever since Terran was young,
the Office of Future Affairs had labeled him, watchful and
interested, so he studied to be a manager at the School for
Managerial Behaviors. We had separate studies and separate
lives. On vacations there were so many age-divided activities
we could go the whole week without seeing each other at all.
Though we were related, he was mostly a stranger.

Once he had reached his teen years, however, I'd glimpsed
things about my brother that *did* interest me. Like the way he
watched the protesters, in a quiet and thoughtful way. How the
night Frederick reprimanded me for missing school, he came
and sat beside me—not talking, just *near*. Now that I

questioned everything, I wanted to know what fascinated him about growing plants. Did he really like digging in the dirt? Why did he like to build things? He asked questions about our world too, but never directly of anyone, and never expecting an answer. His questions went like this, "I wonder why the ground is covered with plastic and cement everywhere, and no dirt. I wonder why we did that?" And, "Isn't it strange we don't have trees here?" He asked the ether, not demanding a response, which is why I suppose he was never sent from the room for asking. The most he ever got back was a shrug of the shoulders, or an exaggerated "humph," and that seemed to be enough for him.

I decided that I wanted to get to know him, especially considering I didn't know anyone in this whole world very well. Maybe I just wanted to tell someone about the books. The Library was a secret I was tired of keeping, a big secret, and not always a happy one. These books were changing me and revealing that there were many different ways to live. I felt confused by the way we chose to live here in New City. If we had every option open to us, why did we dress this way, with so much effort? If we could eat anything we wanted, why did we eat these bars? If we could invent sky projectors, couldn't we have come up with a way to make the stars come back? I felt disgruntled, and wanted someone I could talk to about it all.

So, for his seventeenth birthday, I took him to the Library for the first time and read him part of a book called *Harry Potter and the Sorcerer's Stone*. He was practically breathless as he listened, and when it was time to go home for dinner, told me it was the best present he'd ever been given. "I am kind of depressed though," he added.

"Why?"

"I'm seventeen now. I guess my Hogwarts invitation is

never coming." He grinned at me.

"I know what you mean. I've read a pile of books, and all of them are about experiences I'll never have." I dramatically sighed.

That evening, as we left the gates of The Old Time Museum, the guard leaned toward me and said so quietly that Terran couldn't hear, "If you'd like to join the next protest, meet tomorrow at six behind the Old Stadium." He left without waiting for an answer.

My hands trembled as I started my car and drove Terran to his birthday party. Could I go to a protest? Would I? And if I did, why?

wishful thinking

The next day I was apprehensive as I dressed for the protest. I pulled on a pair of loose green slacks with azure piping that I hoped would be understated enough. I chose a blouse of cream with a scarf of brick red. This combination was not approved by Jonathan, but I definitely wasn't looking for approval. What *was* I looking for? I stepped back and looked at myself in the mirror. The colors clashed badly. I had hoped the combination would look brown. I squinted my eyes and concluded this was wishful thinking, at best, but at least none of it was pure white. I pulled on my exercise shoes, certain that heels wouldn't do.

I headed toward the abandoned buildings of Old Town, turned right onto Main Street, and passed the Old Stadium looming on the left. Desolate and abandoned like everything else in this part of town, its lights still brightly blared to appease our fears of the dark.

I parked and walked across the giant lot toward the stadium entrances. As I reached the western side, I could see a crowd of people. I approached unnoticed until I was close enough to make them out individually. Everyone fell silent, and looked me over. I was nervous, really nervous. My legs were shaking, and I perspired in a way I had never experienced before. Sweat was rolling down my side. Tears welled up, of course. Great, now I was thirsty, too.

There were close to a hundred people dressed in shades of that odd brown color. Everyone looked at me in an expectant, but hostile, way. I tried to gather my nerve and explain why I was there, but there was no reasonable explanation. Thankfully the guard pushed his way through the crowd and greeted me warmly. "If you're here to protest, we're happy to have you. Please stick with the group, don't tarry at the edges, and don't get separated, or you'll risk arrest. We lost two people during the last protest." He turned to the crowd and said, "She's from New City, and a reader in the Old Town Library." This seemed to appease their general curiosity, but it did nothing to calm my own. Why was I here?

A few hundred more people showed to march. They pushed and jostled. I was never in a disorderly crowd before. These people were *all up* in my personal space. I never realized how much I liked my space before, and severely missed it when it was gone.

Large signs were handed out that said, 'Foods Should Come from Farms Not Factories,' and, 'Real Food isn't Square,' and 'Pink isn't a Flavor.' This was all news to me. I just ate the bars and yummy sprinkles. I never thought about what food was made of, only which flavors were my favorite.

I was given a sign, and someone gave me a shirt in the same drab color to wear over my own. I gratefully took it because I definitely didn't want to be seen. It was clear now, with the crowd around me, that my color choices had been completely wrong. I felt completely wrong. I didn't blend in, and I had no idea why we were protesting. I held half a sign that said, 'Control the Food=Control the People,' in big letters. Who could I ask what that meant? My father, or maybe the guard? The other half of the sign was held by a dainty woman in her thirties.

"Where are you from?" I whispered.

She answered, "Manufacturing City #45609," and looked straight ahead, not inviting any more questions. The drumming and the staccato thumping mimicked my heartbeat. It made it impossible to stand still. We bounced in our place, in time to the beat, and waited until our line inched slowly forward. We advanced en masse through, and then out of, the deserted Old Town, and then marched into New City. I followed the crowd and chanted timidly. The procession twisted and turned, up and down the streets, as we chanted, marched, sang, and danced.

I felt more comfortable and shouted slogans at the few people who watched from their windows. I was cautious not to meet their eyes, careful not to be noticed. Mostly though, the streets were clear. The inhabitants of New City were inside, safe, tucked away from the night and the strangers that noisily protested outside.

"No Factory Yuck in our Meals!" I yelled, feeling courageous. Then I heard screaming of a different sort, loud and panicked. I glanced around wildly, looking for the source. The sound came from the front of the march. I stood on my toes, almost wishing for my absurdly high heels. There was jostling up ahead, so the people in front backed up. The ones right in front of me shoved and almost knocked me over backwards. There was chaos as someone beside me fell. People were pushing from every direction. The drumbeat stopped, and I felt lost, confused, and immobile. The woman I was walking with dropped her end of the sign and yelled, "Run, police!"

I twisted in mid-stride and shoved forward to keep the

man in front from falling on me. Arms were swinging up ahead and I heard more yelling and screaming. I turned to run, but my foot was stuck under someone's body. I pulled it free in a panic and ran. I made a hasty decision not to go back in the direction we had come. Instead, I bolted straight down a side street, pulled the borrowed shirt over my head, and tossed it away.

I ran down two city blocks and up another side street. I never stopped, though it felt like my heart might burst. My mind kept repeating, 'Don't get caught. Don't get caught. Don't get caught.' The repeated plea was a new beat to follow. *Don't get caught.* I raced into the parking lot of the Old Stadium, slowed down, put my hands on my hips, and tried desperately to catch my breath. I leaned against my car, grateful for the cool comfort of its chrome and glass. I could see a small group of protesters gathered again at the starting point. They looked disheveled and unorganized, and there were far fewer of them.

A couple rushed by and said, "They got at least four of us." They rushed on to notify the rest of the group. I decided to drive away before the police followed someone here. Definitely before that.

All the way home I just kept thinking about how dangerous that had been, and for what? Something I didn't even understand? What would I have done if I had gotten caught? Who did get caught, and what would happen to them? I thought about where that woman had said she was from, a Manufacturing City? Where in the world was a Manufacturing City?

When I walked through the front door, I knew I was in trouble. Frederick jumped to his feet. "Where have you been? Your phone's location tracker had you in Old Town near the stadium, and walking through the streets?" His voice was loud, perhaps louder than *ever* before. He gathered control of himself and asked, "You remember, don't you, *we* don't go out at night?" There was a *big* emphasis on the *we*.

I couldn't believe I had forgotten to turn off the location tracker. Tears splashed down my cheeks as I said, "I marched in the protest."

A strange look crossed his face. "You did *what?*"

"I protested. I'm sixteen, so I can do what I want." I tried to sound braver and more self-assured than I felt. The tears made this very difficult.

Frederick sat down heavily in his chair. The look I had witnessed a minute before disappeared and was replaced by his placid, explaining expression. "I want you to listen to what I have to say. First, protesting is trouble, and the Congloms and the Government don't like trouble. They want to close the protests down, and protesters are being arrested and *disappeared* all the time now. Please, don't go looking for that kind of excitement anymore. Second, what you were protesting doesn't even make sense."

He sat for a minute and ran his hand through his hair. "For thousands of years people lived off of the foods they grew on farms, *in the dirt.* This growing of food would sometimes succeed, but there were famines and droughts and plagues and disease. Humans fully believed they were at the mercy of gods. Most of us have since seen this is no way for rational people to live. Medicines and pesticides were produced which extended our lives, extended the growing season, and made everything better. Foods were changed at their genetic level, and vitamins, minerals, proteins, and all the good things your body needs were added. The flavors were enhanced to make the food especially pleasing. You love your sweetener, right?"

I nodded, feeling chastised. "And Terran loves his nacho cheese flavoring. Whatever we want, whenever we want it. Food is better now. It tastes better, and with vitamins added, our health improved. Most importantly, there is no more starvation here anymore."

"What do you mean by disappeared?" I asked, harking back to his first point about the protestors.

He sighed. "I don't know, probably sent somewhere else. Ultimately, they aren't seen again by those of us that matter. I don't want that to happen to you." He seemed unable to meet my eyes.

I asked, "Can I be excused to go to my room?" Sylvia bustled in and gave me a tray with my fourteen pills in different colors on it. I took them while still distracted by the conversation. As I got to the door to leave, I turned back. "About the farming and the food, you mean everyone, *everywhere* has enough, right Frederick?"

He sighed again. "No not everyone, but we're improving the food, adding to it. Someday the whole world will have enough to eat. I really feel we're getting close now."

"Okay." I walked up the stairs, while swallowing back my tears.

like we have

When I got to my room, I searched on the computer for anything about Manufacturing Cities. They were defined as "Large cities in which new food and new products are manufactured for the Conglomerates in improved ways: See Development Cities and Marketing Cities." So, I searched for information about Development Cities. I found out those were "Large cities in which new and improved products were developed for the Conglomerates with new methods: See Manufacturing and Marketing Cities." So I searched for information about Marketing Cities, of course, and it said, "A large city where new and improved products are packaged and advertised: See Development and Manufacturing." There was no information about where the cities were, or any explanation why I never met anyone from there. Everyone in New City was from New City. I guess I never thought about that before. Now I felt like a big idiot for never noticing.

That night I lay in bed for hours going over and over this all in my head. Our water is clean, but perhaps their water isn't. Our air is clean. They probably won't buy the filters. We aren't aggressive. We just have defensive weapons and use them sometimes, but only when absolutely necessary. I've been assured of that, right? We aren't starving. Is it possible they are? Over and over these thoughts kept swimming in my mind. The next morning I woke up at dawn and watched the sunrise for the first time in my whole life. It was a glowing orb in a grey and murky sky. I've got to admit, it was a bit of a letdown from what I had imagined. The books I had read made it seem like it would be amazing.

I went into Terran's room and nudged him awake. He mumbled a groggy, "What?"

I sat on the edge of the bed, stared out the window, and said, "Terran, the protesters are trying to tell us things aren't okay in other places, even though everything is okay here. Whenever I ask Frederick for an explanation, he agrees things aren't okay for everybody. What I want to know is where do these people come from? Why don't we hear about them? Why don't we see them? Why don't we study this in school? And why the hell haven't I asked these questions before?" I plopped back onto Terran's bed, just missing his legs, which he quickly pulled up. "I'm disgruntled." I stared at the ceiling and furiously twirled my hair.

"Wow, you really know how to wake someone up." Terran sleepily rubbed his head. "I've wondered about all of that too, Stelley. The things the protesters say are the opposite of what I know to be true. Someone must be lying. It's confusing. I watch the protesters and wonder what their lives are like. Do they live on farms?" We both fell quiet. I stared blankly at the ceiling. He held his groggy head in his hand.

I became irritated. I had questions and wanted answers. The only person I could ask was Terran, and what did he know? Less than me, apparently.

Terran said, "I guess we'll never know most things, huh, Estelle? I mean everyone seems content with the way things are now, or they go along without thinking. Like the zombies in this book," he pointed at one of the small pile he had on his bed, "they have no brains."

"Do all the books you bring home have wizards or monsters in them?"

"This one has vampires," he said with a smile.

I wasn't ready to laugh. "Make sure you hide these books."

"Estelle, do *you* ever wish you didn't have so many questions, that you could just be content with things too?"

I knew he didn't really want an answer, but I could still feel myself getting testy. I sat up and looked directly at him. "Are you suggesting you want me to give up or something? Because it sure sounds like what you're saying."

"No, Estelle, that is seriously not what I'm saying. I'm just asking if you ever think it would be better...oh forget it." He tried to appease me with a smile. "You know me, I just want to dig, right? You know what I'd really like to do? Plant a tree and watch it grow. I think it would be amazing to have a tree that lasted my whole lifetime and kept going through the lifetime of my children and maybe even my grandchildren. Everyone could call it Terran's tree long after I'm gone. That's what I want. I'm a simple guy, really."

"Yeah, I know," I said, smiling as well. "I'm the complicated one."

He climbed out of bed, threw the top covers over my face, and headed to the bathroom to get ready. Boys had almost as much to do to get ready as girls. Their current fashion included layer upon layer of clothes, all belted, buckled, and buttoned. They wore their hair long but swept back from their face; their sideburns trimmed just so.

I looked down at myself. I had barely slept, but had done that little bit while still in my clothes. Oh well, I'd change into something spectacular to detract from the bags under my eyes, and I'd program my hair style-a-matic to create a complicated and extreme coif in an attempt to look more marvelous than I felt.

During school I asked my teacher about the different cities. As if it was common knowledge, he said, "The world is made up of giant interconnected specialized cities that have separate Corporate Conglomerates which control their specialization. Does that answer your question, Estelle?"

"Yes, but how are those cities different from here? Do they have less than we do?"

"Because they have different specializations, they have different characteristics, but the overall structure is the same. Okay?" He sounded testy as if he had better things to talk about, when in reality we were discussing color choice and the creation of fashionable culture.

I asked, "And what about the in-between places, like The Beyonds?"

"What do you mean, the in-between places? What are you talking about?"

"What's there?" I didn't mean to be so persistent, but I wanted to know.

"I don't know. I suppose the in-between places are full of the old products and trash, though I never gave it any thought. Why in the world would you wonder about that? Let's please go back to color choices." He said this as if it was all explained, and that was that, but I couldn't stop myself.

"Why is this class about color choices a whole semester long? Aren't color choices inconsequential when there's so much more to understand about our world? Do you even know where our clothes are made? Do any of us know?" I could see from his face I was about to be sent from the room again.

"Color choices are an important issue in our culture, Estelle. We all care about fashion; it's what makes us good citizens of New City. Who *cares* where our clothes are made as long as they're made well?"

"I care," I said. My voice was barely audible.

"I wouldn't worry about the *people*. I'm sure the people are content. They make useful things for us, *and* they get our castoffs when we're done. I'm sure they consider themselves lucky."

"Wouldn't they rather have things that are new, like we have?"

"I think you had better go to the Office now and discuss any concerns you have there," and with that he went back to addressing the class.

As I gathered my things to leave the room, I glanced over at Jack. He looked directly at me, and turned back to the front of the room. Tears welled up in my eyes because the look on his face wasn't a look of shyness, or curiosity, or sympathy, and definitely not friendliness. It was contempt, pure and unmistakable. My future-husband didn't like me, not one little bit.

can't see

When I was sent to the Inquiry room my multiple choice questionnaire asked the following:

> Are you bothered by this year's choice of Azure Blue as the Color of Record? If so, which runner's up colors would you have chosen?
> - Royal Blue
> - Denim Blue
> - Sky Blue
> - I'm not bothered by this year's choice of Azure Blue.

Then the question:

> If a community wants to express their unity, then fashion is
> - A formulaic rule for getting along
> - A complementary form of communicating balance
> - A unifying political structure
> - All of the above

Later in the day I found a definition for Great Historical Protests that said, "In the past protest was an expression of dissent against a government or other entity that assumed power and control. Protest is an archaic form of expression, long unused because the current state of representation and power in New City and Environs is voiced by the people through the marketplace. There is no longer any need for oppression *or* dissent." That seemed odd, since the night before I had been in a protest in the streets right outside.

The definition included a list of famous protests, such as Gandhi's Salt March, the Boston Tea Party, and the Orange Revolution. These people had decided not to cooperate with oppression anymore. Their disobedience became movements. Their movements made their societies change. I had never heard about any of this in my Historical Facts classes, and everything I read now made me want to know more.

Exploring deeper, I found the term 'civil-disobedience' and the name Henry David Thoreau. I recognized that name because I had recently leafed through his book, *Walden,* at the library. The quote read, "Most of the luxuries and many of the so-called comforts of life are not only not indispensable, but positive hindrances to the elevation of mankind." I read it over a few times and sat back in my chair and mulled it over for longer. Thoreau had also written an essay called, *Civil Disobedience.* Could I find it at the library?

When school was over for the day, I left for the Old Time Museum. The parking lot was mostly empty, and as I went through the gate, I stopped to speak to the guard. "I'm Estelle Wells," I said.

"Good to meet you, Estelle Wells. I'm Anthony Heaps. That was awful last night, huh?" he asked.

"Yeah, is everyone okay?"

"Not really; they arrested four protesters. One was a good friend of mine." He looked down at his hands.

"Will they get out? What happens to them now?"

"I don't know. It's like they're just gone. There's supposed to be a trial, but it won't be public, so we don't know if its happened yet, or not. We've been asking around, but it's difficult to find out where they are and what's happening with them. We're worried that if we contact the Justice System, we'll get implicated and possibly arrested, too."

"So, you might never see them again?" I asked, horrified.

"Maybe, probably, I don't know…" His voiced trailed off.

I asked, "Are you from New City?"

"Yeah, I'm from here. Why?"

"So, why do you protest?"

"When I took this job here at the Museum, I found myself with too much time, way too much time. I thought about the how our world is and compared it to what I knew about life a long time ago. I read books, from the um, *library,* and realized there was an awful lot wrong with the city I live in. I met people from all over, and I just became the kind of person who wanted to try to change things." He shrugged his shoulders.

"Do you think things are changing?"

He seemed almost startled by my question. "Yeah, they're changing. It doesn't seem like it's getting any better, but I figure if more of us protest, eventually the citizens will listen. They'll have to."

I nodded my head, though I wasn't sure. It didn't seem like anything ever changed.

"Hey, do you want to come to the planning meeting tomorrow night at the stadium? It's safe. We need to talk about it all, new protests, and how we carry on."

"Sure, I'll be there. I need to go now, um, read."

"Of course," he said and politely left me to my mission. It only took a few minutes to locate the book, *Walden.* I stood there at the shelf and read. It was complicated, difficult, and sometimes confusing, but despite all of that, as the story unfolded it felt like this was *it*. *The* book, just sitting on this shelf, waiting for *me* to come across it. I shoved it under my clothes and snuck it home. I read most of that night, until I fell asleep exhausted.

When I woke up the next morning, I felt jubilant. It was as if I wanted to know unnamable things, and here they were, the *answers*. I read while I got dressed for school the next day. I risked taking the book to school and read whenever I could find time alone. To top off my rule-breaking, I missed dinner with my parents to go to the planning meeting of the protesters. My parents were going to completely freak out. That was one thing I knew, but I wanted to know more.

I hoped attending this meeting would help me learn more about the protests. I wanted to ask about their end goal. Where did they come from? What was life like there? Were they scared? Where did the protesters go when they were arrested? And had any of them read about Henry David Thoreau? I needed answers, so I couldn't worry about Frederick's issues with me being out at night. I would remember to turn off my phone's location tracking and explain it to him later. I'd be able to get him to understand. At least that's what I kept telling myself.

I was one of the first to arrive at the Old Stadium and joined a few others in leaning along the barricades around the entrance. By the time the meeting was scheduled to begin about sixty people were gathered. I noticed the new arrivals gave me a wide berth. Probably my attire again. I tried to dress down, but I was still excessively, and dramatically, dressed compared to the company I kept.

A young blonde man in his mid-twenties moved to the

front and gestured for conversations to cease. I felt excited that I'd get some explanations.

"Everybody," he said, "is worried about our fellow protestors. We will let you know when we hear how they are. If you think about it, the police are only arresting a few people at a time. They're just trying to scare us. The odds are good most of us will be fine and that protesting is still safe. So, while we wait to hear how they are, we should keep planning, okay? The next protest is about the animals. The habitats are shrinking every day, and there aren't many species left. So let's come up with some sign and chant ideas."

I forgot all about my other questions because I was so stunned. The animals? Was this a repeat of the first protest from years ago? I looked around at everyone wondering if they were wondering what I was wondering. If these people risked their lives protesting this issue, and nothing got better, then what was the use?

People yelled forward things like, "Animals deserve protection, too," and "Wild is Better." I was confused. Heat crept up my face and my head was spinning. What was going on? I absentmindedly twisted the strap of the bag slung across my back and remembered the book *Walden* was inside. I guess it gave me courage, because without knowing what I would say, my arm shot up in the air. The young man at the front looked at me expectantly, and everyone turned to stare at the New City girl with a question.

"I don't understand. When I was younger there was a 'Save the Animals' protest, and my father told me the animals were all safe and protected and ..." The crowd laughed.

The young man had a bemused look on his face. "Let me get this straight. *Your father* told you the animals were fine?" The audience cracked up.

I looked around for any compassion, and finding none, asked, "You mean they aren't?"

More giggling and whispering from the crowd. "We've lost hundreds of species and massive amounts of habitats. It's only getting worse. Maybe your *father* was talking about the *zoo* animals."

"There are other animals besides zoo animals?" I said under my breath and hoped no one heard. My throat tightened, and tears threatened to pour down my face. The crowd finished laughing and redirected themselves to the urgent issue at hand. I was grateful the attention was off of me, so I could feel sorry for myself. I was a naïve idiot. I didn't know anything. I didn't understand what was being protested and apparently believed everything I was told. I felt awful and totally mortified.

I quietly cried, letting waves of shame crash over me. Splash! They had the extra benefit of quickly washing away my embarrassment. I got angry, really angry. First, at these protesters, who didn't seem to care that at every protest people were being *disappeared*. *They* were making fun of me? I didn't even know the people who were arrested, and I was worried about them. These people didn't know how hard it was to stand here in a bleached white shirt. I had left my comfortable home, where *everything* was the newest and the best, to come here to be with these people who came from who knows where. They were making fun of me? How dare they?

My arm shot up again, as if it had a mind of its own. Uh oh. For the second time that day, all eyes turned to me. I stuttered for a brief second, and then said, "If the first 'Save the Animals' protest happened years ago, and animals are still disappearing, and habitats are gone, and…" My voice trailed off while I groped for eloquence. "Well, I don't see what the purpose of protest is. It's inconvenient for the inhabitants of New City sure, but other than that everyone just closes their doors. They ignore you. No one even cares if protestors are disappeared. Have you seen the new polls? We, I mean *they*, want all the protestors arrested. The numbers aren't small, and they're growing. It doesn't seem like protest changed their minds about anything except treating you more harshly. If it just pisses people off, isn't it futile?"

No one laughed this time. They murmured to each other and turned to the young man in charge. He pulled himself up to his full height and said, "Protest is required when resources are squandered," and changed the subject. Who could blame him? I doubted if anyone there knew how to answer my charges. However, I was beginning to know. Yes, I was beginning to see.

I turned to leave the meeting. I pushed my way to the back of the gathering as I heard someone ask whether they could petition the Congloms for a permit to protest. Permission to protest? How was that even logical?

I found myself in front of Anthony, the guard. Crap. Would he be pissed off? Would he think I'm an ungrateful guest and an insolent question asker? He whispered, "It's not futile if we reach one person, Estelle," and pointed right at me. He turned his attention to the front. The crowd moved to disperse, and I was swept along until I found myself free in the parking lot. Whoa, that was intense.

I was hot, flustered, breathing rapidly, and upset. I stood for a few minutes in the parking lot trying to figure out what to do next.

Then I experienced what some might call a moment of clarity. A fully refreshing, cool breeze blew past me and rustled my hair. I took a deep gulp and filled my lungs. I let the air slowly out and walked. I went across the endless empty parking lot, past my gleaming car, and out into the middle of the road. I paused and stared up at the hazy grey sky, then walked south toward New City, straight down the middle of the empty street. When I reached the crossroads of New Time Street and Best Boulevard, I stopped in the center and looked up at the sky.

Tonight's display was polka dot. The choreographed patterns were multicolored and constantly bounced along the top of the high-rise buildings. It was Friday. I wished desperately to see a star, or even the moon, but now it could only be seen a few times a year. I searched the heavens trying to make something visible, anything. It's not fair. It's not fair that it's all so bright that I can't see.

the enormity of it all

The things in my blue porcelain box had become more precious to me than ever. I took them out and handled them whenever I needed to ponder something, which was often. It helped me to imagine that I was the box, and inside were the things I needed help with. I would pretend the origami bird, the thimble, and the heather all had the power to fix the parts of me that were bothersome, that I struggled with, or that my Behavioral Counselor called my *issues*.

The silver thimble stood for crying. I was sick and tired of the tears, and yet they flowed right when I needed to seem strong and in control. They made me feel weak and out of control. I hated them and the subsequent snot, because they made for an embarrassing spectacle. So, now when I felt close to tears, I would say to myself, *Only enough to fill the thimble. Only that, and no more.* I hoped this would somehow manage to control them, but it didn't really work. I tried though, I did try.

The heather, I thought of as my future. Not the one that had been planned for me, but something else, something vague and unplanned. I didn't intend to deviate from the future that was laid out for me, but I did have a vague desire, someday, to see the place where wild heather grows. Okay, not to just see it, but to lay down in it. I imagined it must smell heavenly to recline in a field of growing flowers. This idea was unformed though, because I didn't even know where that field existed. It was a hazy dream, like my hazy sky.

The origami bird symbolized my questions. Such as, how in the world did someone fold a bird like this? And how long would it take to make a thousand, which is how many the article said would have been folded for a wedding? Just the origami bird alone raised a hundred questions right off the top of my head. So holding it was like holding every question, about everything in the world, right in my hand. I imagined that if I held them, then I controlled them. If I focused on the bird, I could maybe keep from blurting questions out in class, or at the dinner table, and maybe if I could control the questions, maybe I could get to the answers on my own.

On this night, as I sat in the road with my face to the sky, I didn't have my blue porcelain box of precious things. Still, my intricate knowledge of them helped me as I formulated an idea. I imagined holding the origami bird. I slowly pulled the folds apart, noting where the creases were and which direction the folds went. Keeping track of all of it in my mind, I pulled the paper apart until it lay flat. That was my idea, my big plan, a flat piece of fancy, overly creased, possibly ruined paper. I took that pretend origami of an idea and asked questions of it from every direction, and I folded it again. At one point, my imagination forgot how to fold one corner, and the paper threatened to become one giant mess of an idea. For a long moment, it seemed almost impossible to continue, because it was so unwieldy, confusing, and terrifying. I had to remind myself that I hadn't ruined the bird. Calm down, if my plan is terrifying, maybe it's not a good plan. Maybe it's best it's ruined here, in a heap of crinkled imaginary paper. I didn't want to give up on it though, so I asked more questions and figured out more answers, until I folded it expertly back. Checking it's creases, it's logic, it's soundness, until I had that piece of paper exactly back as a beautiful delicate origami bird. I had an idea. A *big* idea, and it was formed and faultless.

I took that idea and held it up to the light. Metaphorically of course, though by this time the hazy glow of a sunrise washed over the world. I had forgotten to sleep. I had also forgotten to go home. That light washed over my idea and made the golden accents of the bird's paper, and my deliberation, shine. There was absolutely, positively, no downside to my idea, except, of course, the possibility of arrest and disappearance. However, on this new morning, when I had a Big Idea, those misgivings seemed inconsequential. Totally unimaginable even. In the morning light, I felt like every possibility was hopeful and wonderful. Now that the plan was a fully formed Big Idea, it just seemed so workable. I reiterated to myself it was a no-lose proposition.

I shook my head to wake myself. I was sitting right in the middle of the street, and the light glowed even brighter. That was all the light I could bear. I stopped considering and walked up Best Boulevard toward home.

When I walked in, every light was on, but there was an eery, expectant silence. I put down my bag and started up to my room, only to be greeted by Frederick on the stairs.

"Hello," he said, "are you okay?"

"Yeah," I said, and we were quiet as we paused there, him half down the stairs, me half up. "Frederick..." I started.

He interrupted to say, "Why don't you go and get cleaned up for school, and we'll talk over breakfast."

"Okay," I walked past him up the stairs. I showered and felt revived, although I hadn't slept. Renewed and excited, I looked forward to the day, even though I knew I was about to have a difficult conversation with Frederick.

When I sat down at the table Frederick had my book *Walden* in front of him. "Where did you get this?"

"From the Old Time Museum, I took it from the library." He peered at me for a long, long time.

"You know, I never read the book, just the one quote from school. Perhaps you might be interested in knowing your grandfather was named after Henry David Thoreau." I started with surprise. "So this author must have been well thought of in our family at one time." His voice trailed off. I didn't know what to say. "Estelle, is this about the protests?"

"Yes," I said, "and no. I can't really explain it." I looked down at the table. "I'm just confused about what I want to do."

"What you want to do?" His voice was quiet, but then he repeated it louder. "What *you* want to do." He repeated it a third time. "What you want to *do?*" It was loud enough for everyone else to hear. Luckily, Terran and Sylvia came into the room, and Frederick recovered his manners. "So you don't want to be a scientist? Maybe I was wrong about that. Perhaps you could work directly for the Congloms or in the Governmental Oversee."

"Frederick, I just don't know if I want to be *anything*. I think I just want to *be*." Silence ensued, I swallowed and could have sworn it echoed.

Sylvia said, "You're probably very tired, but Estelle, there's something we need to talk about. I didn't want to bring this up now, when you're obviously going through something, but this was sent yesterday."

On the table she placed a letter that read:

Dear Estelle Wells,

It is incumbent upon us to inform you that Jack Maranville has filed a Stay of Betrothal, Form 8 and asked for a hearing to be scheduled for Dissolution of Betrothal Contract, according to these complaints:

Anticipatory Complications, form 317-b

The hearing has been scheduled for next Tuesday. Please bring all pertinent background information and be ready to discuss the case at 11:00 am, room 11, Corporate Hall of Partnership Agreements.

If dissolution is granted, a new betrothal will be arranged within one week through the Office of Future Affairs and Behaviors in your school district. Your Doctor will be given a copy of this correspondence and forms, so that medicine can be adjusted accordingly.

On behalf of the entire Office of Future Affairs and Behaviors and the Ministry of Medicines, we would like to express our condolences at the possible dissolution of your future relationship. Please be prepared for the upcoming hearing.

Sincerely,
Samuel Flanks, Office of Betrothal Dissolution

Crap, just sixteen and in a messy divorce. What the hell? Jack never even spoke to me, just decided I wasn't good enough for him? What did he think was wrong with me? Wait, what was wrong with me? I had never even heard of anyone else having their marriage contract dissolved, had I?

Sylvia broke into my reverie. "What's this about, Estelle? Do you know why Jack would do this?"

Frederick looked stern. "What's going on with you, Estelle? Jack is from a good family. He's a *Maranville*. They're an important family in marketing and public relations. I looked at his records; he's going to *be* someone in his family business. He would have made a great husband. How did you blow this?"

"I don't know. I never even spoke to him." I bit my lip to hold back the tears.

"Never spoke to him?" Frederick and Sylvia spoke in unison, which frankly freaked me out.

Sylvia leaned onto the table and looked me in the eye. "This is a very serious situation, Estelle. At this hearing, things could come out about all of your questions and your endless crying. This could go down on your personal record. If Jack dissolves your engagement, with *cause,* another husband might not even be possible. In which case, you would be considered an 'unsuitable match' and left *unassigned.* Do you have the ability to grasp what being unassigned means? It means your work choices will be severely limited. You won't have children. Your homes, your things, none of it will be..." Her voice trailed off. She was dismayed and exasperated. Sylvia was having trouble describing the enormity of it all, but I got the enormity, I did indeed. I just couldn't imagine what could be done about it.

Frederick turned to Terran and said, "You've been through the betrothal process. Your future-wife, Janice, is working out well. Do you have any words of wisdom for Estelle?"

Terran looked like he didn't want to get involved in the conversation. He looked at the table, the chair, anywhere instead of directly at me. "I don't know. You have a long time from when your match is selected to when you have to get married. You don't have to worry about it too much, but at least talk to them occasionally."

Sylvia looked incredulous. "You're supposed to talk, to get to know each other, to make plans. What am I going to do with both of you?"

We all sat for a minute mulling it over. Frederick said, "Today at school I want you to speak to Jack. You need to ask him to withdraw his forms and give you both more time to get to know each other. At the very least, you need to ask that he let you apply for dissolution as well, so there won't need to be an airing of grievances. If the dissolution is mutual, he won't need to state a cause. Would you be okay with that, Estelle? Did you want to marry him?"

I looked at Frederick surprised. Was he seriously asking me if I was okay breaking off a marriage contract with a boy I never even spoke to? Like it was a delicate subject?

"No, Frederick, I'd be okay with breaking it off with Jack. I'll talk to him about it today at school."

Frederick changed the subject. "Your seventeenth birthday is coming up. What kind of party would you like? What presents? If we plan, we can make it much better than last year's. We've got some new things at the Institute you'd probably like to have..."

I interrupted and turned to Sylvia. "I know what I want for my birthday."

"Anything, Estelle, you'll be seventeen, such a grown up. It's special."

"I want you to sign over the leases on our old houses and buildings." Frederick's breakfast bar hit the table.

"What?" They both asked at once. Speaking in unison was a new thing for them, and here they'd done it twice in one conversation.

"Well, we have the four big rambling houses in Old Town that aren't used any more. I want my name on the leases. I want them."

"What do you want with old houses? They're useless. They're no good. When you turn twenty, you'll get a new house in the latest style, with all the best innovations. I can't, for the life of me, understand where your head is these days," said Sylvia, curtly folding the package her breakfast bar came in.

"I just want them. You said I could have anything, and

that's what I want. They're just empty. Put my name on the leases. That's what I want."

They looked at each other, and Sylvia said, "Well... I guess it won't hurt anything for you to own them. For the life of me, I can't figure out what you would do with them...I don't know. I'll have to think this over." Then she asked, "You don't plan to live in them do you? Because they aren't new, they aren't improv..."

"Sylvia, I *promise* I wouldn't live in them, okay? I promise." We gathered our things for the day.

"Well, I still have to think about it."

"Okay."

As we walked out the door, Frederick asked, "Where's your car? Don't you like it? You'll have a new one for your birthday of course. You're going to love the new model we're working on."

"I parked it. Don't worry. I'll get Terran to give me a ride to it after school. Okay, Terran?"

"Yeah," he said looking at me inquisitively. He had to be curious about what was going on with me, but he wouldn't have long to wait. I planned to ask if he would help when he picked me up after school. I wanted to protect him from the dangerous parts of my Big Plan, but he was integral. Without him, it would never work.

We separated for our day.

something else

"Hi, Jack." Shocked, his head jerked around. I had come up from behind because he was definitely trying to avoid me.

"Um, hello?"

"I'm Estelle Wells, you know, your future..." It seemed weird to say it aloud, so I couldn't finish. I hoped he would help me through this awkward conversation. I dropped down beside him on the bench.

"I know who you are." His voice dripped with condescension. Nope, no help at all.

"I thought maybe we should meet before the hearing, have a conversation or two. We need to make sure we aren't making a mistake by breaking it off."

"I'm sure I'm not making a mistake. You're clearly not my style."

What style would that be, total jerk? Man I was so glad I wasn't marrying this guy. How had the system put us together in the first place? I knew I needed to stay cool though; I needed him to do me the favor of letting it be mutual.

"So what are you looking for in a partner? If not my *style?*"

"I want someone to help me advance, to get ahead in business, to go *along*. Not someone who has to be difficult all the time."

Difficult, me? Because I asked questions? And cried and had issues, and never even said hello before today? Okay, now that I thought about it 'difficult' might be a good word to describe me.

"Why do you have to ask so many questions all the time, anyway? It's not how you're supposed to act. Can't you see that? Don't you know everyone is staring, noticing you?"

"I guess I can't help it. I want to know why things are the way things are. Don't you ever wonder what stars look like, or where the protesters come from, or why we don't get to read full books? I look around and everyone seems kind of blah, like no one cares about anything, you know?" I looked at him to see if he did know, but he just stared straight ahead. "Don't you ever wonder what it must feel like to fall in love, Jack? I've been reading about what life was like generations ago, and boys and girls fell in love with each other. They had exciting, wondrous, sometimes painful love affairs. I wish I felt anything half as deeply as the characters in the stories I've read. Why don't we feel?"

Jack looked at me, as if mulling this all over. I knew he didn't have an answer though. How could he? Looking away, he said, "Maybe you need your medicine adjusted." The malice was gone though. He was more relaxed, maybe even thoughtful now.

I decided to plow on undeterred, though my voice was shaky. Would he react compassionately to tears? I doubted it. "I'm interested in someone very different too. I'd like a partner who questions things, and is, um, understanding of me."

"Good luck with that."

"Yeah, my dream guy might be hard to find, especially when the Office of Future Affairs did such a poor job putting us together." He cut his eyes at me. The thought hadn't occurred to him yet. What if his next match was just as disagreeable?

"I'm thinking we could file a joint dissolution, and tell them *together* that they screwed up by matching us. We should tell them the *match* didn't work. Then there's no blame." He looked at me again, full on this time, with an eyebrow raised, incredulously.

"Why in the world would I let you say you want to dissolve the relationship with *me*?" His color heightened. "I can easily prove you aren't acceptable, just by showing them your school records and your medical records. I can bring in a couple of witnesses. It'd be easy. I don't want *my* name dragged through the mud."

"Yeah, but you're doing it to me! What if after you make your case, they find me unmatchable?"

"What do I care?"

"Well, here's the thing, the Office of Future Affairs is never wrong, right? Everyone knows that. So if you and I are matched together, and you make me sound difficult during the hearing, don't you think it will follow you? Won't people wonder if you're difficult too, in some way because you were matched with me? What if you prove I'm not marriageable, but they don't let you change your answers on the questionnaire? You might end up with someone just like me, *again*. How would that look?"

"I truly doubt I would end up with someone like you again. That's not possible."

"Wait, why not?"

"Because think about it, Estelle, have you ever seen anyone else get kicked out of class for asking so many useless questions?"

For a second I could feel the blood rush to my face. I was

about to tell him he was a total ass—but I clamped my mouth shut, took a deep breath, and glanced at him just in time to see the corner of his mouth twitch a little, the beginning of a smile.

"I guess I have been kicked out of class a lot, haven't I? The most of anyone, really? Cause I wouldn't know; I'm in the office so much."

"Maybe William Loftin has you beat, but he's a boy, so its safe to say you're notorious for your gender. Also, it's safe to say they wouldn't match me with William." Now Jack had a full-blown smile across his face. We looked at each other long. Could this be my first friend, the boy I'm breaking up with?

He asked, "What do you propose?"

"If we both file form 894, Misplaced Betrothal, and ask for a dissolution together. If we tell them *together* the match didn't work, I think they'll grant us a dissolution. They won't even need a hearing. The best part is, I think they'll let us redo the questionnaires. If anyone asks about it, we can say the matching didn't work, there was a glitch or something. So we're both in the clear. Trouble is you'd have to figure out what you answered wrong on the questionnaire that got you matched with me and answer it *right* this time."

He laughed and jostled my arm. "This time, I'm answering everything the opposite, just to be safe."

"Me too." I jostled him back and we were laughing, and yes, it was almost how I imagined friends would be.

"All right, definitely. I can go to the office today after school. Meet me there, and we'll file them together?"

"Yes, that seems like a classy way to end our relationship," I said.

"Okay then," he paused for a moment. "How do you know all of this Estelle? How'd you figure it all out?"

"Maybe you haven't heard, but I ask too many questions." I smiled.

He returned my smile, picked up his things, and walked to class. Maybe the Office of Future Affairs wasn't wrong about us after all. We might have made an okay match if our end goals weren't so different. Hopefully, Jack's next match would be a good one, everything he wanted: success, goals, a bright, comfortable future, but not me. Definitely not me. If I answered the questionnaire again, I didn't plan to wait for the results. What I planned was something else entirely.

that deep spark

After school, I met Jack at the Office of Future Affairs. He greeted me warmly, and we leaned over the counter together and asked the receptionist for the forms we needed to dissolve our betrothal. She handed them to us with a quizzical look on her face, and then I spent the next few minutes trying to figure out how to fill them out without a pen. I checked the same pockets twice. Jack watched me silently, a smile spreading across his face. He slowly took two pens out of his pocket and put them in front of me, giving me a choice. Here's something I now know about my almost future-husband, he has a ready smile and carries two pens. I carry zero. We completed the forms, glancing at each other's to make sure they were filled out fully, signed them and turned them in together.

As we left, on the steps outside, Jack said, "So, here we go again. I come in next week to fill out my questionnaire, and hopefully I'll be matched with someone a little less interesting. I hope she's as beautiful as you, though." Jack said I was beautiful. Why were we breaking up again? He turned to walk away. "I'll see you at school tomorrow." He headed to his car, as I watched him go.

I walked over to meet Terran at his car. "Was that Jack?" he asked.

"Yep, the husband that never was. We just dissolved our betrothal together. It's done, and maybe we're even friends, I think."

"You, with a friend? I guess there's always a first time."

"What, you have friends?" I half-teased, kind of wondering if he might.

"Yeah, I have friends." He stated it simply and quickly switched the subject. "Where's your car?" I told him it was at the old stadium, and he looked at me quizzically. As we headed there, I filled him in on what had happened the night before.

"Wow!" he said, to which I agreed. Yes, *wow*. I asked him if he could get access to one of the big bulldozers, or a back hoe, or maybe both, from the Old Product piles. "Yeah," he said, "I've done some work there for credit. I have keys."

"Could you get one for a few days?" I asked.

"Yeah, Estelle, probably." He looked at me over his driving arm. "What are you planning?"

"You know the leases I asked for? I'm going to demolish all those houses and build a farm."

"A farm? Like with crops and animals?" Terran looked confused.

"Yeah, a farm. I'm going to demolish the houses, break up all the cement and plastic on the ground, dig up the dirt, plant some seeds, and grow some food. You know, a *farm*."

"But...but..." He looked at me and raised an eyebrow. He was quiet for a moment thinking, and then he jerked his head back to size me up, as if he just met me right there in the car. "This is not at *all* what I *ever* would have dreamed you'd say. A farm? A *farm*? But then again," He talked to himself. "Dirt, huh? I could get involved if there's dirt. I guess, yes, definitely if there's dirt."

"Yeah, there should be dirt, lots of dirt. I don't have any

specifics yet, but that much I know. I also know I can't do it by myself. There is a problem, though, a big one. There's a very real possibility we could get in big trouble. Really big trouble. We'll risk arrest, and we might even get disappeared. I've been asking around about what disappeared means, and no one really even knows. So this is a big deal. It's huge what I'm asking you to do with me. You'll be giving up your clean clothes, your comfortable bed, and maybe ultimately *everything*. I really shouldn't even ask you to, but I don't have anyone else. So Terran, are you in?"

Terran stared off into space for a second and said, "Yeah, I'm in. What else am I going to do with my life? I definitely don't want to do what everyone has planned for me so far." He grinned. "You know you don't just need a bulldozer, you need the Scorpion."

"What's a scorpion?"

"Not a scorpion, *the Scorpion*, and it's the most awesome machine. It will do everything you need it to do."

"Can you get one of those?"

His eyes went far away dreamy. "Yeah, I can get the Scorpion. It'll be fun to drive it again."

I laughed at his facial expression. "You sound like you're in love with it!"

He laughed back, and we sat and talked. We were parked in the huge empty parking lot in front of the old abandoned stadium, staring out through the front windows of the car as I told him everything about my plan. We discussed the details, and he added creative thoughts and ideas from his own life experiences. Terran was undaunted by my worry we would be arrested, and he thought the best plan would be to carry on as if we believed we wouldn't be.

"Wishful thinking," I called it.

"Confidence," he assured me.

Terran's way of thinking through an idea didn't involve origami birds, his was more like digging. He went through the layers of a question and came to an idea from down deep, long buried, finally revealed. It was fascinating listening to him think it all through, and I knew then we would make a great team.

He was excited about being active again, wanted to work with his body, to move, and run, because New City, sadly, didn't have many opportunities for exercise. Last year, when he had been employed down at the Piles, he had used the heavy machinery and labored until he was exhausted. That was last year though; this year he was on his career track and working his mind. My plan might not succeed, but it included hard physical labor, so he was all in.

"Estelle, remember the present Frederick gave me for my birthday, that game? The one where I put on the suit, and it felt like I was floating in outer space?"

"Yeah, when he gave it to you, he turned to me and said, 'Estelle, you'd love this game it has *stars!*'"

"He was wrong. You would have hated it. Totally."

"I know. He completely missed the point that I want to sit and look up at the stars, not careen around inside them."

"I only played it once. It made me dizzy and gave me a headache for hours. I felt terrible, but I feel that way a lot; like my brain is murky, and I'm half asleep. I feel slightly confused almost all the time. Do you feel like that?"

"Yeah, I feel like, I don't know the right word, maybe suppressed. Maybe the right word is *even*. I feel really blah. Unless I'm doing something I'm not supposed to do, then I feel better."

"Oh, *that's* why you're such a troublemaker." He laughed outright, then added, "I used to think it was normal, but when

I worked last year, really labored, I had moments where I was clear-headed. It seemed like the more I sweated, the better my brain worked. I definitely like that better. I wonder if a farm will fix my brain?"

"Who knows? Maybe our brains are past fixing. Jack seemed to think so." I chuckled, remembering the look on Jack's face when he said I was clearly not his *style*. "My brain might be broken, maybe I can't change that, but I can change my circumstances. I can change what I wake up and do tomorrow. Maybe that's enough."

Terran nodded. "Yeah, maybe that will be enough." By the time we were done with the plan, The Big Idea wasn't only mine, it was ours.

"We're ready, huh?" I asked.

"Sure. You know, this plan means giving up your things? You love your car, and your toys, and you really love your clothes. You adore Jonathan, your designer. How can you give any of that up? Much less all of it?"

"I don't know, maybe I can't. It's scary to think about walking away from it all. Last night, I kept imagining a closet in the corner of the farm with all my things inside, and my car parked out front. I would have to remind myself that I was giving all those things up. Maybe we can build me a big closet? And do you think Jonathan will design farmer clothes?" We both laughed.

"I am kind of mad at him because of these stupid high heels." I held up a foot and waved it around. "How are you supposed to walk in these? They're ridiculous!"

"So what you're saying is the shoes were the final straw? You didn't want to wear high heels, so you decided to break the law and become a farmer instead?"

"Yep. It sounds ridiculous when you say it out loud

though." I added, "It'll be hard to give things up, but maybe they'll be replaced with new things I like. I just don't know what they'll be, yet."

"I know. You're going to fall in love with the Scorpion," he teased.

"What about you? Can you give up all your things?"

"I think so. I'm willing to try. Hey, let's go over and look at the lots. I'd like to see what we're talking about."

We drove over to the old houses our parents had owned, and their parents before them. We sat quietly before the vastness of the prospect and took it all in.

The houses were all lined up in a stately row and filled an entire city block. Over the years, improvements had been made to the first house; it was the most different in size and shape. It rambled and spread out over the pavement-covered lot. After that, our forebears decided to move to new houses instead of renovating the old. They leased those old houses to people that couldn't afford the newest improvements, and they built and moved into a new, bigger, more improved house. The next three houses varied from each other in smaller ways, as improvements were designed faster. Just before Terran and I were born, everyone decided the whole city should be given up and the New City built.

Just like here in Old Town, the workers laid foundations and then the brightly colored plastic and cement pavement. It was a sprawling layer that covered every square inch of land. The goal was absolute cleanliness while everyone worked and eventually lived there. Then the construction crews built all new houses and buildings for everyone and everything.

Frederick and Sylvia were newly married when construction started, so they lived together for a few years in

Old Town, while the New City was built. Sylvia remembered those years as full of privations and want, even though their house was one of the largest and had every improvement available. Frederick teased her that he was inventing as fast as he could. She teased him back that he didn't invent fast enough.

When New City was completed, I was very young. A holiday was declared while everyone in the city moved from one place to the other. It wasn't a long or arduous process; Frederick and Sylvia just gathered us up, put us into the car, drove over to the new house, and moved in. We only brought the clothes on our backs and a few things we didn't want to immediately replace. Of course, later I found out that Sylvia had bundled up my blue porcelain box of precious things, and apparently Frederick had brought his grandmother's book of the stars. I find it difficult to imagine what made them move those things from one house to another. Could it have been nostalgia? What else could explain it?

Everything else my family needed, or could imagine, had been created new and was installed. The Congloms and the Institute had been in development overdrive, and the city flourished with jobs. The whole decade was a renaissance of shopping, planning, and inventing.

That was fifteen years ago. Now the Congloms and the Institute were developing new building ideas for the next move. In fifteen years, there would be a finished new New City, just to the east of this one. We planned to completely desert an entire city again, in our quest for newer and better. I shook my head as if wiping the thought away. Maybe what the citizens of New City needed was a different way to live, instead of a new and improved *same old way*. Is it possible to convince an entire culture that different can be better? Probably not. It worked in the past, in other times, with different cultures, but change couldn't possibly happen here. Our way of life was too entrenched. I couldn't imagine this culture being any other way, and I was *disgruntled*. It was difficult enough for *me* to look at these old houses with possibility after a lifetime of looking at new as better, and *I* was the one with the Big Plan. The only thing I could do is change myself. That was all I could hope for.

Here was a problem, though. How could I change me, if I wasn't sure who I was? Were my thoughts and emotions truly mine? Did I ever feel really good, or terribly bad? I cried sometimes, but my Behavioral Counselor and my Doctor called it one of my *issues*. They wanted me to get it under control, but how could I control what threatened to overcome me? Being overcome is *exactly* a lack of control.

I had never seen anyone in deep love, laughing uproariously, crying in desperation, screaming in hysterics. I read about these things, but I had never witnessed them, never cowered in the corner from the sheer magnitude of it. My father almost yelled once, but had controlled himself quickly, surprisingly quickly, considering I marched in a protest. Why wasn't he angry? Why wasn't anyone ever angry? Why wasn't I angry now, wondering about all of this? Then again, there was that furor at school, when William yelled, and the teachers dragged him down the hall. William's anger was an anomaly though, the only outburst I'd ever seen. Terran had just told me that he lived in a fog and was never fully *aware*. It was the medication that altered us, I was sure of it now.

Whenever I cried, it was because I had questions. Whenever I questioned our culture, and cried, there was a corresponding adjustment of my medication. It was so clear the medicines were directly related to my emotions and my behavior, that I couldn't even believe it had taken this long to figure out. It was obvious they were changing me, the me that should truly be mine.

Was that deep spark, the one that gave me volition and ideas, a smaller flame than it might have been? Would it have been a full-blown raging fire had I lived in a different time? If I'd been born to another woman, in a different place, would I be joyfully frolicking in a life of my own making? Perhaps reclined in a field of heather staring up at the stars?

I had questioned the medicines before. I had asked my mother and my Doctor which pill was for which ailment, but it's a revelation that they aren't *for* ailments. Those pills were there to make me different. It was like emerging from a fog to realize I wore swim-goggles, and that's why I was seeing so funny. Maybe it was time to take these goggles off. It was a terrifying thought though; if I stopped taking my medications, what would I see?

We sat for some time, both of us caught up in our own thoughts, until Terran broke the silence. "We have *too* much work to do."

"That's an understatement."

"Oh why wasn't I born with superpowers?" he said, and we sat for another hour creating a list of what we would need, and when.

The next day was my birthday. As a gift, Sylvia gave me the leases which gave me ownership of our old houses and the land they sat on. She said in a grandiose way, "I'm not sure what she plans to do with them, but I'm sure it will be something that will move her career goals forward. She's been stuck in a bit of a rut." She continued like I wasn't even in the room, "It's high time she moves away from the negative space she's in and sets her sights on being successful! Tomorrow, she gets her new betrothal assignment, and everything is moving forward as it should be."

She didn't realize how right she was. I did plan to move out of this negative space, and move forward. I figured though that our versions of forward were very different from each other.

Frederick showed me my room was now newly decorated in a beautiful deep azure blue. My window seat was still there; the pillows were now long cylindrical shapes. I fingered the pale blue piping on the pillows and ran my fingers along the window sill.

"This is really beautiful. I think it might be my favorite color, ever." I felt melancholy, like I was saying farewell.

"Beautiful like you," said Sylvia, "and the color matches your eyes. If you're going to sit there all the time, you might as well look good." She attempted to be humorous, but I didn't feel like laughing. I wouldn't be sitting here all the time, not once I began my big plan. It felt hypocritical, almost treasonous to enjoy the gifts when I knew I wouldn't be living with them much longer.

"Thank you Sylvia and Frederick. It's all really, really beautiful. Jonathan got it perfectly right." I felt tears waiting right behind my eyes.

Sylvia said, "That's why we pay him so much. He's the best designer around."

"Yeah, but thank you, for the leases, and everything."

Frederick said, "It goes without saying, Estelle. You know only the newest and best will do."

I nodded. "Thank you," I said again.

Frederick and Sylvia turned from the room and left Terran standing there. I threw myself back onto the pillows in the window seat with my arm over my eyes.

Terran asked, "Mind if I hang out for a bit?"

I peeled my arm up. I had almost forgotten he was there. "Sure. Maybe you can help me get out of this mood. Seeing this window seat all newly decorated...It hit me that I'm planning to leave all of this behind."

"To leave Sylvia and Frederick behind," he corrected. I nodded. "Changed your mind?" he asked.

"No."

"Good, me neither. What are you reading? Want me to read to you for a little bit?"

"Yeah, that would be great." I went to the back of my closet and brought out a book. "I'm on chapter three." I curled up at one end of the window seat, while he sat at the other. Terran began to read.

to somehow ease

Later that night, Sylvia brought in the little tray with my fourteen pills on it. When did the number swell to fourteen? How did I not notice? I said, "Thank you." I probably said it too brightly, because I eager for her to walk away. I told her I'd bring the tray back down in a minute when I was through taking them. I repeated that I would take them in a second when I was done with what I was doing. Why couldn't I stop talking nervously?

Once she left, I dumped the pills in the trash chute. I tossed some tissue down after it, betting it would cover the pills in case anyone looked. Of course nobody would look because no one would ever think of going off their meds. Definitely not without a doctors supervision. What was I, crazy?

8:00 pm - felt fine, just getting tired.
9:30 - laid down, stared at the ceiling.
10:15 - still staring.
11:30 - anxious. Was I doing the right thing?
11:45 - okay, this was ridiculous. I was tired, but couldn't sleep. I got up and brought my box of favorite things to bed. I stared at them instead of the ceiling. At least that was a bit less panic

inducing.

2:00 am - wondered if I could slide down the trash chute and figure out which pill was the sleep pill. Apparently, the pill that induced sleep was highly important.

3:20 - tried to figure out if there truly were voices coming from outside on the street. Every time I looked out the window, there was nothing there.

7:15 - awoke for school. That was good news. It meant I did sleep at some point.

I laid there for a moment and took stock:

- Eyes were stinging
- Arms felt really, really, really long, and heavy
- Heart was racing
- Mouth felt like I was chewing velvet, really disgusting smelling velvet
- The smell in my mouth kind of made me want to throw up
- Add nausea to the list.

There was only one thing to do, and that was get ready for school. I took a good long look at myself in the mirror. My hair was damp from a sweaty sleep. I programmed the style-a-matic for a dramatic up-do, but couldn't sit there long enough for the style to be completed. I just sprayed everything that had been done so far and hoped it was good enough. It wasn't, not by a long shot. My hands were shaking and I was seriously nauseated. I needed to sit down. Whose bright idea was this anyway?

I programmed the Make-up Printer to airbrush my face with a color that would make me look less green. Maybe Outrageous Orange or Prettily Pink? I decided on the orange, to ill-effect. Come to find out, orange completely clashed with sickly pale. You'd think with all the classes I took on color choices, that I'd be able to come up with the perfect accent for pallid, but I seriously lacked the skills I needed. I removed the orange and decided on azure blue, since it was trendy right now. At least it had that going for it. The machine added filigrees all around my hairline that I hoped would take the focus off my face, my sad sickly face. I took stock in the mirror. The dark circles around my eyes weren't accentuated, too much.

I went into the bedroom and laid down until Sylvia softly knocked on the door. She entered with the tray of my morning medicines. I jumped up to put on an outfit for the day. I picked a stylish bodice with a short train I hoped wouldn't attract any extra attention. I tried not to meet Sylvia's eyes, but she was intently looking at me. "Sleep okay, Estelle?"

"Yeah."

"Thinking about your Betrothal Contract appointment today? It'll be okay. This time you'll just make a point of *speaking* to your future-husband." She dropped the tray of medicine down on my bedside stand, squeezed my shoulder affectionately, albeit awkwardly, and left.

Oh man, was that pile of beautiful pills tempting. At the moment I felt really horrible, maybe-I-wont-survive-the-day horrible. I grabbed the tray and slid the pills into the trash chute before I had a minute to reconsider. I looked like crap, but I was headed to school.

The first few hours passed slowly. I was in turns sweating profusely, then chilled through. I was slowed down, then my heart raced. Every system in my body seemed to be going haywire, and all I could do was grip the edge of my desk and hold on. Why didn't I just skip school? I didn't want anyone to be worried about me, or suspicious, definitely not before some crucial parts of The Big Idea were in place. I knew that was *why* I came to school, but even so, coming was a huge mistake. Now I had to get through my new Betrothal Contract meeting, and this agony, before anyone asked questions. I definitely didn't need any trouble. Terran and I had too much to do.

There was a big problem though, a Giant Whooshing Sound in my ears. That. Wouldn't. Stop. Whooshing. How could I act normal with a wind-tunnel inside my brain? Couldn't everyone around me hear it, too? I tucked my head down and tried to stay out of everyone's way.

After lunch, which was practically inedible because I was so nauseous, Jack passed me a note:

Are you feeling okay, Estelle? Good luck finding your future-husband this afternoon! -Jack

Oh, Jack was the kind of guy that asked how you were doing and wished you luck. He was almost my husband and now...oh no, tears threatened to pour down my face. I held on and bit my lip. I tried to think of The Big Plan until the tears subsided, but I could tell they were waiting right behind my eyes.

I managed to make it through the rest of the day and then half-stumbled into the Office of Future Affairs. Stupid heels. I was sent through to the Inquiry Room where I dropped into the chair closest to the door. The frigid air was cold on my feverish skin and I shivered. The screen said, "Hello, Estelle. Welcome back." Shut up, stupid box. The marriage questionnaire appeared for the second time in my short life.

"How important is dependability in your future

relationship?" it asked. I thought about how Jack carried two pens and sent me notes asking how I was doing. A tear splashed down on my arm. I struggled to keep from flat-out wailing.

The questions were completely irritating. How do I know whether I'd rather have someone who is considerate, or introspective? Aren't they almost the same thing? And why would I know, when I've never been married before? I answered them as quickly as possible, not caring about anything but getting out of this cold room. The screen said, "Thank you, Estelle. Your Behavioral Counselor will have your results in just a few minutes."

I lurched into the waiting room and fell into my favorite chair. Why did I pick a bodice dress this morning? I had hoped it would give me a modicum of control around my middle, but instead it threatened to suffocate me. I struggled for a second, trying to get a buckle loose and more air into my lungs. I leaned back and took a deep breath and felt a little better. Maybe I could just sleep here. I opened an eye to see people glancing nervously at me and turning away, embarrassed.

With a slam, the boy named William walked in. "Me again," he announced. The receptionist looked irritated. He smiled broadly, fully at ease with how uncomfortable he made her. He turned to take in the scope of the room and noticed me in my corner chair.

He had a completely different course-list in school, so I had never seen him up close before. Except, of course, for the day he barreled furiously through the school halls, looking unkempt and half-wild. Today, on closer inspection, he looked handsome and competent. He sauntered toward me with an air of cocky confidence. His eyes, though, were kind, and when they met mine, seemed momentarily concerned.

Sidling over, he sat down just inches away, leaned back in his chair, completely at ease, and asked, "What are you in for, Comrade?"

I attempted to smile in spite of the whooshing and the head-splitting ache that had developed in my temples, an ache probably caused from answering that inane questionnaire. I feebly smiled. "Betrothal Appointment."

"Yep, I've been through that process. My formerly betrothed is a fine upstanding citizen of these parts. She's beautiful and quiet and applied for a dissolution right away, like a smart girl, and so I'm languishing in my 'unassigned' status. I'm *unmatchable* apparently." Speaking louder for the receptionists and really everyone in the office to hear, he said, "The good news is, I'm still available ladies!" He glanced around the room and smirked at me conspiratorially.

His hair was long and dark and loose, like he had run his fingers through it and decided that was good enough. He had a wide smile, but when he wasn't smiling, had an intensity to his eyes and a way of looking down his nose that I guessed some might think was arrogance and self-importance. Maybe his withering look was why he got away with being so much trouble to everyone.

I closed my eyes in an attempt to keep the room from spinning around me. I felt untethered, like I might float above the chairs, and frankly, I didn't think I would like the view. What would I see, a handsome boy sitting beside a profusely sweating, shaking, nauseous girl?

He looked strong, so for a brief moment I thought about asking if he could please lift my hands up off the floor. They were entirely too heavy for normal hands. Whoosh! I needed to concentrate to keep from spinning out of the room. On question 10, should I have answered confident or assured, or wait, maybe I remembered it wrong, and what did it matter anyway? The quiz was done, my future-husband picked.

I glanced sideways at William. He looked intently at me while leaned back, relaxed and completely sure of himself. My heart fluttered faster. I had never seen anyone act like this boy, like he was from a different planet. I would have found him fascinating if he wasn't attracting so much attention my way. People were looking at me, and I was barely holding it together.

"Who are you, by the way?" he asked in a quieter tone. His voice filled my head and sent a vibration through my whole body.

"Why do you keep asking so many questions?" I closed my eyes as another wave of nausea washed over me. I opened one eye. He was still looking, so I said, "Estelle Wells."

"Oh, right, the notorious Estelle Wells, finally we meet." He held out his hand to shake. "I didn't recognize you in your current state." He waved in a gesture that let me know he saw exactly what I hoped no one could see, that I was clearly having a difficult day. My guess was that my current skin color was a bright, perhaps, neon green, and the blue filigrees were not helping at all, *decoratively*.

I limply gave him my own hand to shake. "Yep, that's me," and then when I pulled back, a new feeling rushed through my body. In waves, it came from my feet and threatened to bring the soles of my shoes up and through and out. Death by high-heels! Before I could figure out what could be happening, my entire body convulsed, lifting me almost out of my chair. Everything I had choked down for lunch came back up the opposite direction, and I threw up all over the floor, right between, on, and around my shoes. Some chunks even came up and out of my nose.

"Oops," I moaned, in what might have been the world's biggest understatement, because even in my delicate condition, it was clear my vomit was all over his shoes. His formerly shiny shoes. I held my head down between my knees, wishing I could just fall through the floor where my puddle lay.

Through the whooshing sound, I could hear the staff of the Office mount the emergency signal. They came around the desk and called for the cleaning staff. The receptionist clucked disapprovingly. "You'll just have to miss your meeting with your Behavioral Counselor, Estelle. We can send you the decision at your home, I suppose. Why don't you head directly over to the medical offices?"

While everyone fussed and fidgeted over me and my mess, William leaned in and whispered, "Don't let them take you to the medical offices. Tell them your ride's outside and will take you. Go out as quickly as you can. I'm calling Terran and telling him to come for you." How did he know Terran? I numbly nodded, understanding enough to stumble outside. I declined all offers of rides and doctors and cleaning. I somehow made it out into the parking lot and thankfully, fresh air.

Minutes later, Terran's car spun around the corner and pulled up in front. He rolled down the window and said, "Sis, you look like hell."

"How do you know William?" I sank into the passenger seat.

"We're friends."

"Oh, well, I just threw up on your friend." I moaned as I leaned back on the seat and tried to close my eyes to somehow ease all the pain. Trouble was, the tears were coming, and there was no way to stop them now. I slid into despair, tears pouring out of my eyes. I sobbed like my heart was breaking. Ah, so this was really feeling. I was swept away again in a torrent of pain.

Terran was terrified. "Are you okay, Stelley? Maybe taking your meds again would be a good idea."

"Yes–and no–and oh–I don't know," I said between sobs. "It's part of the plan. I can't go back. It's crucial! How am I going to get in the front door like this?"

"I'll help you up to your room, and I'll try to distract Sylvia and Frederick, but Estelle, you *really* look like crap. Can't you stop crying?"

"No," and then I was fully submerged in grief, torrents of grief.

I shoved it down while I walked to my bedroom and collapsed on the bed. Crying and crying, my emotions swung from despair that this was too difficult and it was impossible to go on; to anger that I had to go through this just to be able to feel something again; to sadness that I was so alone, in everything, alone. I forgot, in my despairing solitude that Terran was right downstairs making a million excuses why I needed to stay in my room. He had my back, but I couldn't see anything friendly, or helpful, or loving right then. All was pain.

Sylvia brought up my tray of pills as I lay on the bed, face deep down in my covers. I said, "I'll take them in just a minute." I hoped she would leave, but of course she stood there staring at me.

"What's going on, Estelle?"

"Nothing." My voice was muffled. I tried to make it sound normal, but it was difficult from inside all my bedcovers.

"It's not *nothing*. Is this to do with the betrothal assignment? If you messed up the quiz, Estelle, I...I don't know what I'm supposed to do with you! Why can't you just do what you're supposed to do and stop being so difficult. Why can't you just be normal?" A question to which I had no answer. A loud sob escaped me. Why *couldn't* I just be normal?

Sylvia backed out of the room, taken by surprise at the grief-stricken sounds I made.

As night came on, I pulled out my box of lovely old precious things and sat in my window seat. I stared out at the projected swirls in the sky. The whole world was spinning, and I wanted to get off. I could hear whispering outside my room, discussions I couldn't make out and didn't really care to try. I was just–too–sad. Tears rolled down my face, and sobs racked my body. Exhausted, I fell on the bed, ready to sleep, but succumbed to something less than sleep. It was more like just not being awake any longer.

That was the state I was in when the strong gripping hands of strangers pulled me by my upper arms to a standing position and onto a stretcher. I was lifted up and carried out to an awaiting ambulance, and rushed through the city to the hospital. Luckily, in my sad, sad state, I didn't even care.

fully understanding

The next three days were filled with bursts of bustling medical personnel, followed by long stretches of deep sleeping and even longer stretches of falling into sleep and struggling back out of it. I laid there in a half-awake state most of the time, neither talking nor fully understanding what was being said.

Terran wasn't there until day three. Whatever the cause of his absence, he was there when I woke up. He looked tired, but he was probably worried about me and our plan and whether he was in trouble for running interference. "Hi, sleepy," he said when I was finally, fully awake.

"Where's Sylvia and Frederick?"

"Work. I'm supposed to call them when you wake up, but I figured we might want to discuss some things first."

"Do you know what they've been giving me while I've been here?" I worried all those hours of withdrawal would be for naught.

"They've concluded that you had a reaction to a few of the medicines you were on, specifically the one prescribed a few weeks ago. Apparently reactions are common, so they've taken you off almost everything, except the basics. Those they've been giving you with shots instead of pills. I heard all of this because two nurses were talking in the hallway. I pretended to be busy and listened in." A broad smile spread across his face. My brother, the quiet one, loved to get away with things.

"Do we know what the basics are?"

"Nope, but because they don't suspect you've gone off your meds on purpose–why would you? They're going to quit the shots and give you the meds in pill form, once you wake up for real. I figure I can smuggle them out in the trash. You can wean off everything over the next few days while in their care, just in case you go totally freaky again. It will probably work, as long as you can act normal. Do you *think* you can act normal?"

"I don't know. What's normal? I wonder if I've ever known what it is."

"Estelle, I've got something to tell you. I know it's going to upset you, but I have to."

"Well, it can't be worse than what I just went through."

"You know that porcelain box, the blue one?"

"Yeah," I closed my eyes, as a sinking feeling washed over me. I was sure I knew what he would say.

"The night you came here, Sylvia threw it away."

I nodded, because of course she did.

"I found this, though, and saved it for you," He pulled out his wallet where he had tucked the tiny origami crane. I felt a tear roll down my cheek. I didn't think I could ever cry again, and here it was happening already. I held the delicately folded bird to my chest, knowing there was no need for words.

"Okay, now I've got to call Frederick and Sylvia and tell them you're awake, and let the doctors know."

"Thanks Terran, I don't know what to say..." I stared up at the ceiling, feeling the now familiar sadness threaten to engulf me. Then I felt it pull back, not spilling over the banks of my life, but contained within, safely. I looked at him for a minute and noticed he didn't look so well himself. "What's going on with you?"

"Well, I figured while everyone was focused on the drama-queen, and not thinking about me, it'd be a good time to stop taking my medicines. So, you know, it's been painful, unbearable really, for the past three days. Not as bad as you though."

"I'm the drama queen, huh? That's what we're calling it?"

"Totally. Of course, you were taking more than double the meds I was. However, that doesn't make me sound quite as heroic, so I'm leaving that part out." He smiled widely at me and we sat for a second, fondly looking at each other. He leaned forward, squeezed my shoulder, and said, "It's good to have you back, Stelley," and left the room.

I fell asleep, the first non-fitful sleep of the past five days.

a million miles

A few mornings later, I was still supposed to be recuperating in bed, but instead I went with Terran to the main office of the Old Product Piles. He was greeted as a former summer intern. Then we asked for fencing, some random tools, and the Scorpion. It was an audacious request, perhaps best described as *unprecedented*. While the guys working the desk conferred, we talked loudly about 'our *mother,* in the *Government.*' The Supervisor came over to ask questions, but we showed him the leases and made up a story about it being for a school project. Delivery was ultimately arranged.

The following day, and for many more days, we skipped school and installed a chain link fence around the town block that contained our old houses. No one missed us. Terran was so quiet and easy-going no one figured him for a troublemaker. Plus, he was nearing the end of his school years, so they assumed he was doing something he was supposed to be doing. Me, I think they were happy to be rid of. It was helpful for everyone that I not show myself after the way I looked that last day, and by now the story about me vomiting on William's shoes had reached epic proportions. There was no way I would go back there, hopefully ever again.

Frederick and Sylvia were cautious around me. They

checked to make sure I was okay every few minutes when they were around, but when they were away, I was out of sight, out of mind. I could get away with just about anything because they were, frankly, tired of being bothered by my *issues*. In their medicine-laden lives, they didn't have the tools to cope with or control things that were out of the ordinary.

While Terran and I were working on the prologue to the Big Plan, a new white envelope from the Office of Future Affairs came addressed to me. My new husband assignment, just great. Thing was, I cared not one whit what name was inside, so I took the unopened envelope and hid it in the back of my closet, at the bottom of a small stack of books with my origami crane.

Jack sent me a letter a few days after my release from the hospital:

Dear Estelle,

Heard about the excitement at the Office of Future Affairs. You definitely like to keep things interesting.

I guess you received your envelope by now. I wondered if you're more satisfied with your new betrothal assignment? I got mine a few days back. We should get together soon and talk, once you're feeling better. I'll see you at school soon I hope.

Your former future-husband,
Jack

Sadly, I didn't plan to see him again, and definitely not at school.

A few weeks later, Terran and I were ready. Fresh and clear headed, we had the energetic excitement of people who were making a new start. Our heads were full of plans, and our bodies were ready for the difficult labor ahead. We were happy and satisfied the preliminary work was finished.

I found four outfits in my closet to take with me, though they were hardly acceptable for hard labor. They consisted of a few pairs of slacks and some loose shirts, and would have to do. Brilliantly colored, with ruffles and flounces and ribbons, they definitely weren't farmer clothes. In my imagination, I had planned to look like a farmer, but I just didn't have the outfits. I was disappointed, but pretended to be beyond caring. I didn't want my clothes to be important anymore.

I took my newest pair of exercise shoes, and without a bit of regret, said good-bye to the too-high heels that filled the shelves of my closet. Jonathan would never forgive me for what I planned to wear from now on.

We gathered the bedding and pillows off of our beds and stuffed them into boxes to use for padding and warmth. We collected as many food bars and sweetener as we could without raising suspicion. Terran went to one of the vacation outfitters and bought two hammocks that the salesperson assured him were merely *decorative* and not to be actually *used*. Terran also managed to secure ten buckets with lids for our water supply.

The fence was fully installed. The Scorpion was parked on the lots. The extra tools: wheelbarrows, gloves, and shovels, and all we had bought and gathered from home were delivered and waiting within the locked gate. We were ready.

We met before dawn in the hallway by the front door. We were sneakily quiet, so we wouldn't wake Sylvia and Frederick.

"Good morning, sleepy head," I whispered, noting Terran's extremely rumpled attire.

"I figured if I dressed fast enough, I could sleep a little more." He yawned to prove how tired he was.

"It's four in the morning. I don't know why you're so tired," I teased, while I took my keys and my phone and placed them on the small table by the front door.

Terran also emptied his pockets onto the table and said, "I'm going to miss my car. You're sure I can't take my car?"

"I'm sure, and don't forget the Scorpion is waiting for you."

Terran smiled, but he still fingered the keys in our little assortment of belongings we were leaving behind. "I wonder if Sylvia will be sad when she sees this pile?"

"Probably," but he needed reassurance, so I added, "We're only going a few minutes away. Old Town, it's practically next door."

"True, but this is Sylvia we're talking about. Where we're going might as well be a million miles away."

"Like the stars, huh?" I opened the front door to leave.

the magnitude

Terran and I weren't home when our parents woke. The citizens of New City who lived near the edge of Old Town woke up to the loudest crunching sound they had ever heard. They came out of their homes and traveled toward the sound. The sound was me, or rather us, Terran and I. We were inside the fence we had erected around my four old houses, a tall chain-link fence, gated-closed and locked to be on the safe side.

People gathered all around, but not too close because of the horrendous racket we were making. Terran was up on the Scorpion, a machine that was a sight to behold. It had six wheels that rolled it along and six legs that telescoped out and clamped onto the ground for stability. On the back was a weighted, swinging tail, that could arc and crash into and break things. On the front were two big claws that could punch, shatter, push, and then grab and remove anything you wanted. In the middle was the driver's seat, swinging around as the machine changed directions.

News traveled fast and our parents arrived. I was later told that Sylvia screamed that we were going to be hurt, or get dirty. I guess that's probably the first time she had ever made a sound like that, and I'm so glad I couldn't hear it over the noise we were making. Frederick gripped the fence, just watching.

When it came time for me to drive the Scorpion, I quickly discovered it was *not* like driving my car. There were buttons, levers, and pedals that all had to be operated at the same time. My seat could arc around from forward to back, or could be stationary while the whole machine twirled around me, tail coming to the front, or claws. Terran gave me a quick tutorial and stood off to the side and let me practice a few times. I put the tail out over the house and pushed the controls to make it swing down. The plan was that it would break through the roof and bust down the walls, but I repeatedly swung it down too meekly and overcompensated and missed the house altogether.

Terran was a good and patient teacher, but there was an audience watching, staring, *judging,* as I jerked around on the seat trying to get this giant machine to act in a reasonable way. I decided to try it with the claws in front. With the lever, I drew them back and punched them forward, and a lengthy crack appeared in the wall. Terran waved and hooted excitedly. I moved the claws into position and shoved the wall over.

"You did it Estelle! You did it!" He jumped up onto the front of the Scorpion and applauded. "Now you just have to get smoother and faster." I rolled my eyes at him. "No worries, do what you just did, but better this time." He turned to jump off the front of the big machine and then turned back. "And be careful not to hit that wall." He pointed at a back section of the house. "It's got plumbing running through it. If we want a working bathroom, we need that wall attached to that bathroom to remain standing, okay?" He pulled his ear protection back over his ears and jumped off the front of the Scorpion.

Yeah, okay. I just had to learn to drive this big confusing machine, in front of a whole crowd of people, while making a horrific racket, and not mess up. Thanks for reminding me, big brother.

Once a wall was on the ground, we would drive the Scorpion forward and push the large debris—lumber, walls, and furniture—into a pile. Bathtubs, shelving, and anything too big to push had to be picked up in the claws and moved. Everything too small for the Scorpion had to be picked up and carried.

The noise was terrifically loud, even with the ear protection we wore. You could feel the vibration through the soles of your feet. We called it *shaky feet* as a joke, though it didn't feel very funny.

Once I got the hang of the scorpion, Terran and I traded the driver seat all day. One of us drove as the other picked up the small pieces and moved them to the far corner. When the rubble carrier was exhausted, we traded jobs.

We were the most interesting novelty in town, until just before sundown when everyone headed home, but we kept wrecking until we were so tired we could barely move. We sat and ate some food bars and marveled at how good they tasted because we were genuinely hungry after a long day of work. I didn't even need to dip my food in sweetener this time, though that was probably because I was too exhausted to remember where I put the packets.

"Where are we going to hang the hammocks you bought?" I asked sleepily, while looking at the massive destruction all around us.

"Good question." Terran looked around him, too. "We could attach them to one of the other houses. That way we'd be away from all this wreckage."

I yawned. "I was really looking forward to sleeping outside and away from civilization. I kind of imagined we would be on an empty lot by tonight."

"You and your wishful thinking. We definitely aren't on an empty lot. We're still in the shadow of three and a half houses. This is a trashed lot, a destroyed lot, an unbelievably large pile of debris on top of a lot, but definitely not an empty lot."

"I don't want to sleep in, on, or attached to any of the standing houses as a matter of principle. What about hanging them from that partial wall over there?" I waved halfheartedly in the direction of a bit of the first house we hadn't pushed over yet.

"Don't know, and I'm too tired to check." We both chuckled at our plight.

"What about right here?" I looked down at the pile of old house I perched on. It would probably be the worst place ever to sleep, but I was willing to try.

"That simply won't do, not for our first night." Terran stood up with a groan and pushed and pulled on some of the wall sections that were still standing near by. "Nothing is strong enough to hold the weight of the hammocks." He stood thinking with his hands on his hips. "Okay, here's the plan. For tonight, we'll tie the hammocks to the Scorpion and to the bathroom wall; it's still structurally sound enough. Tomorrow we'll have to pick a couple of walls to leave standing for our hammocks because I don't want to sleep that close to the Scorpion every night. It's greasy and smelly, and frankly, I've had enough of it today."

In answer, I pretended to snore and then pulled myself up with a groan to help him hang our hammocks. True to my promise to Sylvia that I wouldn't sleep inside my old houses, we slept outside for the first time in our lives.

Frederick waited quietly at the fence, until we hung the hammocks, and then slowly walked away.

The next morning we woke with the sun, ate some more of the provisions, and began working again. Crowds gathered, less than yesterday, but still lots of people. Frederick resumed his position, this time in a chair. It was unsettling how he sat just watching us. I knew he had never missed a day of work, and this would make two days in a row. I glanced toward him once and thought there were tears on his face, so I didn't look again.

At about midmorning, a group of officials from the Conglomerates and the Governmental Oversee came to the fence with Sylvia in the lead. She stepped forward and banged with a rock on the fence for my attention. I walked toward her attempting to look more confident than I was.

"Yes, Sylvia?" I asked.

"Estelle, Dear, just how long do you think you are going to carry on with this charade?"

"What charade?"

"We get your point. The People-in-Charge should do something about these old structures. They aren't fit to stand. Now that you so eloquently made this point, you can come home."

I stared at her incredulously. "I'm not making a point. I'm not acting out. For the first time in seventeen years, I'm doing something real."

"Estelle, I want you to listen to me. The Congloms want to bring you up on charges. Your father can't sleep. We are a laughing stock. Are you even taking your medicine? You must stop this nonsense." She tapped her finger on the clipboard she carried for emphasis.

I looked over my shoulder and noticed Terran had stopped the Scorpion. He stared straight ahead, pretending to be emotionless.

"Sylvia, City Document # 678.92, article A, says anything

can be done to property in Old Town as long as it is new and done by the owner. Document # 9056.01, subsection B, says improvements may be made to any property that does not have a structure. Nowhere does it say that you can't knock down buildings..."

Sylvia blurted in, "Because no one does anything this foolhardy, we don't need to have a law about it!"

"That's precisely my point." I walked back to Terran. Out of the corner of my eye, I saw Sylvia speak to Frederick for a few minutes. She walked away, leaving him on his seat.

Terran and I worked the rest of the day, demolishing the house and shoving all the broken parts into the corner of our fenced in area. We stacked and separated the long pieces of wood for later use, and removed the bits of rubble that could be recycled into a shelter. Most of our pile could be reused, so the trash heap diminished in size as we worked. Any leftovers were busted into small pieces destined for the Useless Products Piles.

The sun went down, and the dwindling crowd dispersed. As dusk deepened, Frederick got up and quietly walked away again. Terran and I worked until it was without a doubt the end of the day, though it was difficult to tell because every street light around the block and every parking lot light at the stadium nearby were blaring on. Light gray and quiet, it was peaceful enough to signal the end of a busy day, and at least here in Old Town, there weren't projections on the sky, just a bright nothingness. I was thankful for that.

We made a small fire from some of the scrap wood. It was the first time in my life I ever sat near a fire. I ate my dinner entranced by the dancing light. I softly talked over the day's work with my brother and then, mesmerized by the warmth and comfort of the firelight, fell asleep.

On the third day, our idealism had been completely exhausted out of us. We laughed at the hilarious enormity, the *magnitude,* of our undertaking. As I passed Terran with a pile of debris on my shovel, I asked if we had completely lost our minds. To which he retorted, "Who's bright idea was this?" Then we jokingly called it, "Our Bright Idea." The joke never got old because we were laughing and happy for the first time in our lives, even though we were also bone-tired and astonishingly achy.

We quickly learned that crunching into the side of a house with the Scorpion, working with the heavy machinery, swinging a sledgehammer, the noise, the destruction, it was all deeply satisfying. We both couldn't wait for our turn to drive. I gave vent to seventeen years of suppressed rage. I didn't even know I had so much built up inside. We also learned we needed a lot more people to help.

We were more tired than we had ever been, ever. This wasn't just an hour on a treadmill. The work started at sunup and ended at sundown, sometimes later, and the work was endless. Anyone–the people watching all around the fenced perimeter, the police driving by slowly, and me and Terran–could see that. We were *never* going to get this finished alone. A few days in, and we thought we might not be capable of any of this at all.

Our provisions dwindled. The amount of food we were used to eating was inadequate when working a twelve hour day, and working unceasingly hard.

We also feared that at any time we would be arrested. Terran wasn't so sure, he took the police cars driving by slowly as a sign they weren't ever going to intervene. I was sure. I was sure one of these days, one of those cars would stop, and we would have to deal with what happened next. I wished I knew what that would be, and when, so that I could be ready and not taken by surprise.

In my conversation with Sylvia, I had shown off everything that I had discovered about my rights as a leaseholder in Old Town. If someone confronted me with new objections, *real* legitimate objections, I would be at a loss. There were still three houses left, and a whole bunch of rubble. To top it off, Frederick resumed his seat. He looked horrible, like he hadn't slept since we left. Maybe he would stay there until we came home. Maybe he would dwindle away in front of our eyes to make a point. Maybe his presence would make me rethink this, make me falter and quit. I tried not to look over at him, but I couldn't help furtive glances. What if he never talked to me again?

Terran said it didn't matter. "Frederick should be happy, if we're happy. Things will go back to normal in a few days." But Frederick passed almost a week of missed work, and then more.

This was a part of the plan I hadn't fully considered. What were the consequences for our parents? Would they lose their jobs because they have unruly children? Would they lose their standing in the community for raising such outlaws?

A week on, only a little over twenty people came to watch. Maybe the others had gotten bored. Maybe they assumed we would be stopped soon enough, so they lost interest. The ones that stayed were probably waiting to see how our story would end and didn't want to miss any gory details. Frederick was still there all day.

We were almost done demolishing the second house. The mess

was unbelievable. In the afternoon, we heard a commotion near the far side of the fence. It was William Loftin yelling for our attention and motioning for Terran to come talk.

I tried to figure out how to hide behind a pile of debris. Okay, I'll admit, I ducked and hid. William was the last person I wanted to see, mostly because I vomited on his shoes, but also because that week of my life was still so painful and raw I didn't want to think about it. At all. I was moving on, happy and healthy. Why would I want negativity? Then again, wasn't that why I quit the medicines, so I could feel everything, deal with all of it?

So yeah, I had almost convinced myself I should come up from behind the pile and say hello and probably even, *thank you, for saving my hide that day,* but I chickened out. William was over there in his clean, new, stylish clothes, freshly washed and smiling casually. Whereas I was in an outfit I had been wearing for three days. I hadn't washed in a proper bath in a week, just spot washed in a bucket of water. I was not talking to William, definitely not, ever.

After they conversed for a while, Terran came over with a smile spread across his face. "William offered to come over with a big truck tomorrow to take our trash to the Useless Product Piles. He likes to be involved in subversive movements. Did you know he protested a few times?"

"Really?" I searched his face to see if he was teasing me. "Really, William protested?" I was astonished. I had comfortably assumed I was the only New City resident who was disgruntled, besides the guard from the Old Time Museum, and Terran, of course.

"Sure, Estelle, I know a few students who protested." In a playful way, he said, "You would have known that if you had gotten to know anyone. No, you had to be a bookworm, reading outdated books with pages, from beginning to end." I guess he made a good point. How would I know what anyone else was up to?

"I listened to Sylvia's admonishments not to be weak, not to make friends. Remember how she said, 'never look to the left or right, but straight ahead, because that's where you're going. Don't let anyone distract...' I was still doing that. How did you make friends?"

Terran looked at me for a long moment. "You know I was about to tease you that it was because you're young, and I'm old, but I can see you're seriously asking. About a year ago, William came up and just started talking to me. He talked to lots of people in our wing at school. He'd invite us to sit together during breaks, and he'd start discussions about things and ask about us, until eventually we all talked. It's William's fault I have friends."

"Fault, huh? I guess we both need to thank him." This was a lot to mull over. There were others who had protested. There were young people who had friends, who talked to each other, that were disgruntled, too. This was only the first of many surprises for the day.

"Oh, and by the way, he says, Hi." Terran looked at me with a teasing grin that spread to laughter because of my dismay and discomfort. Hi? What did William mean by, Hi?

new set of hands

At sunset, when we expected Frederick to get up and walk away as he had every day previously, he instead walked up to the fence and motioned ever so slightly. I didn't want to go. I was sure he would, could, talk me out of my Bright Idea. I walked slowly, head down, across the pavement to where he stood. The light was dim, but I could still see his hair tussled and large dark circles around his eyes.

"Hi, Frederick," I said, trying to keep it simple, less uncomfortable.

"Hi, Estelle." He stood there, as if speechless.

I nervously fidgeted and tried to figure out why in the world he would come up to the fence and call me over and not have anything to say. What is going on in his head? He's gone *crazy*, and he's trying to take me with him. I shifted from foot to foot. I'm not going to say anything, I'll wait him out. Time will stand still, but I'm not going to talk when I don't have anything to say. I looked at him. He looked off at the sunset, staring as if through it, with a peaceful look over his face. I reached up and touched his hand, and his reverie broke.

"Estelle, is there anything I can get for you? Is there anything you and Terran need?" After seventeen years of being given the newest, the best, and the most improved products from this man, I think this was the first time he had ever asked me this simple question. I knew the answer, an amazing first for both of us.

I reached into my back pocket where I had the Manufacturer's Catalog of Old Town Implement Replicas, a catalog made to fill the Old Time Museums which existed as tourist attractions in every city. My catalog was rolled, bent, dog-eared, stained, and damp from sweat. I wondered if he'd refuse to take it. I squeezed it small and passed it through one of the chain link holes. "If you really mean it, Frederick, I circled some things in this…"

He took it from me and absentmindedly said, "Tell Terran I said good night," and walked away in the direction of home.

I told Terran about our exchange, and we both agreed that we had no idea what it meant, but we had a fire and tired muscles and stomaches that needed to be filled. Again we deeply slept. I loved the soft sway of my hammock, slung between the two hooks. I was gravity-less, sleeping on air. The night was so quiet and peaceful. I couldn't help but wonder why anyone ever slept indoors.

The next day my father showed up and waved again. Did he order what we asked? I walked over. "Good morning, Frederick."

"Good morning, Estelle. I brought you these." He held up a huge carton of food bars. I unlocked the gate and he passed it through. "Oh, and these." Out of his pocket he pulled a large handful of sweetener packets. I laughed as he filled my arms. "These are for Terran." He put a handful of cheese flavor packets on the very top, until I could barely see over it all.

"Thanks. Did you make an order? I have money in my account."

"Not yet, but the catalogue made me understand a lot more. I'll do it tonight." There was a long pause. A few of the flavor pouches slid off the top of my armload, and he caught them as they fell. "I'll let you get back to work." He closed and locked the gate for me and walked away.

I rushed back to where Terran was working. "Look what Frederick brought us!" I poured the pile into one of the empty buckets.

"That's great, but what does it mean? Why is he sitting here every day? Why isn't he going to work? Is he mad at us? What about Sylvia?"

"I don't know. I didn't ask him about any of that."

"You didn't ask him? You just took the dinner bars and walked away? Seriously, Estelle? I don't think you get to go to the gate anymore."

"Did you see all the cheese flavors?" I smiled ingratiatingly at him and batted my eyes. "He confused me with the sweetener packets."

Just then there was a honk at the gate. We both turned. William had driven up in a big truck.

I looked at Terran with wide panicked eyes. "I'm *not* opening the gate. You said I'm not allowed to go to the gate anymore, so I'm not going. In fact, I'm not speaking to him. As a matter of definite fact, I am going over and working in the far opposite corner." I glanced at the truck just in time to see William honk and wave exuberantly at me. *Eek!* I turned tail and scurried to the corner. I wasn't proud of this at all.

Terran went to the gate and opened the lock and let the truck in. Then he let me know that we were *all three of us* going to load the truck *together*, so William could drive our trash to the Piles. "He's here to help, Stelley, and you're going to need to talk to him at some point."

"I can't," I said with a melodramatic wail. "I threw *up* on him. My face was a color of greenish-gray that was decidedly not fashionable, and he's so handsome and clean, and now I'm covered in dust and sweat and I stink. Have you smelled my..." I stopped short. I had the unmistakable feeling that somebody else was close enough to listen. "He's right behind me, isn't he? He can hear me?"

"Yes," said Terran with a big smile. "So, William, have you met my sister, Estelle?"

I gave Terran the best I'm-going-to-kill-you look that I could muster and turned and held out my hand. There was William, oh so handsome and close enough to, to, well, to throw up on. Would I ever get over that?

"Yes, we've met," said William with a smirk. Great, now I had two teasing, smirking, jokesters to deal with.

To get past the awkwardness, I got down to business. "Should we start with that load over there?" I drove the Scorpion, while William and Terran loaded the debris by hand and wheelbarrow into the truck. William made trips in the truck to the Piles. The Management at the Useless Products Piles had never received bits and pieces of broken and crumpled debris before, but, happily, they weren't able to find a restriction against its being there, so they allowed it in. Being the first to do anything this bizarre continued to work its advantages. We were outside of the law.

William went home at dark, after we took stock of what we'd accomplished. The new set of hands had given us a fresh perspective. There were still two buildings standing, but clearing the rubble of the first two houses showed us that we were capable of demolishing the rest. William's arrival made what seemed impossible before, almost seem possible.

When William came back the following day, we really progressed. By the end of the week only one house was left, and the pile of trash was completely gone. With three of us, the sorting of the recycle pile went much faster. We had become old news, uninteresting, at least to the masses. Frederick was there, still dressed in his Institute uniform even though he hadn't been to work in a long time. Did Sylvia know, and where was she?

My relationship with William was tepid at best. We barely spoke, and I was discombobulated whenever he came near. While we worked, I listened to him and Terran banter back and forth and crack jokes. Sometimes, I desperately wanted to join in. I couldn't though. I was still entirely too embarrassed and willful, I guess—if I totally come clean. I stayed clear of any conversations with him.

It was easy enough to avoid William because we were consumed with work the whole day, but after he had gone home at night I would ask Terran questions. What did he say at this time, and that moment? When did you meet? What is he really like? One night, Terran laughed and shook his head.

"What?" I asked, irritated that I didn't know what was funny, and suspicious I was the cause.

"You! You should just ask William this stuff yourself. You should talk to him, Stelley. He's *nice.*"

I opened my mouth to make an excuse, but clamped it shut again. I had no excuse. I was behaving ridiculously. I made a deal with myself that I would strike up a conversation with William the next day. The day after, at the latest. Definitely by next week.

My procrastination ended the next morning, when William used the same tactic I had used with Jack, and walked up behind me. "Um, Estelle, can I talk to you?"

I swear I almost had a heart attack. "Sure?" I said it like a question hoping he might rethink and say, 'never mind.' He didn't.

"I know when I came to help I only talked about it with Terran. I also know this is kind of all your idea, and so I feel bad I never asked you if it was okay. I should have asked. I'm asking now. Do you mind if I stay and work for a while longer?"

I looked right at him. It was the first time I had let myself do that since we met in the Office. "No, I don't mind at all. Having you here has helped enormously, and I don't know what we would have done without you."

"Oh man, I'm so relieved to hear you say that." His eyes looked around the land, taking in all that we had accomplished. Then he turned to me and said, "I was so nervous about asking. Petrified, actually."

"Petrified?" I repeated, "To talk to me? Why?"

He looked at me incredulously. "Because you're *Estelle Wells,* look what you've done."

"I'm really just a girl, and Terran is here too, and..." I tried to come up with an excuse, to cover my embarrassment at being singled out.

He smiled at my consternation. "You don't get it do you? I know Terran. He's here because he loves the work, but ask him and he'll say the idea is all *you.* It *is* all you. I can see it when you look out over these lots. Like you're thinking it over, and through, planning what's next, and you're worried about it all."

"So, why are you here?" I asked, intrigued by this insight.

"Me? I like the idea." He looked down at the shovel. He held it loosely, like he was judging its heft. Then, as if he was talking to it, he said, "We've got work to do," and walked over to the Scorpion where Terran waited.

The rest of the day, I tentatively talked to William. I joined in his banter with Terran, and laughed at their jokes. By the end of the day, the awkwardness was gone, and William and I were friends.

William offered to stay, indefinitely, or, "At least until we break through the pavement, because Terran's excitement is so contagious."

We talked about going ahead and cutting through, but Terran wanted to have everything ready, the houses completely gone, before the next phase. He was like a kid with presents, ready to tear into them, but wanting the excitement to last.

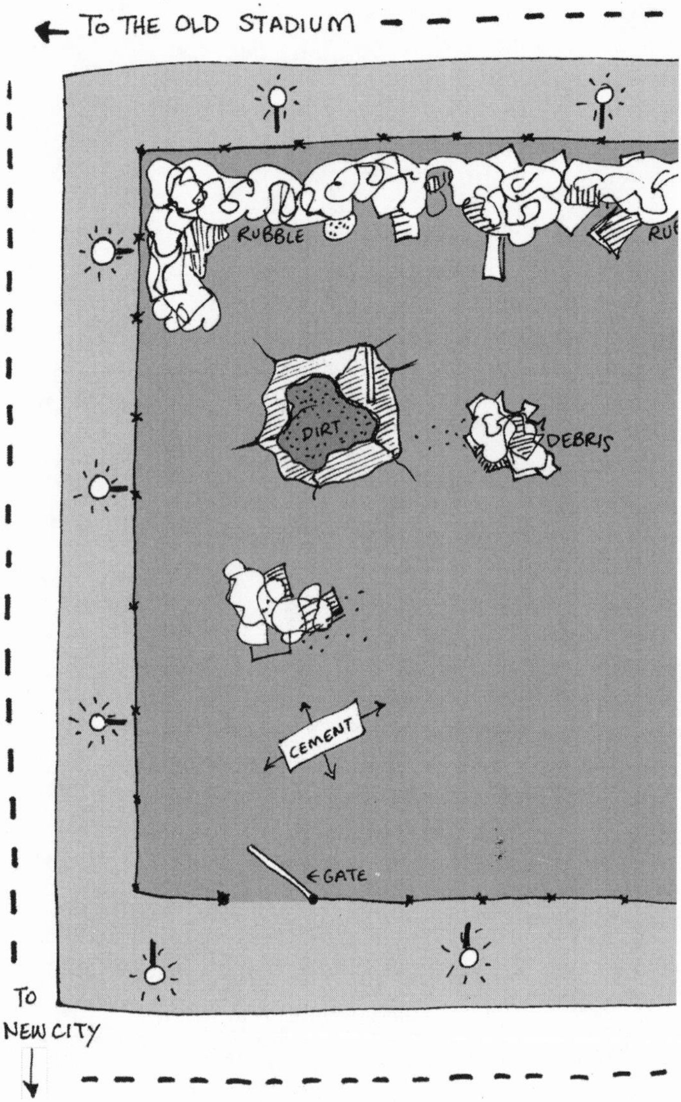
TO THE OLD STADIUM
RUBBLE
DIRT
DEBRIS
CEMENT
GATE
TO
NEW CITY

through the gate

We were ready. The houses were demolished. The debris was sorted. Most of the trash was removed.

We had left two small structures standing in the far northeast corner. One had two partial walls that formerly belonged to the second house, and were just the right distance apart for our hammocks. We built up their weight bearing capability and added hooks. There wasn't a ceiling. It effectively cut off our view of the spectators at the fence, but we slept under an open sky. We placed our fire pit within view of an open end.

The other structure was a half-broken wall that had the kitchen sink and part of a counter connected to a bathroom that had four walls and a ceiling. The bathroom had a door, making it the only place you could go for privacy on the whole piece of land.

Spreading out to the south and west from those two structures was a bright-green, cement and plastic, ground-covering. It covered everything in Old Town and New City and had been created to prevent any dirt or plant-life from coming to the surface. We knew breaking through it wouldn't be easy.

At midmorning we planned to bust through a two foot by four foot area. William sat on the seat of the Scorpion and aimed the claws downward, using the lever marked *dig*. The claws hammered into the ground, and after two loud strikes, there was a deep crack that splintered out in all directions. We cheered with excitement. William climbed out of the seat, and the three of us kneeled down at the edges of the cracks and pulled up chunks and pushed them to the side to peer at what was underneath.

It took a few minutes for our eyes to adjust and realize it wasn't dirt. Terran's face was crestfallen. We pulled up more chunks that broke fairly easily once the structural integrity was gone. We took a few minutes to investigate what was underneath. It was another type of surface, a medium-grey in color, that looked like rock and, as far as we could tell, stretched in every direction.

I sat for a few minutes holding a few chunks of our green pavement. Terran got up and walked around, hands on his hips, mumbling to himself. William knocked and tapped and kept investigating. "It looks like an older cement covering. Yep, definitely. See this white-painted stripe?" He pulled up more chunks of the green, "It's a road or something, maybe an old parking lot. Imagine that, Estelle, your farm is built on an ancient historic parking lot!"

I groaned, the last thing we needed was more cement. Terran walked up with a shovel and attempted to break through it. The shovel didn't even make a dent, "That sounds thick," he said, defeat in his voice. "Do you think the Scorpion can get through?"

"We have to try, right?" William strode over and climbed up to the seat. "Just past, *dig,* is a setting called, *crush.* I'll try it. If it doesn't work there's still, *pulverize.*"

We all put on our hearing protection, and Terran and I stepped out of the way. The sound the Scorpion's claws made when they attempted to crush through the grey cement was so loud and unnerving that, after a few seconds, we had to stop. Even with ear protection, the noise was so intense I heard it in my bones. I stepped forward and was so disappointed to see a teeny, tiny dent.

Terran said, "The supervisor at the Piles told me *not* to use the higher levels on the Scorpion. He specifically told me not to take it past, *dig*. He said that would be plenty enough to get through the ground-covering."

William climbed in the seat. "He didn't tell me though. I'm going to *pulverize*." He worked at the controls for a moment while Terran and I stepped way, way back. The Scorpion's feet clamped down on the ground covering, the claws centered over the area, and crashed down with force and power and repetition. The claws hammered over and over and over. William kept adjusting the Scorpion and moving to different areas, pulverizing a wide berth. I guess he figured if it was going to be that loud, he should get as much done as possible. After about ten minutes, he stopped the machine.

Terran and I stepped forward and leaned down. There were deep cracks all over the grey cement. We were in. Terran reached down and pulled up a big chunk. It was full of rocks and about six inches thick. He passed it to me so I could marvel at its density while he pulled out another and another. Underneath was what we had been looking for.

The dirt was dark, black, and ominous, and before I could get my eyes to adjust, Terran had plunged his full arm in. He pulled up a handful and put it on his lap. He smeared some on his face like the war paint we had read about in books. It stunk terribly. I covered my nose and he laughed in a raucous, uproarious way that, in our former lives, we had never heard anyone do. In this life, we were getting used to the sound of our laughter.

What was that smell? I was unsure about touching it and trying to get used to the idea that my brother was covered in it. We'd been warned about this stuff since well...since forever, and that smell was *absolutely* not okay. I was definitely not touching it. Could I farm without touching it? Terran reached over and wiped a dirty finger across my nose and cheek. *Gasp!* It was cold, and slightly wet.

"I'm going to kill you, Terran," I said, right as William dug up a bit and tossed it merrily in my direction. It landed on my shoulder and stuck to my white shirt. Ha! Just like that, I looked like I came from The Beyonds. Jonathan would kill me. I dug in without thinking and sent a handful sailing over to my brother. He responded in kind, then threw some at William too, and before we knew it, all of us were covered. We were filthy, like never before. I had it in my ear.

Terran said, "Look!" and reached into the pit and pulled out a writhing earthworm.

"Seriously? You're touching it?" He grinned, enjoying my shock. "Its a slimy, creepy, yucky creature. Please don't come near me with it." I shuddered. I *might* have to touch dirt, but I *wouldn't* touch creatures.

Terran said, "You know what this means? It means our dirt is healthy, even though it's been covered all these years."

The first life on our land. Terran jumped to his feet and did a strange jig-like dance. I looked at William and said, "He's completely out of control."

"Totally," he agreed, and we both jumped to our feet and danced with him. We held hands, kicked the air, jumped, and occasionally yelled, until we fell to the pavement, laughing. We put our feet in the hole, and burrowed our toes into the dirt, our faces turned to the sky.

Slowly we got our breath back and our euphoria drained away. The moment was over, and we were self-conscious again. William sat up on his arm. "I'm tired of being constantly watched. It's like we're a tourist attraction or something."

Terran remained flat on his back. "They're thinking, 'Hey look at the crazies, opening up the ground, touching the dirt. Bring in the Medical experts! We'll need to convene a special Institute Committee to study these kids who dared to touch dirt and earthworms.'"

I leaned up on my elbow. "And Frederick won't stop staring at us. Yell, scream, or be like Sylvia and forget us, but don't just stare at...hold on."

Frederick got up from his seat. It wasn't sunset, what was he doing? He unclipped his Special Head of New Development credentials from his pocket and placed them on the chair. He took off his Institute coat and folded it neatly and placed it on top of the credentials. He took off first one shoe and then the other, and his socks and pushed them into each shoe, and picked them up in his left hand. Believe me, I know these details because by this time Terran, William, and I were watching, dumbfounded. He walked up to the gate and stood there expectantly.

Terran said, "What the hell?" and walked to the gate. He and Frederick talked while he undid the lock. Then Frederick walked in through the gate and came straight toward us. I jumped up, but he seemed to take no notice of me. He stepped right into the pit and stood there as a smile slowly crossed his face. "It smells. I had no idea it would smell." Terran re-locked the gate.

A few moments passed while Frederick stood with his feet in the dirt. He leaned over and grabbed some and looked it over, rubbing it between his thumb and fingers. Then, with his feet still in the dirt, his toes occasionally wiggling, he told us he wanted to stay, to help. He said it had taken him a while to figure out what we were doing, and even longer to decide why, but the dance in the dirt had made it impossible for him to stay away. This was Frederick, a man who did everything he was supposed to do, choosing to break the rules with us.

I asked him if it would be difficult to leave everything behind, and he said no, with us in here it was much harder to stay outside, but he had to admit, walking through the gate had seemed like an insurmountable task. "Well, Frederick, we're glad you're here," I said, and we went back to crunching pavement and moving debris.

We were removing the top layer of our civilization, and the underneath layer of an older civilization from our piece of the world. It was brutal work, but also exhilarating and rewarding. Our reward was that this had become our land, not our old houses, or our cemented-over lots, our *land*. It belonged to me and Terran, and now probably Frederick. It belonged to William now, too. He was that fond of it, and after that dance in the dirt, I wasn't uncomfortable with William anymore at all. The land brought us together, working on it made us all friends.

back to wondering

Now that there were four of us, the work went much faster, but it was still exhausting. A whole town block of contemporary cement had to be busted up and moved with the Scorpion. The land that was covered in the old grey cement had to be pulverized. The cement chunks, green and grey, were pushed and piled into stacks all around the perimeter and sent by truckloads to the Piles. Even with the Scorpion working full time, there was still plenty that had to be moved by hand. The work was backbreaking.

As more dirt showed itself we would step into the holes and pull out handfuls and smell it or pretend to bathe in it. The dirt made us even sillier than before. Even Frederick had a sense of humor, come to find out.

The following afternoon Sylvia came to the fence. Frederick walked over to meet her, and they talked quietly, too quietly. They parted and Sylvia drove away. Frederick walked back across the land with his head down. He walked slowly. Terran asked, "Is Sylvia going to come too, Frederick?"

"No, Sylvia isn't going to come. She still doesn't understand. I guess she's been working for the Congloms for so long, she just...Well, she misses having us around, but she just can't drop what she does."

"Oh," I said.

"Don't get too mad at her. She's spending her time keeping the wheels of government machinery out of your hair. Oh, and Estelle, she and I think you should know that Jack and his family are helping your cause. The Maranvilles are very important people, and they've written a defense of you to the press. Sylvia says they've been pulling strings with the Congloms on your behalf. They're why no one has come to cause real trouble for you."

"Jack Maranville, and his family? Why? What? Why in the world?" I had been absentmindedly eating a snack bar and dropped it in my consternation. Now it was covered in dirt *and* sweetened sprinkles. Oh well, I ate it anyway, a true sign of how adapted to the dirt I had become, but also a sign of how distracted I was by this information. Why would Jack and his family be helping me?

"Sure, Estelle, the other night your story was on the news and they interviewed Jack. He's acting as your press agent. They go to him when they have questions about you."

William said, "I saw him on the news the other night, too. I just assumed he's a friend of yours. He certainly spoke with familiarity."

"Yeah, I guess he's a friend." Maybe, sort of. Did former, future-husbands count as friends? If you only spoke to each other a few times? I couldn't figure this all out. Why was his family helping me? They had absolutely no connection to me whatsoever. The dissolution of our Betrothal Contract was mutual, so what happened to me from that point had nothing to do with him. It didn't make any sense, but yes, no one had bothered us, and we wondered why. Were Jack and his family the reason? Who could I ask? In all my consternation, I was distracted from Sylvia's absence, but I could see Terran was really bothered by it. I put my arm around him consolingly and tried to get back to the present subject again.

"So there's nothing we can say to persuade Sylvia to come here?" I asked.

"Well, look around kids. What exactly are you offering Sylvia Wells; a hammock, a fire, backbreaking work, and the threat of arrest for a cause she doesn't believe in? I'm not thinking she's coming, even if she misses you. That's just the way it is." Frederick sighed, not quite consoled himself.

"She also gave me this." He gave Terran a white envelope.

Terran looked around at the group and took a deep breath before opening it. He tore open one end, pulled out a letter, unfolded it, and showed it around the small circle. "My future-wife is dissolving our betrothal."

"You could talk to her." I said, "Like I did with Jack, ask her to make it mutual."

"Mutual? Nah, this is good. I'll be unmatchable."

"Sylvia might be able to pull some strings though," said Frederick.

"No, I'll just stay unassigned. It's okay. It's better this way." He looked decided, like there was no point in arguing.

"What about your future? What about both of your futures?" asked Frederick. "I don't think either of you are thinking about what's next, after you're done with this."

"This *is* my future, Frederick," said Terran simply, and we didn't speak of any of it again.

Because night was coming on, we cleared up a little bit of what we had done that day and headed over to the area where we kept our fire pit. It was time for our evening relax and unwind, my favorite part of the day. Most of the time William left for home just before dinner, but tonight he stayed and ate with us.

Terran got out the dinner bars and my sweetener packets for the evening meal, and we lounged around enjoying the fire and a lively, meandering conversation. After a long evening, William mentioned going home to sleep.

"Your parents are probably worried about you, huh? Do they wonder where you are?" I asked.

"No, they don't care what I do with my life. I'm free to go where I like."

"Are you worried about walking around out there?" asked Frederick.

"You mean the dark, or arrest? I haven't been afraid of the dark for a long time, and I'm just a peripheral person on this farm." He smiled teasingly at me. "I'm not the person who planned to tear down old houses. My defense is I'm just *helping*." Terran and I laughed, but Frederick looked thoughtful.

"Do you kids have a contingency plan for arrest?" Frederick asked. "Have you considered the very real possibility that there could be trouble?"

"Not really," I said, "or rather yes, but I can't plan for something I don't know will happen. What would the plan look like anyway? Every time the police cars drive by the fence I think, *this is it. Here we go,* but I don't even know what happens to someone when they're arrested. It's all just so abstract that I can't even think about it. Terran and I decided early on we should just live like we don't believe we're doing anything wrong."

Terran said, "If I remember correctly, you called it, wishful thinking."

"Yeah, wishful thinking. That's my plan."

"So the Maranvilles keeping the Congloms out of your business is crucial if you think about it," said Frederick. We sat in silence.

What were Jack's motives? William proved he was wondering the same thing, and asked, "So who *is* Jack to you anyway?"

I looked at Terran, who looked at me. It was kind of hard to explain, especially because telling him Jack was my former future-husband might remind him of the forms I was filling out in the office that day. Which would definitely remind him of me throwing up on his shoes. I did not want to remind him of that, not when he was playing along like it had ever happened. Terran just sat there, letting me explain.

"Well, when I turned sixteen, Jack was assigned as my future-husband."

"Oh..." William's voice trailed off. After a moment of musing, he asked, "Is he planning to come live here too?"

"Oh no, that's just it, he didn't want to marry...I mean, we didn't want to marry each other, because we were too different. He wanted success. His family works for some of the biggest brands in marketing and PR. They're important. He's going places, and me, well, you see where I went." I sighed deprecatingly at the dirt smeared on my clothes and the pile of rubble I sat on. The nicest thing I owned right now was my hammock. I really liked my hammock, blue and green woven fabric with fringe down the side. Just thinking about it made me look over at it lovingly. Man, I was ready for some sleep. I was also, admittedly, trying to distract myself from the conversation I was in. I couldn't believe I was discussing Jack with William. "So we applied for a betrothal dissolution together about two months ago."

"So, why is he on the news talking about you?"

"Yeah, good question, Stelley," said Terran.

"I don't know, I really don't."

William stared off into the fire, and we all sat in silence for a while. Looking into the fire was a new joy, watching it change shape and dance across the top of the wood. It enthralled me watching the changing colors. I loved how when you were sitting around a fire, all the pressure to speak was gone, but the inverse was also true. Something about the fire and the surrounding stillness made conversation easy. Not this one though, not with William, not tonight.

William took a piece of wood from beside his chair. He pushed it into the fire, stirred up the coals, and built up the flame, and said, "All right, I'll see you tomorrow. Good night." He walked toward the gate.

"I think I'm going to turn in too," said Terran.

"I'm as tired as I've ever been, so I better turn in too. Good night, Estelle, Terran," said Frederick as he went to get his bed ready.

"I'll go to sleep in a bit," I replied, and went back to wondering what was going on with Jack.

what's being said

As we were gathered in our usual morning huddle to go over the plans for the day, we were interrupted by a shiny car pulling up in front of the fence. Jack stepped out, walked up to the gate, and waved silently to me as if I should have been expecting his arrival.

"What the..." I walked to the fence. Why was he here? Well, at least now I could find out why he was helping me, but did I really want to know? Was it too late to turn around and pretend like I didn't see him? One of the best things about my life now, was that it was protected from the outside world. I was safe. I didn't like having my Bright Idea interrupted, even for a moment.

"Hi Jack. What are you doing here?"

"Hi Estelle. How are you?" He answered, without really answering. His eyes darted across the cement, debris, and dirt behind me. The look on his face made me feel self-conscious. Yep, I lived on a pile of rubble. "What did you think of the press we've been getting you?"

"I haven't seen any press, I don't know..."

Jack squinted his eyes, "You haven't been watching the news? You're all over it! You're the hottest thing going right now."

"Why, I don't get what...? I don't have a TV. I haven't watched TV since I left home."

"Whoa, that's extreme, Estelle. While we're on the subject, that's an extremely interesting look you've got going there. What is it, mud puppy?" He grinned disarmingly.

I returned his smile. "I'm looking pretty grungy, huh?"

"Grungy, yes. Pretty, not so much."

"Very funny. So why don't you tell me what's being said about me, in the news?"

"Well, at first no one understood what you were doing. There was serious talk of having you arrested. It came forward that you'd been hospitalized recently, and Leo, my father, realized that if we didn't spin it quickly you'd be labeled a crazy. You know what happens to crazy people, Estelle, they *disappear*. Leo asked me if I thought you were crazy, and I told him no. I told him you liked to be different, to ask questions of the status quo, to be difficult, but you weren't mentally unstable in a bad way, no. So, he took it to the papers that you were this hot, hip, avant guard, artist type, and you were creating something *new* in Old Town. They're eating it up, Estelle. Everyone wants to know everything they can about you, and what you're doing. No one is talking about arresting you anymore."

"Oh, well, so why haven't they just come and asked *me* what I'm doing? Why not talk to me directly?" I was still confused about his motives, and what he knew about mine.

"Oh, Leo's got the press totally controlled. He's giving them bits and pieces of information, only what they need to know, and no more. It's much better for your brand that people get to know you *slowly*."

A sleek little car whipped around the corner and pulled to a stop right in front of us. A young, impeccably dressed woman stepped out. She wore an azure blue outfit and had a diagonal stripe of brown across her chest. The fashionable side of me noted the brown color was new. When did it come in style? Had I been gone that long? As she approached, the small crowd of people parted to let her through, then closed tightly around us, hoping to hear what would happen next.

"Hello, you must be Estelle Wells. I'm Valerie Triumph." Oh, I knew who she was—an incredibly famous newscaster. Was she seriously here to talk to me? "It's great to meet you. Thank you for agreeing to speak to me *exclusively!*"

I cut my eyes at Jack. "No problem."

"We've been interviewing Jack about you. He's filled us in a bit, but we'd like to hear directly from you now. What exactly are you doing here in Old Town?"

"Um." I looked back at the land as if I was asking it for help with the answer. I struggled for a few seconds trying to find the right words. What I was doing here was ultimately too big to say. So I gave her the shortened version. "Creating a farm."

"A farm? Like a food growing farm?" I think I surprised her, because she lost her ability to form coherent questions.

"Yes, food and animals, and I plan to build a shelter over there." I pointed toward the fire pit. I expected her to turn and follow my gaze, but instead she looked straight at me, not caring where my shelter would be.

"There are farms out in The Beyonds, or so I hear. The Congloms have mega-farms farther away in the grain regions. Why don't you leave the farming to the professionals and go back to living a normal life?"

"Because I like this life. I like living here with friends, building and digging. I plan to someday grow things."

"In the dirt?" She smiled at me in the endearingly

condescending way she smiled at all of her interviewees. It was the smile that made her famous, and it usually meant her questions were going to get difficult. I didn't like having it aimed at me.

"Yes." I wiped the sweat off my forehead, possibly accentuating the point with a filthy smear. "Right here, on the edge of New City, in Old Town."

"Why right *here*? Why not somewhere else, far away, where your dirt won't *get* on everyone?"

Startled by her directness, I faltered for a second. "Because here in New City we all live the same way. We all go to school. We all get married. We all go to work. We all exercise three times a week at the gym. We all eat the same brand of dinner bars. I read some books a while back…"

Valerie broke in, "You read books?"

"Yes, I read…"

"Where did you get books?"

"From…" I looked around wildly. What if I gave away my secret library and couldn't get books anymore? What if I got the guard in trouble? She scrutinized my face.

Jack expertly pulled me by my elbow away from her and said, under his breath, "Just get back on topic," and turned me back toward Valerie.

I smiled, attempting to divert her attention. "I was *reading,* and discovered there are many other ways to live. I learned it's possible to spend the day working with friends, to grow your own food, to sleep outdoors. This is just one of the other ways, but I wanted to try it."

"Why right here, Estelle? That's what I'm asking. Why are you doing everything you can to be different, right *here* where everyone can see you?"

"I'm hoping other people will see there is no one right way

to live. That there are many different paths to happiness, and the path chosen for us doesn't have to be the one we choose."

"Hmmm, very interesting. So your little farm isn't just an experiment for you, it's supposed to be an abject lesson for us as well." She looked at me like it was a question, but I could tell she didn't want an answer. She moved on to the next topic. "So was Estelle Wells *unhappy* with her life before the farm?"

I looked down at the ground, feeling insecure. "Not unhappy, but it just seemed like I wasn't experiencing anything at all."

Valerie looked at me with eyebrows raised. "Well, you are young. You have your whole life ahead of you. However, if you want experiences you could go on a fabulous vacation. I hardly think you need to dig in the *dirt,* or be *different,* to have a full life."

"I don't think I'm all that *different* from anybody else. I just figured something out. Maybe I'm just the first person to figure it out."

"You're new and improved." She was gloating. I could see from her excitement she had discovered the title for this interview.

"No, it's not really that at all. I'm not new and improved. I'm just a normal girl, questioning her way of life."

"Have you always been a questioner, Estelle?" She leaned in with her other signature move, the earnest peer.

"I guess."

"Because I'm not, and I would think most of my readers are decidedly not, *questioners.* We *like* our New City lives." She nudged Jack, conspiratorially. "I'd also like to think we're *normal.* Which would make you absolutely not normal, but then again, you might say, being a *questioner* is normal for *you.* Very interesting. How long will you be working on this project?"

"Um, well, I was thinking, until I'm finished." I didn't know how to answer this question. I felt like I had been walloped on the head by a board I didn't see coming.

"Oooooh, very enigmatic!" Her voice was almost a squeal. "Do you have anything to say to your fans? Any advice, or words of wisdom?"

"Well, I guess you should do your best to understand what's going on around you. Ask about things that don't make sense, try to get to the truth of..." What was I babbling on about? Valerie looked at me expectantly, eyebrows raised. "Everything," I said.

Jack stepped forward. "That's probably good. Right, Valerie?"

"Yep, perfect!" She shook my hand warmly. "Thank you," and headed to her car. As she climbed in, she took a small towel out of her purse and wiped the hand she had used to shake mine. She didn't just wipe, she rubbed it vigorously all over, making sure she got the grooves. Her back was to me, but I couldn't take my eyes off of her.

While I watched, Jack said, "You did great, Estelle. I hoped to prep you more, but she was early. You did really well though." He smiled at me affectionately. "So now you're safe from arrest, you could go home and back to school. You could work, um, here on the weekends, right?"

"No, I'm planning to live here. This is a home I'm building, a farm."

"Oh, sure." He shook his head like he was trying to keep this disturbingly strange thought from sticking in his brain. He looked over the still mostly cemented-over land for a few minutes. I watched him for any sign of distaste, or anything, but he just seemed calm and uninterested. I reminded myself he was massively medicated. I'd forgotten what it was like to talk to people like that. He asked, "Do you have your medications, enough food? Can I get you anything while you're working on your 'project'? I'd like to help."

"I'm not on any meds anymore," I said. He looked at me sharply, obviously upset. "And we have enough food for now, but if I need anything, I'll let you know. Hey Jack, I have to ask, why are you helping me? Why are your parents helping me?"

He squinted his eyes at me intently. "Because you're my future-wife, Estelle, of course. Saving you, saves me." He turned around and went back to his car. I stood watching him go. No, you silly, I'm your *former* future-wife.

I turned and let myself back through the gate. I walked across the land toward Terran and William who were pretending they weren't *dying* to know what had just happened.

About five steps in, I heard a noise behind me and turned to see Jack getting out of his car again. He put a note or something into the chain-link fence. He waved goodbye abruptly turned, and walked back to his car and drove away.

What did he leave? I stepped back to the fence and pulled the white envelope through the links. It was a strangely familiar envelope, addressed to Jack Maranville. Inside it said:

Dear Jack Maranville,
  According to your personality, aptitude, and behavioral exam, we are pleased to tell you that of the 10 types, you are a #3-managerial. As you learned in your Types of Personalities class, the #3-managerial personality matches best with a #8-creative. Taking into consideration your aptitude, your behavior, and your future plans (form 84.B), we have paired you with:

Estelle Wells, also of Education Section 7, currently on sick leave

On behalf of the entire Office of Future Affairs and Behaviors and the Ministry of Medicines, we would like to congratulate you on your future relationship. May your wedding be joyous and your marriage be comfortable.

Sincerely,
Clarise Jordon,
Counselor of Future Affairs, School Section 7

Oh man. What had before been an impossibility, was now, absolutely true. Jack was my future-husband, *again*. If I had bothered to open my white envelope when I received it, instead of putting it unopened into the back of my closet, it might have made me falter in my Big Plan. The Office of Future Affairs really *was* never wrong, and here they picked me and Jack to marry, *twice*. Maybe, probably, they were right after all, or were they? Jack was in agreement, or, at least, he wasn't fighting their decision. He was helping me, and even seemed to enjoy my 'crazy' idea, at least from afar. Maybe, probably, I really *was* supposed to spend my life with Jack.

a lot to learn

Slowly I turned to walk back to Frederick and Terran, who were now at a full stop, leaning on their shovels, waiting to hear what had happened at the fence. I'd been there for less than a half hour and had a million things to tell them. I planned to start with, "I thought I wasn't supposed to go talk to people at the gate anymore. Why do I have to be the spokesperson?"

I was about a hundred feet across the land before there was a commotion at the gate, *again*. Voices were raised, so I turned to look back at the crowd. A young woman waved and yelled, "Estelle, Estelle Wells!" It was the first time someone in the crowd had made contact. Startled, I went over to see what was up.

When I came close, she said, with a broad smile, "Hi Estelle, I'm Merrily Jones, but everyone calls me Mj. Anthony, from the Old Time Museum, sent me to see you. He said you needed my help, so here I am!" Totally confused, my auto pilot took over and I opened the gate to let her in. She seemed trustworthy, in that she looked like no one I had ever seen before.

Mj walked through the gate with a pouch strung across the front of her body. A squirming pouch that must have contained something alive. It was definitely alive. I could barely pull my eyes away from it, but I had to investigate this entire odd person. Tall, and slim, her hair resembled thickly knotted ropes and was piled high on top of her head, held in place wrapped around a stick, a *leaf-covered* stick. There were flowers stuck here and there throughout. She wore a pair of pants that came up and over her chest, and strapped into buckles over her shoulders. They were brown, the color of the earth. She had a short-sleeved shirt underneath, also in a brown color, and a brown leather back pack. On her feet were the most wonderful boots, black and big, with even bigger, sturdy soles. I glanced at my own shoes, small and made of all-new, breathable, lightweight materials. They were made to feel like nothing, which was completely inadequate when working around heavy machinery. I knew my shoes were all wrong, but her boots, *they* were perfect.

We walked a few feet away from the fence for verbal, if not visual, privacy, and stood there for a second, sizing each other up. She still wore a big beaming smile.

"So, you're friends with the guard?" I asked.

"Well, kind of. I order things I need for my farm through the director of the Old Time Museum. She can get anything you need through her catalogs, by the way. A few times a year I show up there to pick up orders and I usually stop in to say hi to Anthony. He told me to come see you, said you needed my help," she repeated.

"I'm not sure I understand. I need help?"

"I grow things," she said plainly.

"Oh," I said, as if that explained everything. I still couldn't stop staring at the fabric pouch she had wrapped around the front of her body. It was dyed in an explosion of color; red, blue, purple, green, and was tightly tied on her back shoulder. As she recounted how she happened to be standing on my land, the pouch kept moving. What was in there? It made a mewing sort of sound, and I had to ask. "Do you mind...what's in your, um, pouch?"

"My baby."

"Oh," I said again. Why couldn't I come up with anything more eloquent? "Shouldn't a baby be in an incubator, or a nursery?"

"Wow, you sound just like the civvies at the gate. They were harassing me about it, too. No, babies are meant to be with their mothers. I'm her incubator *and* her nursery. I totally thought you'd be more, I don't know, *enlightened*," she replied, looking at me with squinted eyes, as if sizing me up.

Humph, I was enlightened. Whatever that meant. "I was just wondering why you have the baby *already*. Why it's not still in a nursery when it seems so small." I'd frankly never seen babies that little before, but I definitely didn't want to seem unenlightened, not in front of this regal, foreign creature.

"Estelle, don't you know where babies come from?"

"Yeah, I know." I smiled, attempting to cover my lack of savvy. Of course I knew where babies came from, incubators, right?

"So you grow things, like what exactly?" I asked, changing the subject. I could see Terran, William, and Frederick coming to join us with quizzical looks on their faces.

"So everyone, this is Mj. She came to help. She *grows* things. Mj, this is William, Terran, my brother, and Frederick, my father."

"This," Mj added, pulling down the front of her fabric pouch, "is Beatrice." The men paused for a minute, seemingly speechless. Like me, they were confused by the presence of a baby–here–outside.

Terran recovered first. "Hi Mj. What can you grow?" He

turned and said to the group, "Let's take a break. We can eat lunch and hear all about Mj, and why she's here."

Once settled in our fire pit area, Mj launched into her story. "I live in The Beyonds, a few days walk from here, near the Mountains of Discards. Many people live in, and right around the Mountains. They scavenge and pick and put together lives from the refuse of the civvies." She looked around and seeing our blank faces said, "That's *you*. My family though, we live a bit further out and we farm. We have a few acres, a house, livestock..."

Terran said, "You have animals? What kinds of animals?"

"Horses, chickens, cows. I come to the edge of New City, to the Old Time Museum, about every six months to pick up our orders of supplies. Sam, the woman who curates the museum, can procure anything you need for a farm, *anything*. So, recently I was there, and she told me about your little revolution, your civvie farm." Mj looked at me and smiled.

"I asked the guard about you, Estelle, and he told me you were a protester. He said you question everything, and you read a lot. I figured you were my kind of people. Anthony told me he didn't think you knew much about farming though, 'only what they read in books.' So I asked him if you might want help, and he reckoned you might. He says to tell you that everyone is rooting for you.

"I went back home and finished up what I needed to do for the season. My Mom, Dad, sisters, brothers, and my husband Adam are there, so everything will be handled while I'm here to help you get started. I can spare two weeks," she finished as if it was all settled.

It was. I had assumed if we had land, and the desire to grow things, that things would just grow. Listening to Mj describe her life in a place called *The Beyonds*, a place I had barely even heard of before, made me think that maybe I was a tiny little bit idealistic. If this land was going to support life, perhaps Mj had just the kind of help we needed.

My lunch was my usual bar, rolled in four packs of sweetener. Mj's was contained within a handkerchief. She placed it onto our table, opened it up, and revealed the contents. Revealing isn't the right word, because she had to explain too, "These are apples. This is cheese, salami, and some slices of bread." She didn't share, and we didn't ask to try. It was all way too natural looking. I was sure it was probably contaminated.

To be conversational, I asked if Beatrice ate apples, too. I knew babies were fed from bottles here in 'civvies' world, but who knew what they fed babies in The Beyonds?

"Beatrice doesn't have teeth, Estelle. She drinks milk, from my *breasts*." I choked on the bar I was eating. That was not at *all* what I expected to hear. I thought I was so liberated from civilization, but I was still just a civvie living on a cemented over lot in Old Town. I had a lot to learn if I wanted to become someone different, better.

All afternoon, we shoveled and broke up cement, while Mj walked around with a notebook, pencil, and some small tools. She walked the lot, back and forth and around. She looked at the lights, where we slept, the fire pit, and where we kept the water buckets. She cooed and talked to her baby as she quietly walked all over. She added her plan to our plan and made it all bigger, better, and much more *planned*.

That night, around the fire, she told us all about where the garden should be. She told us we should reuse the cement chunks by building them into a low, stone-style wall around the perimeter, because someday she hoped we would no longer need the chain-link fence. She thought we could plant hedgerows around our private areas and put paths around and through the fields. She told us we were going to want a pond and that chickens, ducks, rabbits, and goats would be a good start for livestock. The conversation was long and varied. Her plans got us all thinking and talking about what our future looked like, above this once cemented-over land and under this pewter-grey sky. Our future was growing green, earth brown, sky blue, and I hoped someday, twinkling black.

"So Mj, tell us a story about what life is like in The Beyonds," asked Terran, fascinated by these strangers in our midst.

She sized us up for a minute, probably wondering what she could tell us without spending all night attempting to explain. How could you explain things to a bunch of civvies? "Sure, but we have a tradition back home that a story is repaid with another story. I get to pick who goes next."

She smiled and began, "Everyone back home calls me, Little Traveler, because I never want to stay in one place. I've loved to roam ever since I was a little girl. It's mostly safe in our farming community, but there are forests and discard piles bordering it on two sides. My family didn't want me to wander too far, so mom and dad tried to curtail me a bit with a walk around the perimeter of the farm. They showed me the boundaries and urged me to stay inside them. Trouble was, I'd lose track of what I was doing and keep walking until I found myself way farther away than I was supposed to go.

"Then my father took me on weekly walks from our land out into the woods and the piles. All through the walks, he would point out landmarks and sights. Within a year, I could go anywhere, almost any distance, and find my way back. At the time my chores were to help with the kitchen garden, care for the chickens and goats, and help in the kitchen at dinnertime, but my afternoons were free, and I could wander."

"How old were you?" asked William.

"I was eight by then." We looked at her in amazement. An eight year old in New City was barely competent to tie her own shoes. It would be totally beyond her grasp to travel alone and have chores. Wouldn't it?

Mj continued, "They hoped I would stay within a three mile radius at that point, and I did, mostly. Okay, my circle got wider and wider, but I tried to stay put. I really did." She chuckled to herself. "Until I was fourteen and convinced my older brother, who was sixteen, that we should try riding one of the trains."

"Oh, no," I said. This was all just too much. I wasn't sure of many things, but I knew that fourteen year old children shouldn't ride trains.

Mj continued, "There was an area of our community that bordered the train tracks, and I crossed them all the time. Once a day the train went through–slowly–so as not to disrupt the farming too much. I figured we could jump on, ride for a couple of miles, and jump off while it was still slow. That, my friends, was a miscalculation.

"Chris jumped on the train first. He threw out his hand to me, and I swung up easily enough. Then we sat there, our legs out the open door, the wind in our hair. It was so amazing. We don't have many cars. There is only one in our whole community, so we'd never gone that fast. We enjoyed it so much that we lost track of the time, and the train started going faster, and faster, and faster. We knew that home was a long way back. If we had jumped, we would probably have gotten killed."

Most of us gasped or groaned. "What did you do?" I

asked, almost breathless.

"We waited, and occasionally Chris would tell me he was going to kill me if we survived. I really couldn't blame him. Right at the edge of the Craggy Mountains, the train slowed down to make it's climb. We saw our chance and took it. We held hands, jumped into the bushes, and laid there while the train continued rolling on past. It took us two days and nights to walk home. It was easy enough. We just had to follow the tracks back, but there were all kinds of unsavory characters that followed those same tracks. We had to hide a lot, sleep in the woods, and forage for food and water. Let's just say it was an adventure."

"Man, your parents must have been furious when you got home," said Terran.

"They were mostly relieved. There was abundant celebrating." She looked at all of our incredulous faces, "What?"

"You didn't get punished?" asked William.

"Why would we get punished? For doing what was in our nature? That's absurd." We looked at each other in amazement. "Now, along with my chores, I'm the person that goes to the edge of New City every few months to procure stuff for my community. That's why they call me the Traveler, and that's ultimately why I'm here."

"Did you ever hop a train again?" asked Frederick.

"Well, I promised my family I wouldn't anymore, and I think I had a good taste of it. Ultimately though, I prefer the pace of walking, and walking for a few days is something I still love to do." She added to Beatrice, "Don't we little Beatrice? We love to walk, don't we?"

She shook herself out of her distraction. "Okay, Frederick, your turn."

"Hm, what would you like to hear?"

"I know," I said, "tell us about when the stars disappeared."

"Are you sure, Estelle? You've heard this before. You don't want a new and improved one?" I gave him a pleading look, so he told the story.

"My mother was named Cora Snow. She was born to an amazing woman named Alexandra Snow, my maternal grandmother. Alexandra was an astronomer at one of the Space Institutes. Her focus was mapping the stars with giant telescopes. The institute also sent up space ships and investigated other planets and solar systems. Alexandra loved the night sky, almost as much as this one." He pointed with his thumb at me.

"In her lifetime, she discovered a big and significant star system, and it was named after her, the Alexandra System. Estelle loves that part, right?"

"I've searched the records, and I haven't seen much about it. I'd love to know where it's located, in the scheme of things," I said.

"Yes, you would want to know." He looked at me as if I was insufferable, but I knew he was joking. "When Cora was a little girl, she hoped to work at the Space Institute too, but by then there were some major problems with space exploration. Most people were afraid to go out at night, so they didn't care much about what was out there in the dark. If they had cared, it wouldn't have mattered much, because light pollution was bad, almost everywhere. No one cared to look up at the sky anymore. Politicians stopped talking about space, and the Congloms stopped paying for exploration. Slowly the space ships were all landed and the telescopes closed down. There were no careers left for astronomers. Happily Alexandra was an

Old One and missed the demise of her profession. Cora gave up the idea of being an astronomer and was given a job in Development and Marketing. Same place I work. I mean, *worked*.

"When I was young, I went through a phase where I wanted to be an astronomer. If there had been stars to gaze at, of course, but Estelle is driven to see the stars. She's been talking about them almost since she began to talk. I'm sad she's alive during these Dark Ages."

"The Dark Ages, that's funny," said Mj, enjoying his play on words.

"What do you mean, the Dark Ages? There's light everywhere," I asked.

"Dark Age is a historical term. It was first used to refer to Medieval times, a long, long time ago, but was also used to describe a few periods since then. It doesn't describe the light outside as much as the light in here." He tapped the side of his temple.

"The thing about Dark Ages," said Mj, "is that the people living in them don't *understand* all the things they don't know. Like they're in the dark, or asleep, and can't wake up."

"That's an apt description of us, huh? Even with all of these lights," added William.

"I saved a part of the story, that Estelle never heard before. When Alexandra died, Cora was melancholy for a while. One day I asked her what was wrong, and she showed me a letter that was found in Alexandra's things. It was a love letter, and it contained a poem written for her called, *The Stars of Alexandra*. Cora let me read the letter and keep it for a while. I remember the feeling it conveyed to this day, romantic, exceedingly so. The man who penned it swore his undying love and begged Alexandra to marry him. Cora pointed out that it wasn't written by the man who Alexandra married, Cora's father. Someone *else* had loved her desperately and tried to talk her out of marrying the man she was betrothed to by contract."

My great-grandmother was in *love*. "What happened to the letter, Frederick? I want to see it," I said.

"It's been long purged, out with the old, in with the new." We all sat in quiet for a few moments, thinking about Alexandra the Astronomer, the stars, and the long-lost poem.

"Frederick, were you happy to be married to Sylvia?" I asked, forgetting I was in a group and carried away by the idea of love.

"Yes, sure, though it might not look like it now that I've moved to a dirty future-farm with the kids. Yes, happy and thankful. If it wasn't for our betrothal, we wouldn't have had both of you."

Mj asked, "But why couldn't she just marry who she wanted to marry? I swear you civvies are so weird!" She threw up her hands in feigned disgust.

"Well, she had to follow orders, and as you all know, the Office of Future Affairs is *never* wrong," he said, reciting the oft-heard phrase. I wished I could ask Alexandra if the Office *had* been right all those years ago.

While we talked and told stories, we passed around the baby. Everyone held her for a while and enjoyed the comfort of a sleeping baby who trusted our arms. She was so heavy. I couldn't get over how tiny, perfect, and solidly real she was. William stayed late to listen to stories and discuss plans and hold Beatrice and coo sweetly to her, before he headed home.

Right before bed, Mj asked, "I've been wondering something. Why do you call your mother and father by their first names? Do all civvies do that?"

Terran and I looked at each other, and I answered, "Yeah, what would we call them?"

"Mom and Dad, or Mum and Pop, or I don't know, Ma and Pa."

Frederick said, "Our culture believes using labels like that would emphasize the relationship over the independent person."

Mj nodded her head as if that explained everything.

I asked, "What do you call your parents?"

"I call them Mom and Dad," said Mj. "We call everyone who's a parent mom or dad. It feels weird to me to call Frederick by his first name. I keep wanting to call him Dad."

"Well, since we're challenging everything about the 'civvie' lifestyle here, I give you permission to call me Dad," answered Frederick, in a magnanimous voice.

"What about us, Frederick? Do *we* get to call you Dad?" asked Terran, with a huge teasing grin.

Frederick responded with, "I don't know son, that would sound weird coming from the likes of you."

"I'm definitely calling you Dad, from now on. Okay Frederick?" I asked, teasingly.

That night Terran gave up his hammock to Mj. We worried for a minute about where Beatrice would sleep, but Mj said she would sleep right beside her, and so she did. The night was peaceful and quiet for everyone there. Everyone except for me, because the last thing Mj said before bed was, "You're going to need water, Estelle. You can't have a farm without water."

How in the world would I get water?

kinds of people

Over the next few days, the five of us settled into a flow and built a two-foot high surrounding wall out of the chunks of cement. Stacking the rocks was meditative and finding the right pieces to balance, and stay balanced, took concentration. It was an improvement over the loud work we were doing before, but still backbreaking. I never wanted to lift and carry a rock again.

Mj planned over her catalogues, created orders, measured, and deciphered. Every now and then she would wander over with enigmatic questions, like, "How many eggs do you think you'll each eat in a week?" And, "Will you use goat milk to drink, or will you use it mostly in cooking?" Questions I had no answer for and only barely understood.

I learned quickly to say, "What do you think, Mj?"

She would answer with, "Probably one egg for each, a day, will suffice, at least at first," or, "once you fall for goat milk, you're going to love it. I better get you the best milk goats." She would wander off with her pencil scribbling in the catalogues.

On the second night when we were gathered around the fire again, Mj asked, "Fancy another story?"

We resoundingly said yes, and she said, "When her last baby was out of arms, mom decided to teach herself how to knit. A family down the street had sheep, and after shearing, they would spin the wool. Mom traded milk from our cows for some of their yarn even though it was a creamy white and not at all her style. She gathered up herbs, berries, and seeds, for their coloring properties, and spent a week or so dying it. Her hands and arms were purple. Purple! The trouble was, she didn't dye the yarn all *one* color, so she could knit a *sophisticated* sweater. She dyed yarn every color under the rainbow, and I swear there were some colors never seen before, anywhere."

Mj's laugh was a bird's twitter, with an occasional snort. "Tee hee hee shnurgle, tee hee hee shnurt." I giggled because it sounded so jolly. Terran had the beginnings of a laugh on his face.

"Mom was so proud when she started knitting. Trouble was, she'd never knitted before, and she doesn't like to follow directions. She's too *arty* for that. So, though she worked on that sweater daily for months, it came out, let's just say, *interesting*." Mj had to pause to laugh-snort for a second, completely overcome with hysterics. "When she was finishing it up, we all wondered who would be the lucky winner of that sweater. Nobody wanted to be the person who would have to wear it–probably *everywhere,* so we wouldn't hurt her feelings. It was a riotous *explosion* of color." Tears ran down Mj's face. She finally recovered herself enough to squeak out the end.

"With great fanfare Mom presented it to *Dad.* She said, 'Here, Dear, I knitted you a sweater,' and gave him a sweet little kiss. There was nothing he could do but put it on," Mj dried her eyes. "The sweater was tighter in the top, around the ribs, and was bulbous around his waist. One sleeve was longer than the other, by about two inches, and the neck hung loosely," Mj had to pause again to tee-hee-hee-snort more, unable to talk through the hilarity. "You know the best part? When Dad walked out into the room, Mom said, 'Perfect!'" That did it, we were all laughing in hysterics, tears running down our faces.

"I'd love to meet your mom," I said, when the laughter wound down.

"She walks to the beat of another drum, that's for sure." Mj smiled affectionately. "I think she'd like to meet you too, and maybe knit you a sweater!" She collapsed into a sideways heap of twitters and shnurftle sounds.

I said, "I have to hold my sides because I think I might explode!" It felt so good to laugh like this, why didn't we do it all the time?

When we were all calmed and quiet, Mj said, "I'm thinking William should tell the next story. I want to hear about how he came to be here."

William said, "Well, I have to go back a few years, and it's not humorous."

"That's all right. All stories are good stories when they're told around a fire," Mj coached.

He nodded. "If you insist." He paused, seeming to search for the words, "When I was twelve, my family went to the shore for a two week vacation. Have any of you been to the shore?" Only Frederick had, so William carried on with a description first, "It's difficult to get used to a horizon line of water and a big, big sky. You can't even imagine the sky. You're literally at the end of the Earth. It's unsettling and miraculous all at once. When I saw it, I couldn't leave the beach. I sat in the sand and stared out at the ocean, wondering, watching, and dreaming. Every day I went there as soon as I woke up and stayed all day. On the third day, I walked until I rounded a bend and left the–I guess Mj would call it–civvie beach, and found myself in the company of locals. I hung out with them for a while, and a guy named Kelly offered to teach me to surf."

William asked, "Have you ever seen surfing?"

We had all seen surfing in videos, or photos, so he continued, "I picked it up in a few days and surfed the whole rest of the vacation. It was one of the best two weeks of my life.

"I talked about surfing, the beach, and the ocean all the time after that. This was a huge mistake because my parents, John and Marie, didn't approve at *all*. I guess they thought it was dangerous, or dirty, or didn't like the local kids, or whatever. When they planned another trip to the shore the following year, they came up with a plan to keep me from spending so much time in the water."

"Oh no, what did they do?" asked Terran.

"They adjusted my medication. They gave me new ones that made me sleepy and confused. I felt exhausted and cloudy-brained. I slept inside our hotel room almost the entire vacation. I just about missed the beach completely, except for a few minutes here, and there, looking, but not really *caring*. I *miraculously* snapped out of the fog a couple of days after the vacation.

"It wasn't until the following year, when I was fourteen, and we were headed to the shore again, that I realized what John and Marie had done. They had adjusted my meds to make me more compliant, and again, a week before vacation, new medicines were in my nightly cocktail, *again*."

"Wow, you must have been pissed," said Terran.

"Yeah, that's an understatement. I refused to take it to their face. Every time they brought me a tray of pills, I threw the extra ones away, right in front of them. We went to the shore, and I surfed every minute of every day. I came home late and left before they woke up. By the end of the two week vacation, they hated the sight of me, because they couldn't control me.

The best part was I didn't care.

"I stopped taking all my meds the week we came home, right in front of John and Marie. We came to an agreement: we'd leave each other alone, and once I came of age, I'd move away. I figure they're grateful to you, Estelle and Terran, for taking me away almost a year earlier." He smiled at all of us, showing he wasn't at all sad about the outcome.

"They sound like terrible people, and they suck at parenting," said Mj.

Frederick said, "I don't want to make excuses for them, but parents have a tough job. Our babies aren't supposed to ever experience pain, or sadness, or fear. Never anything dark, or dangerous, and no anger. It's difficult work to control everything and to protect kids completely. Some days the easiest thing you can do is make sure the medications keep them quiet, serene, and out of trouble." Frederick looked around. "We've all made that mistake, but I'm glad those days are behind me."

"So, William, do you miss surfing," asked Mj, "and the ocean?"

"I do. It's amazing riding down the face of a wave. The ocean's energy pulses underneath you. It's like you're harnessing its power. I felt competent and alive, like I was truly awake. This, here, feels something like it, toiling for long days with friends. Before I came here, I missed the ocean just about every day. Now I feel content for the first time in a long time." William looked around the fire. "I hope I didn't bring you down too much. I warned you it wasn't funny."

"It's all good," said Mj. She turned to Terran, "Why'd you come with Estelle?"

"Because she promised me a tree with my name on it someday." We all laughed. "My needs are simple, they really are."

Mj got a faraway look in her eyes. "We have a belief in The Beyonds that the world is made up of three kinds of people, and they complete each other. The pattern of three explains all actions and dreams. It corresponds with the body and types of personalities. You have earth people, they follow their feet, are grounded and simple, happy, mostly. There are horizon people; they follow their instincts and guts, they're passionate and usually musical, they struggle, though, against the World. Lastly, there's the air type. Air people follow their head, and they're dreamers. When I came here, I wondered why you three ended up here on this land together, and today I had my answer. You were resting after a few hours of work and sitting in a group. From the distance, I could see Terran looking down at the earth, digging with his toe. William shaded his eyes from the sun, and stared out past the fence, and Estelle looked up at the sky. The three of you embodied the three archetypes."

"That sounds about right, huh?" asked Terran. "So what's Frederick, I mean, *Dad?*"

Frederick said, "I'm just the money guy," and everyone laughed again.

up close

On the third day, Mj came over to where I worked and said, "Estelle, I want to do some shoveling for dirt samples. Can you carry Beatrice in the sling for a little bit?" I scrambled for an excuse, any excuse, because I was clearly not capable. Couldn't she tell just by looking at me? My eyes were wide and beseeching. I searched for a reason to say no, but it was too late. She pulled the pouch over her head and passed it quickly to my front. With one quick motion she looped the fabric over my shoulder, adjusted it across my back, and effortlessly fit it to my body. Beatrice fussed.

"This is a sign she doesn't want me to carry her, right?"

"Just do this," and Mj rocked back and forth in a kind of dance-walk. Okay, it wouldn't hurt to try. I rocked back and forth and felt completely idiotic. "Slow down, you don't want her to get sick." I continued to rock, slowly this time, and Beatrice smiled up at me. "There you go, she likes it," Mj wandered off, leaving me in charge of the tiny baby. I nodded good-bye. I was capable enough to do this, probably.

I needed a break from shoveling anyway, so instead I rocked and walked the perimeter of the fence. I stopped every now and then to look at the land from the edge in toward the middle, a view I rarely took. The land was big, spacious, flat, and blank. It was hard to believe it would produce anything worth all the work we'd put into it. Right now the only colors were brown, bright green plastic, and grey. Would the green of growing things ever exist here? It was hard to believe. Along the way I cooed and talked to Beatrice, realizing I sounded like Mj. Baby talk was an easy language to learn.

Halfway around, I had a view of William, Terran, and Frederick at the other far end. They were tearing out more concrete, a process that was long, difficult, loud, and terrifically tough on the body. My concentration settled on William. How long was he willing to stay and help? I hoped he wouldn't leave, at least not yet. I had grown accustomed to his easy conversation and sense of humor. What would living on this land be like without him? I couldn't imagine it.

He must have felt me looking at him, because he looked up and smiled at me from across the land. It was a big smile, a friendly smile, an almost flirtatious smile.

My reverie was broken by the sight of Jack at the gate. I walked over and said, "Hello, future-husband!"

"You really didn't know? Why didn't you read the letter they sent?"

"I don't know. I guess I didn't *want* to know. I had this all planned, and I was afraid knowing who my future-husband was would change things."

"Well, that explains why you didn't come see me when I asked. I thought you were angry about the outcome, and I'd need to spend some time wooing you over."

"I really had no idea. I didn't even think it was possible for them to pick us, *twice*."

"Estelle, I have to ask, what's that on your front?"

"Oh that's right." I laughed outright. "This is Beatrice, a *baby*. There's her mother, way over there in the corner, Mj.

She's here helping us with the next phase of the plan. Come to find out, I was not ready for that part. At *all*."

"Wow, I seriously have to remind myself to be ready for anything, because whenever I think I've got this whole thing figured out, you're onto some new kind of crazy. *Babies*, out of nurseries!" He joined me in laughing. He was right, this was all completely odd.

"I came because I'm taking the day, and thought I might be able to help. It's why I'm wearing my work clothes." He smirked and looked down. His clothes were azure blue with cream accents. His shoes were light tan. "They're the oldest I have," he explained, chuckling at his plight. "I thought I could work for a few hours, and then you would come home with me for dinner. My parents are dying to meet the famous Estelle Wells. They *love* famous people.

"You could take a shower. I bet you *really* miss bathing." He waved in front of his nose to signal that I stank. It wasn't insulting because it was true.

"I *could* use a shower." Bathing with the buckets of saved water, was getting very old. The bathroom we left standing was also terrifically stinky. So stinky that no one wanted to use it. We had a toilet, but with the city water only coming through the pipes three times a week we had to conserve. That meant flushing every two days. I *really* needed to figure out how to get water here. "Sure, but only if you really work. When you take me home to meet your parents, I want you to be dirty too, to take the pressure off."

"I don't know Estelle. It'll take a lot of effort to get as grungy as you, but I'll try." This was another truth I couldn't deny. Settled, we walked across the field toward the others.

"Hey everyone, this is Jack." I introduced him all around and got him a shovel. Mj came over and took Beatrice, so I could get back to moving cement. We all settled into a routine, though Jack struggled with the physical work and was unsure about touching what was underneath the cement. He looked awkward, attempting to do what we had been doing for weeks. In comparison, we were professionals at cement moving. I noticed William and Terran smirking behind his back.

By the end of the afternoon, Jack did look rather dirty. Far more filthy than I'm sure he had ever looked before. He was uncomfortable and exhausted, and perhaps too gruffly said, "All right, lets go now."

True, we had made a deal. "Sure." He was embarrassed and I wanted to get him away before he betrayed how out of sorts he was after a few hours of hard work. I gathered some things and turned around to a circle of raised eyebrows and disapproving faces.

"Where are you going, Stelley?" asked Terran, glancing at the unhappy Jack.

"Jack invited me home for dinner and has kindly offered me my first warm shower since I came here. I'm taking him up on the offer."

"What if you're arrested?"

"She won't be arrested, my family is making sure of it," responded Jack, speaking for me. I turned and looked at him, unsure that he was supposed to do that. Couldn't I speak for myself?

"*Your* family? Why in the world?" asked William, his voice trailed off, not expecting an answer.

The conversation seemed to be getting contentious, so I finished it up. "I'll be back in a few hours. Good night, everyone," and walked off with Jack.

Once we were outside the gate and in his car, he seemed to gather his strength and good humor. On the way home he ventured a joke about how tired he was, and how stinky, though there was no way he approached the epic filth that was me.

He took me into his family home, showed me to a bathroom, and even provided a change of clothes that his father had bought for me. While I took the most amazing shower of my life, full of floral bubble scrubs and perfumed lotions, he carried my clothes down to wash and took his own shower. He knocked on the door of my bathroom when he was done.

The clothes fit perfectly. The pants were a dark, chocolate brown with an azure blue belt and a white linen shirt. There was a new pair of shoes in a deep blue that encased my feet like they had been made for me. I walked over to the mirror and relished my refection. We had a mirror in our bathroom on the land, but I never looked at myself in it, or at least tried not to. When I did, the face that looked back was almost unrecognizable, dirty and unkempt. I hadn't applied make-up or done anything with my hair beyond a braid in what seemed like forever. Tonight I applied make-up and swept my hair up into a simple hairstyle. I smiled at myself in the mirror. "Where have you been, Estelle Wells?" I felt beautiful for the first time in an exceptionally long time.

I met Jack in the hall and we went downstairs to meet his parents. His father was waiting for us and warmly greeted me when I walked in. "Hello, the *notorious* Estelle Wells, revolutionary farmer, celebrity, and future daughter-in-law." He chuckled as if enjoying the joke and shook my hand vigorously. "Jack told me you were beautiful, but he didn't fully describe your glow." I could feel heat creeping up my face. If I *had* a glow, now it was all covered in splotches.

Mr. Maranville turned to Jack, "Well done Jack, well done."

What was I, a trophy? He addressed me again, "I've seen photographs, but they did *not* do you justice. Drink?" He passed me a blue concoction with smoke drifting out of it, and ice, lots of ice. It was so unbelievably delicious. "You got your clothes I see. They fit well. I had them designed by a fashion designer Maude knows. Just name what you need, Estelle. We're very well connected. We can get you anything you want." He sat back pleased with himself.

"I think we're doing well, Sir," I said, "I do want to thank you for your help, for keeping the authorities from arresting us."

"Well, Estelle, our family is in PR and Brand Marketing. We manage sports heroes, entertainers, celebrities, and conglomerates. We're one of the best families in the business. When I heard that you, the chosen marital partner of my son, were tearing down buildings in Old Town in apparent defiance of the entire world, I thought, this could be the ultimate challenge. Could I turn someone who's questioning the status quo into a celebrity? Absolutely. If I can't do it, no one can!" He enthusiastically clinked his ice cubes in my direction.

My head felt a little like it was spinning, and warmth spread through my body. Oh, remember not to drink any more of that drink. Jack's mother bustled in and shook my hand, introducing herself as Maude.

Mr. Maranville said, "Maude, take a look at this beauty. Can you believe the light that emanates off her? Make sure you tell the photographer to capture that brightness."

Maude said, "I've just been meeting with the photographers. They'd like to do the shoot tomorrow."

"How does that sound, Estelle? Photographers will come and shoot you in the 'wild'?"

I couldn't think of a more terrifying prospect, but I had no idea how to respond. I took another sip.

"Let's head into dinner," said Maude, and I was led through to the dining room by Mr. Maranville's firm hand on my back. Dinner was delicious, the best of everything, and as much sweetener as I could pour onto it. Everyone at the table beamed at me while I coated my food. I smiled a big toothy smile. They looked gloatingly happy, like they had captured sight of a rare beast.

"So Estelle, who do you have helping you at this stage?" Mr. Maranville looked at his wife and said, "To flesh out the story."

"Sure," she said.

"Um, there's me and my brother, he's been helping me from the beginning. He's as much a part of it as I am."

"Did he come up with the original plan?"

"No, but he..."

"He wasn't the creator; that's you. You're the one. Look at you, you're definitely the story. Absolutely." Mr. Maranville punctuated his point with a flourish.

"There's William, a friend of Terran. He's been helping since the first week."

"What's in it for him do you think, fame and glory?"

"I don't know what his motives are..."

"Everyone has motives, Estelle, everyone." He tapped his finger on his temple.

"There's my father, Frederick, he came a few weeks in."

"Now see, there's a fascinating angle. Frederick leaves everything to follow his kid's dreams, quits his important job and leaves his wife. All because his daughter, The Visionary, compels him to follow her. Yep, great story!" Mr. Maranville was pleased with himself.

"There's Mj and her baby, Beatrice. She's an expert at

growing things and came from The Beyonds."

"The Beyonds? Humph, well there's not much story there, is there? When does she leave?"

"A few more days?"

"Good, good. So, is there anything I can get you? Any help you need beyond the creation of your brand?"

"What is my brand exactly, Sir?"

"Why it's you, Estelle Wells, Revolutionary Farmer. Your motto is, *Question Everything*. It comes from a Greek playwright named Euripides, or something. People are clamoring for more. They can't get enough of you!" He raised his glass in my direction, again.

"Thank you, Sir. Um, I, we...we could use some boots. I've seen a pair I like. They're black leather. They go up past the ankles and tie with about seven holes. The soles are thick and wide and rubber. Do you think you could get some like that for us?"

"I could, of course I could, but you don't want big boots. These shoes we had designed for you are the best, lightest, airiest materials, created by one of the most clamored-after shoe designers in the city. These are the best, Estelle, I assure you. Leave a list of the sizes everyone wears, and I'll get them sent to you before your photo shoot." He rose to leave the table and shook my hand. "A real pleasure, you're welcome anytime. Good night, Son," and he swept his wife out of the room.

I turned to Jack with a quizzical look. He replied with, "That's Leo Maranville, so full of ideas no one else gets to say a word. I just nod and smile. Let me walk you back to your land before nightfall."

"You know, now that I live outside most of the day, and sleep outside too, I'm not afraid of night anymore." As we walked outside, I added, "Night isn't even dark. It's as brightly lit as the day. I think it's kind of nice to be outside then, more quiet and still, because everyone else is tucked away indoors."

"So what you're saying is you're trying to be different in every single way, huh?"

"Yeah, I guess."

We talked all the way home, mostly about what it was like to grow up in the Maranville home, where success was measured by how famous you were. Jack knew celebrities, many, and it was fascinating to hear stories about them, even though they were far removed from my own life.

When we arrived at my fence, the crowds were departing but stopped to get a glimpse of me. While I unlocked the gate, Jack stood close, very close, nervously close. I turned to him and said, "Thanks for the evening. It was really kind of you to let me get a shower and clean clothes. It lifted my spirits."

He leaned in, and twirled the hair that was loose at the front of my face, "That's my future-wife, Estelle, even all cleaned up, she still has a hair out of place." As he pulled his hand away, he rubbed it ever so lightly down my cheek. "See you tomorrow at the photo shoot," he said, and without waiting for a response, got in his car and drove back to bright and sparkling New City.

warmth and stillness

Everyone at the fire pit was intent on a long and congenial conversation, so my appearance startled them at first. Then a chorus of hellos and big welcoming smiles reminded me how comfortable it was to be here, around this fire, with this group of familiar faces. Even a long warm shower couldn't compensate for an hour lost from this part of my life.

"Did you miss me?" I beamed at them.

They nodded and proclaimed their despair profusely, and exaggeratedly. I settled into my usual spot.

"I'm clean," I declared. "Smell my arm," I pushed it toward Terran's nose.

"Hm," he joked, "seems to be missing something. Your usual eau de sweat, perhaps?"

Mj looked me over. "Is this how you used to look?"

"Yes, but with fancier everything. This is fairly simple actually. Why?" I felt awkward. Was there something wrong?

"Because you look really beautiful. I didn't realize that was how you looked before. I guess I never realized how much you gave up to do this."

Terran grinned at me, enjoying my discomfort, and told me that Mj was going to go over to the Old Time Museum to place the order tomorrow. "Wow, we're at that point?" I asked no one in particular.

"I'll also go through their supplies and see if there are some things that I can buy from them directly," she said.

"As you know," Frederick said, "I'm putting forward the money needed. You can pay me back when this all gets going." He chuckled, because the risk was high, and the chance of any return low. How in the world would I ever pay him back?

"Uh huh," I agreed. The warmth of the fire had relaxed me so much that I stopped speaking with actual words. "Anything else happen?"

"Well," William said. He drew the syllable out long and hesitatingly. "The situation at home has gotten extremely tough. I thought, if its okay with you, that I could sleep here too. You know, move in."

I looked around at all the faces. They obviously had heard and were waiting for me to have my say. I said, "I thought you knew you could do that anytime. You've worked as hard as we have. It's your home now, too." There was a murmur of assent all around.

"Thanks Estelle, and everyone," he said, eyes turned toward the fire. We sat in silence for a long time.

Mj said, "I told two stories the other night, and I haven't heard one from Estelle yet."

I smiled at my now dear friend, even though she put me on the spot. "Okay, sure." I needed to stall for time. "Can I hold Beatrice? I want to tell her the story." Mj passed Beatrice to me, and I gazed into her eyes as I began, "Once upon a time there was a beautiful girl..."

"Wait a second, you don't get to start yours with, Once Upon a Time. It's not a fairy tale,'" Terran said. "If she starts it that way, I want a do-over."

"It is if I say so, and everyone is going to live happily ever after in it, too." I stuck out my tongue for good measure.

Looking back down at Beatrice, I continued, "The beautiful girl thought her world was terrible because she couldn't see the stars, and she wanted to see the stars more than anything. Thinking the world was terrible made her want to do something drastic to change it. But what could she do? She was just a little, albeit beautiful, girl.

"She tried dreaming that the stars would appear, but dreams didn't do anything but make her sleepless and tired.

"She tried complaining about the lack of stars, but anyone who heard her told her to be quiet. Beautiful little girls shouldn't go around complaining like that.

"She tried protesting. She hoped the terrible world would change, and the stars would appear again, but she realized her protests were futile. Terrible worlds don't change just because a few people yell about things.

"The beautiful..."

"Um, you've said that," said Terran, butting in again.

"Yes, I know, but really, it just can't be said enough," I started again, "the beautiful girl sat and thought about what she could do to change the world, or at least her teeny, tiny part of the world. It came to her when she was very old, seventeen, and wise. She didn't need to change the whole terrible world, she just needed to live the life she wanted in her own small corner of it. So she behaved heroically, and bravely, and started a farm."

"Heroically and bravely!" said Terran, "You're filling poor Beatrice's head with such nonsense." Everyone laughed now.

"She behaved heroically and bravely, and *completely* on her own." I had trouble keeping my laughter in check, over Terran's pretended outrage. "She farmed, and her world wasn't terrible anymore. Now her world was happy. Since happiness had come, she felt certain that somehow, *someday*, the stars would come, too, and she would live happily ever after." I looked up at the sky searchingly, and Beatrice smiled. "I feel sure Beatrice loves the heroic and brave protagonist of my story, even if some people don't." I smiled lovingly at Terran.

"That story was *terrible*. I feel sure Beatrice would much rather hear the part about the incredibly handsome, and long-suffering, brother that had to do everything on the farm while the sister feigned heroic conquests." He smiled lovingly back.

"Thank you for the story Estelle," said Mj. "I think you're very heroic, and I think Terran is *very* long-suffering." She patted her knees, smiled at all of us, and stood up. "Beatrice and I are headed to bed. We have a long day tomorrow. Good night."

Frederick said he was turning in, and Terran said he would hit the sack too. He said, "Literally," because he was sleeping in a sack on the ground, having given his hammock over to Mj, "a sack. I'm going to hit it because it's *hard*. Only for a few more days," and he stood and did a little happy jig, "good night."

William and I sat quietly around the fire for a bit, enjoying the warmth and stillness. "I'm thinking that sitting here around the fire with all of you is the best place on Earth," he said.

"Yeah, me too." There was silence again. "William, can I ask you something? Why haven't you ever asked me about that day I threw up on your shoes? You haven't mentioned it, or joked, or anything. I was *mortified*."

"Because I'd been there before. When I saw you, I knew you were trying to get off your medicines."

"Oh." I hadn't even thought of that reason.

He said, "After I realized how much they were about control, I decided to flaunt my lack of control as much as possible. I relished being a troublemaker, but I was worried I would become, I don't know, irredeemable, beyond hope. In the three years that I was off the meds, I never met anyone else who did it, until that day."

"I went off them because I felt confused, and sort of blah. I wanted to understand what was going on around me. I had so many questions. I still do." I laughed. "I guess going off the meds didn't really fix what's wrong with me."

William smiled. "There's nothing wrong with you. Seriously, you're perfect." I protested for a second, and he said, "Mj was right, you do look really beautiful tonight." I looked at him to see if he was joking, but he had turned back to the fire. "What pattern did they project on the sky in New City tonight, Estelle?"

"It was the awful one with the stripes that sort of slide across the tops of the buildings, so you think you might get dizzy and fall down. You know those patterns are the main reason why I did all of this in the first place."

"Yeah, I know."

"Really? How? I thought that was my secret."

"I kept hearing about you, a girl who questions things and gets sent to the Office almost as much as I did. I was curious. Someone pointed out that Terran was your brother, so one day I sat beside him and asked about you, what you were like. I hope that doesn't freak you out. I was just curious to find out about the only girl who seemed similar to me."

"No, I get it. I was curious about you too."

"Terran said you loved the idea of the stars, that you desperately wanted to see them. He totally admires you. He was the quietest guy in our classes, but the cool thing was that as we got to talking, I realized that he was interesting too. I learned he thought deeply about what was going on. He didn't judge me, and we became friends. I needed a friend, that's for sure."

"While I was coming home, I realized one of the main reasons most people are okay with the projected patterns is because they aren't outside at night. They rarely see them. They're not outside long enough to think about how ugly and discordant they are. They just don't think things through."

"You're right, they don't. The meds are about controlling us, making us all calm, unemotional, and easily managed. The people in charge just want to tell us what to buy, what to do, what to say, and who to marry." He took a part of the stick he held, broke it in two, tossed one end into the fire, and dropped the other by his chair. "I'll see you in the morning, Estelle. Good night."

"Good night, William," I said as he walked away from the fire. Knowing he couldn't hear me, I added, "I'm glad you're here." To no one in particular, I said, "I have a photo shoot tomorrow."

quite the celebrity

About mid morning a truck delivered a large box addressed to me. I opened it to find four shoe boxes inside and an envelope with my name written across the front in a loopy cursive scrawl. I ripped it open and read:

Dear Estelle,
    I just wanted you to know that I'm listening to you.
    Your future-husband,
    Jack

I pulled open the top box, and inside was the pair of boots I had described last night. Black leather, thick rubber soles, and seven eyes. There was a pair for me, Terran, William, and Dad, and, at the bottom, some thick pale blue socks. Those would get filthy quick, but the boots were perfect. I hefted the box and ran with it to where the others were gathered, shouting, "We got boots! We got boots!" Everyone opened boxes and examined the contents. Terran asked, "Who sent them, Stelley?"

"Jack did! His family asked what we needed, and I said boots! The Maranvilles are very well connected, you know. I figured if anyone could get them, they could. What?" I stopped my exuberant chatter and looked around. Terran, William and Frederick had all come to a standstill halfway through pulling on the boots. They all stared back at me. I felt self-conscious and couldn't think of what to say.

Frederick asked, "What's in it for him, Estelle? I can't figure out why he's so interested in what you're doing. Its not like the Maranvilles to express interest in someone like you."

"Like me?" I was irritated by the conversation and the way the boots were being received.

"Yes, *difficult*, like *you*," Frederick explained, "why are they?"

"Well, I didn't know how to say it earlier." I didn't want to say it out loud and definitely not in front of William. "I found out we're betrothed to each other again."

"You what?!" All three spoke in unison.

Frederick asked, "But, how did that happen?"

"I don't know, but Mr. Maranville said because of the um, connection, he figured keeping me from arrest, and even making me famous, was in their family's best interest. They're *helping*," I protested, looking at their skeptical faces.

William said, "Estelle, Mr. Maranville never does *anything* without expecting something in return. Remember that, please," and he put his boots back inside their wrapper and returned them to the box. He walked back to where he'd been working.

Frederick put on the boots, admired their fit, and said quietly, "Tell Mr. Maranville thank you, from me," and he went back to work.

Terran sat looking at me with his brow low over his suspicious eyes. "I thought the whole point was to do something different, to live in a wholly new way, without approval, or control. When did being a celebrity become part of the plan?"

"I don't know. The Maranvilles have kept us from being arrested. It seems like something we should be grateful for, you know, their friendship."

Terran finished putting his boots on without saying a word. His silence felt like an admonition. Then he said, "You've been right about most things—this land, your Bright Idea. I totally trust your instincts. If you think that the protection of the Maranville family is a good idea, then I think so too." He clapped my knee. "You think so?"

"Yes, I think," I replied, looking down at the ground. Did I think?

"Okay, then." Terran looked at his boots and wiggled his feet around. "It's a good fit." He sauntered off to work in the opposite corner. I sat for a while, not noticing my stare into the distance took in the scope of the far end of the land, where William happened to be at work.

I had pulled myself together enough to get back to work, when my industriousness was interrupted again. A van pulled up, and a photographer stepped out. Jack and his mother drove up in another car. I met them at the gate, where Maude stiffly said, "Hello."

Jack warmly greeted me with, "You got the boots, perfect!" He added in a lower voice, "We've agreed with the photographer that you'll answer one question, only one, and you'll pose for a half hour, okay?"

"Sure." I shook hands with the photographer.

While he readied his equipment, he looked me over from head to toe. "What designer are you wearing right now?" I looked down. Uh oh.

"Is this your one question?" I asked, trying to think of a half-intelligible answer. I wore the outfit from last night, but I never asked Mr. Maranville the name of the designer. He'd be pissed. Am I that removed from civilization, that I would wear an outfit without knowing who designed it? I knew nothing about the color, the style, the fabric. How could I have let myself commit that error?

He nodded, so I said, "I don't remember the name. Can you read the tag?" I leaned over, and opened up the back of my shirt collar.

The photographer read, "James Uno. Ah, he's trendy right now. Can you hold that position for a second so I can take a photo?" I kept my awkward stance while he clicked away. The only thing those photos would prove was that I didn't know anything about designer clothes, and I was willing to act foolishly in front of the fashionable citizens of New City.

He asked me to stand just within the gate. He wanted to get the chain-link of the fence in the foreground, me just beyond, and the expanse of the land behind. He told me he was famous for his 'gritty realism' and asked if I'd seen his work before.

"No," but I got why they chose him for me. I was definitely gritty, even with the new clothes.

He told me how to stand, and put me in awkward positions that were supposed to make me look like I was farming. He took hundreds of photographs before he shook my hand and said good-bye.

Maude Maranville said even more stiffly, "Thank you, Estelle," and went to her car.

Jack stayed behind for a minute and teased, "You did great. You have a future as a model, if gritty stays trendy, and this whole farming thing doesn't work out. How are you today?"

"Good. Mj went to the Old Time Museum to place an order for the second phase of the plan. I can't wait to see what she brings back." I looked off in the distance and could see the truck and the guys working. "I've got to go get some stuff done, Jack, okay?"

"Sure, I've kept you from it long enough," his eyes looked toward the laboring men, too. "Mind if I come back and work soon?"

"Of course, we can use the help." We parted ways, and I walked across the land to where work waited.

"A photographer, huh? You *are* quite the celebrity. So, how'd it go?" asked Terran, trying to cut through the awkwardness of the moment. There was no way to ease into hard manual labor right after a photo shoot. I felt ridiculous and embarrassed. I bit my lip because I felt like I might cry.

"It went well. I think it's good to get a bit of the message out, you know. The trouble is he only asked about the designer of the clothes I'm wearing." I tried not to meet William's eyes. I felt like a complete failure. Maybe taking the boots was a mistake, or maybe I missed being a trendsetting teen in New City. I was tired and confused, and no longer sure of my motivations. I looked down and tried to keep back the tears. "I guess I won't know until next week if I sounded like a complete moron, or not."

"I hope you sounded like a complete moron. That way the unsavory types won't keep coming around bugging you for more words of wisdom," said William, with a smirk in my direction. It was clear he wasn't a big fan of Jack.

sure of each step

A few hours later, Mj came back. She rattled on the gate with a shovel, yelling, "I've got presents!" Behind her, was a hand-truck laden with boxes. It was like a birthday, except instead of brightly colored wrappings and logos, everything was bundled up in plain brown boxes.

Mj told us she had placed an order, a *big* order, that would take a week or two to come in. She'd be gone before it arrived, so for the next day or two she would walk us through what would come and what we should do with it. We were all sad at the idea of her leaving. She was a good friend, and it didn't seem like we were ready, or could ever be ready, to be on our own.

We opened the gifts. In one large bundle there were three extra hammocks Mj had found in a closet of the Old Time Museum. "Now you have one extra for your *guest room*," she said, and Terran did his trademark jig of joy. She also brought two pairs of coveralls, similar to her own, that were the right size for Terran and William.

With great fanfare, Mj gave us some pots and pans, plates, and forks and told us they would be absolutely necessary when we made our own food. We laughed incredulously. "No, seriously people, you *will* cook your own food." We acted horrorstruck, so she exclaimed, "In the future! Not now, *someday*. You're clearly not ready yet!"

We all did hope that someday we would cook food we had grown on our land, but that still seemed like such a long way off. It was difficult to wrap our head around how we would get there—growing, harvesting, cooking, and then eating. Maybe we never would. Mj had been teasing us about our food the whole time she was there. Once her own supplies had run out, she had started every meal by saying, "This? *This* is what we're going to eat?"

I would say in return, "Add sugar, it makes it almost edible!" I was going to miss that girl.

Near the end of the packages, she reached into a small box and pulled out a tiny mewling kitten. "I knew, without a doubt, that you needed him. Why don't you ever talk about your pets?"

"Nobody keeps pets in New City because they're dirty and yucky and carry disease," I answered, "right?"

At that, Mj thrust the kitten right into my arms. "Don't be a ridiculous civvie. In The Beyonds, my life is full of animals, livestock and pets. You'll like it, I promise."

I held the kitten awkwardly. What would it be like to share my life with a furry beast? This fur was so soft though, wow, and the kitten was *very* cute. I rubbed its furry body across my cheek and was completely hooked. "I'm naming you Walden."

"So, what's that about?" asked William while settling back with his arms behind his head, "Tell me about Walden."

Mj burst in, "Oh! I read that book, my parents have it."

"Your parents have a copy?" I asked. "The Beyonds keep surprising me.

"*Walden* was a book written by Henry David Thoreau, a really, really long time ago. It's about his decision to leave civilization behind and build a small cabin on borrowed land at the edge of Walden pond. Some of his detractors think he was a fraud because he was still living close to town and could easily walk there, but I kind of think that's the best part." I stroked Walden's back and thought for a moment. "His point wasn't to disappear. It was to show everyone else there was a new–or, sorry, *different*–way to live."

"I bet he didn't risk arrest, though, not like us," said Terran.

"Actually he did, though not for his cabin," I said. William leaned up and rested on his elbow, his face attentive and curious. "Thoreau lived during the time of slavery and decided he didn't want to participate in things his government did that he believed were immoral. He refused to pay his taxes and went to jail. Later he wrote an essay called *Civil Disobedience*, about how important it is for people who disagree with their governments to resist cooperating with them."

William said, "Whoa. I'd like to read that."

"I'll get it from the library if we can ever leave this place again, speaking of being disobedient."

We had one of the best fires that night, our conversation was witty, out ideas grand and expansive. I had little Walden on my lap the whole night. If I got up, I would let someone else hold him, briefly, but when I sat down again, I would remind them, jokingly, "Who *knows* what terrible disease he has," so they'd quickly give him back.

Mj said, "I saved the best for last," and pulled an old guitar out of a bundle. "I have one of these at home, and wished I brought it to play around these wonderful nightly fires. Making friends with all of you..." She choked up a bit, unable to complete her thought. "Estelle, your Bright Idea is everything I thought it was and so much more. I can't wait to come back in a few months and see how it's all going. I'll really miss you all."

She played a lovely song I had heard many times, but never in person, never from someone who was sitting right beside me. Mj played song after song. Some were rollicking singsongs, some soft and lovely, some romantic, many I had never heard, including a lullaby I asked her to play again and again. She said most of the songs came from her home in The Beyonds, but a few were from popular musicians here in New City, songs so popular they had spread to The Beyonds. Mj's voice was so beautiful we didn't dare sing along, until she begged, and then we all sang. We sang in one chorus, then just me–my voice arcing above the others and finishing alone. I didn't know I had a voice, but everyone in the circle murmured appreciatively, and I sat back happier than ever, stroking the warm kitten on my lap. I wondered how I got this far in life without knowing how beautiful it all could be.

The next day we walked the land and received our instructions from Mj. She told us what was coming, what to do with it, and where it would go. She filled us in on every detail and was incredibly patient with us when we were lost and confused by information that was beyond our grasp.

The following day, Mj prepared to leave. I held Beatrice and cooed and fussed over the little being I had grown to love so completely, while Mj gave a kiss and a hug to each of the men. Then she came to me and held me long.

After a few moments she pushed me out to arms length. "This is good, Estelle. What you're doing *here, this* is what's good." She kissed me right on the bridge of my nose, like some form of absolution, and turning quickly before the tears came, addressed the group. "I'll be back before you know it," and then walked out of the gate. I held it open and watched her walk down the middle of the street, calm and sure of each step, carrying Beatrice in her arms.

unrecognizable

The catalogue mail order stuff my father had ordered before he moved in came: tillers, hoes, shovels, seeds. Frederick had ordered everything we asked for and added some of his own ideas. He bought way more seeds than I had thought necessary at the time.

One day Jack showed up at the gate and handed me a copy of the trendiest magazine in New City. I was the cover story. The photo was a close up of me, leaning on a hoe and smiling broadly. The blurb inside was brief but sympathetic, probably because of Mr. Maranville's heavy-handed influence. It omitted that I didn't know the name of the designer whose clothes I wore, which was a relief. It called me a visionary, but claimed my project was about the importance of using the Old Town land in new and improved ways. It wasn't bad press, just not accurate press.

There was a two page photo spread inside of me, in Mr. Maranville's gift clothes, shoveling dirt behind the chain-link fence. Over my left shoulder, in the distance, were Terran and my father, their backs to the camera, loading a wheelbarrow. Past my right arm, in the mid-distance William was paused in mid-dig to look toward me. The sky was steel grey, the cement rock wall starkly defined. The photo was beautiful. I would treasure it forever, this slice of time when we were creating something completely new out of what were skills as old as almost time itself.

After the article was published, the crowd around our fence swelled. People tried to get my attention, but I could never tell why. Sometimes there would be an urgency about them so I would go near, in case they had a question, or wanted to talk about what I was doing. Most of the time they just giggled or seemed embarrassed that I had come when they called. I would go back to my work, and usually it would take a while before it happened again. Then they'd call, "Estelle, Estelle!" I was officially a celebrity farmer. Had those two words ever existed together before?

Mj's order arrived next: more tools, wheel barrows, plans for a chicken coop, lumber, and seeds–boxes and bags of seeds. The order included some trees and a pump for the pond. We slowed things down after the backbreaking work of removing the pavement and building the low layered wall. It was time to till, prepare the soil, and work the land. First, we needed water.

Our land was connected to the city plumbing, and the pipes had water moving through them, but only three times a week. This was Old Town, and no one lived here, so the water was only needed for cleaning or emergencies. Ours flowed on Monday, Thursday, and Saturday. On those days, we would flush the toilet as much as possible, wash our bodies thoroughly, and fill as many buckets as we could. The buckets had to last until the next time. We knew this wouldn't work in perpetuity, we needed water for irrigation, the pond, for showers, for flushing the *toilet*. The stink and filth around here was unacceptable. We decided Frederick should go and ask Sylvia, as a representative of the Governmental Oversee, to let us have water all the time.

He spiffed up as best he could in his new green coveralls that already had dark stains on the knees and sweat stains at the pits. He was unshaved. His hair was tousled, and he had a tan. I thought he looked incredibly healthy, but he was filthy by the standards of our day. He dressed methodically and deliberately, and brushed down the front of his shirt to smooth it as he would have done with his clothes in former days. He said, "Well, for better or worse, I'm off to see Sylvia," and sheepishly grinned. "Do you think she'll recognize me?" We all laughed. Would she recognize him? It had only been a handful of weeks, but we, and our lives, were unrecognizable. He was about to walk right into New City, right up the steps of the seat of government, and right up to Sylvia's desk. We hoped he would be safe.

I took his departure as an opportunity to sneak to the Old Time Museum to gather some books, especially *Walden* and *Civil Disobedience* for William. The crowd at the gate parted to let me pass through and leave and then remained to watch the work on the land.

When I reached the Museum gates, I spoke with Anthony, the Guard, who wanted to know how everything was going. Then he invited me to another protest.

"What are they protesting?" I asked.

"Clean water. We want improved filters, and delivery, and subsi…" That's where I stopped listening, because I noticed the faintest wisp of a cloud settling across the sun. It seemed to lower the temperature deliberately, and I found myself wrapping my arms around my chest and thinking I had never noticed such a sensitive change before. It couldn't have been more than a fraction of a degree and then the cloud moved on by, and I looked back at the guard who ended with, "…the source. So you'll come? You've become a celebrity in the protest movement. No one expected you to go off the deep end."

"I probably won't make it. We have to be careful outside the gates. We could be arrested at any time, though I think we're okay as long as we're on our own property. Besides, we're getting ready to plant."

"Oh, yeah, I heard you've got dirt there now." He gave my dinginess a once over. "I should come by and see what you're up to."

"Yeah, you should come," I said and went to borrow some books from the back room library.

That night, over our dinner bars, my father described his meeting with Sylvia in terse tones. "I presented our case. I said we needed a continuous water source. She told me she would discuss it with the other Water Board members and ultimately the Water and Utilities Conglomerates. She didn't see any problems per se, but told me that I really put her on the spot. She said we would know in a week."

We were silent. None of us wanted to imagine what would happen if they simply said no. William asked if I'd brought the Thoreau books. I passed him the sleeping kitten, went to my bag, pulled out the small stack of classics, and brought them to the fire. I gave William the two books he wanted and put the rest in a pile. Everyone excitedly grabbed at them and traded back and forth, reading from the covers. When we had each settled on a favorite, we silently read with flashlights. The night was occasionally interrupted by someone in the circle saying, "Listen to this..." We read bits and pieces aloud, and then we would go back to quiet again.

Just before bed, as Frederick and I walked to our hammocks, I asked, "Is that all Sylvia had to say?"

He shook his head no. "She told me, 'It's not fair you get to be the crazy one, and I have to be in charge of everything, and be responsible. It's not fair I have to be the one who says, 'It can't be done.'"

"Frederick, you told her she could come with us if she wanted to, right?"

"She knows she can come, Estelle, she just won't let herself. She blames us, but..." he searched for the words to put to the reason, and finding none, we parted ways for the night.

Every week or so Jack would come by to see how I was doing. I would invite him in through the gate, but he never wanted to come all the way to the fire pit area to talk to anyone else, beyond a brief hello. He never showed up ready to work again. I could sense he was compelled to come and touch base, but he was reserved. There were things, like dirt, and kittens, and smirking boys, that he couldn't get past.

Once, when visiting, he asked about the girl from The Beyonds.

"Mj? She went back to her farm and her family."

"That's good, you don't need that type here. This is your project Estelle, it's part of New City. Having someone from The Beyonds..." His face held just a glimmer of disgust. "Just sullies it in everyone's eyes."

"Why?"

"What do you mean, *why*? You know why, Estelle. People from The Beyonds aren't civilized like you and I. They scavenge and live in the discards. They have animals, and if you ask me they aren't much more than animals themselves." He seemed sure of his speech, but faltered at the end, because of the look on my face.

I grew hot, and my heart raced. "Mj is my friend. Her family are farmers. I'm a farmer, and she's no different from me. I would appreciate it if you never spoke about the people of The Beyonds that way again." Jack could see in my face that I was dead serious. I felt angry, angrier than I ever felt before, but proud that I kept it from getting the best of me. I didn't cry, that was a victory.

"Whoa Estelle, I get it. Don't worry, I get it." He looked at me for a long beat and changed the subject. "What are you planning to plant in the corner over here?" I recovered and smiled at him, forgiving him his prejudice. Ultimately, he didn't know Mj, and had just stated what everyone who lived in New City believed about the inhabitants of The Beyonds. My friendship with Mj had changed my opinion, but his remained unchanged. I had to forgive him his ignorance.

Walden came up and rubbed his soft little body along my lower legs. I leaned down to pick him up, and, without considering its effect on Jack, rubbed his soft fur along my face. Jack, looked at me, eyebrows raised. "So this is how you are now? Touching animals, with your *face*?"

"Um, Oops?" I replied, and we both leaned and talked for a while about vegetables and fruits and other things he had never considered before. Things I was becoming accustomed to, and he just pretended to be interested in, to spend time with me.

One morning he showed up and asked if I would be able to go out to dinner with him the next day, "Not home," he added, "without Maude and Leo."

"So this isn't a working dinner?" I teased.

"No, I just want to take you out somewhere elegant, and,

to that end, I have something for you to wear. Maude sent it."

"Your parents are in on this, you taking me to a civilized restaurant? Do they know clean clothes won't make me any less filthy?" I enjoyed the idea of going out somewhere. No, 'enjoyed' wasn't a strong enough word, I *desired*. "Sure, yes, absolutely." I took the bag that carried the new clothes.

I wasn't sure how to break it to the guys, so I waited until the end of the day, and after washing up and changing into the dress, mentioned it casually to Terran as I stepped out of the bathroom door. "I'm going to a restaurant with Jack."

"Wow, Estelle, you clean up real nice and those are definitely not farming clothes. Why go out though when we have all the sweetener you could want here?"

"I'm not going for the sweetener. I'm going for the ice."

"I get it Stelley. Why you'd want to go out, I mean. I just don't get why you want to go with *Jack*."

As we walked back to the fire pit I said, "He's a friend, and he's been supportive of what we're doing."

William overheard my answer and correctly assumed who we were talking about. "Are you sure he's being supportive in the way you need it? Are you sure you understand his motives, Estelle?" I didn't have an answer, though I thought I knew.

William looked me up and down. The new outfit was a lavish linen dress in cream and azure that gradually turned to the color brown at the bottom. I had to tuck the long sweeping train over my arm to keep it from touching the dirt. I felt incredibly beautiful in the clean, gorgeously designed, dress, and felt sure everyone should agree. I wanted to be admired like I used to be. I wanted to be admired especially by William, but this evening, under his gaze, I didn't feel admirable. I felt sort of ashamed, like I was cheating, or pretending to be somebody I wasn't, in my borrowed dress.

When Jack picked me up, I asked him about the brown color on my skirt. He said, "One of the hottest designers right now added the brown to his latest collection. It's an homage to you."

"Oh," I was taken aback. "Oh, I'm that kind of person now? Capable of making the people of New City embrace the color brown? That's a whole lot of power for one person."

Jack looked at me from the side incredulously, "You don't get it do you? You're beautiful and famous. You have a huge amount of power, Estelle. I'm glad you don't know how much, or you might be insufferable." He laughed heartily at my discomfort. I should have enjoyed the compliment, but I was in a sullen, defensive mood. Jack thought I was beautiful. Stupid William didn't know what he was missing.

Dinner was, frankly, terrible. The crowd pushed and jostled me as I left the gate, and then all the way to the car. Why did they want to touch me? When I pulled up in front of the restaurant, the path from the car to the door was surrounded by reporters and cameras. Jack casually put his arm around me and smiled charmingly at the cameras. Out of the corner of his mouth, he said, "Smile, Stelley, these are your fans," and so I did. Though I wasn't happy or comfortable, at all.

Once we were inside the restaurant, we were handled pretentiously and seated with a flourish. The food was the same as it had been my whole life, prepackaged and predictable. I missed eating outdoors, around a fire, with friends. In this restaurant the food tasted more bland than usual. There wasn't enough sweetener in the world to make it exciting, though I tried. The ice was good, though. I ordered a lot of ice and kept it coming.

When the waiters left us alone for a bit of romance, I felt

panicked. What would we talk about? What could we possibly have in common? I talked about what Walden had done the night before, jumping off my lap to fight the light and shadow of the fire, only to notice that Jack looked disconcerted.

"Estelle, I need to talk to you about something. I think its time you went back on your medication."

I said, "Eep," in protest and surprise, but he barged on.

"You don't seem like yourself anymore. You've become *way* too abnormal. I'm thinking you don't ever plan to reenter the useful, normal world. That you intend to live there always."

"I do, Jack, intend to always live there. I don't intend to ever go back to *normal*," It was best to be simple and direct.

"You're famous. You could do anything, be anything, have *anything* you wanted. Leo Maranville has seen to that."

"What I want is my plan, my farm."

"I'm your future-husband, what about that?"

"I think you could come. You could live with me, us, on the land."

"Estelle, don't be obtuse. See, this is what I mean. You need your medication because you're not thinking about your future. I can't live on your land. I'm not a farmer. I'm not going to live like someone from The Beyonds. I'm Jack *Maranville*. I'm going to work in marketing. I have a future and success and incredible wealth ahead of me.

"Well, it looks like we're at an impasse."

"But you're my future-wife, and the system is never wrong." He said it into space as if not expecting anyone to hear it. For the rest of the meal, we sat in silence. We agreed to smile for the cameras on the way out to the car and rode home in silence too.

The crowd at the gate had already dispersed for the night. I said, "I'll see you?"

"Yeah, I'll see you," and his car sped away, leaving me standing alone.

I walked slowly across the land toward the beckoning fire, until I heard a distant drumbeat growing louder and louder. It was a protest coming from the direction of the Old Stadium. William, Terran, and Frederick met me from across the fields, and we gathered with our hands on the fence to watch.

As the first marchers came into view, dancing and chanting, their jubilant mood was infectious. I swayed and bounced. I smiled at Terran and William, forgetting all about my date with Jack. It was good to be home.

The protesters were decorated with blue in their hair and clothes. The signs were bigger than in the past. Many had sparkly blue water drop designs, and a big one said, 'Water filters for every city.' Oh, they were protesting about polluted water, another repeat from years ago.

I asked Frederick, "Remember when you said everybody should have to buy their own filters?"

Frederick sighed, shrugged his shoulders, and said, "I was a different man. It seems like such a long time ago."

"Nothing like bathing in a bucket to make us change our mind about water, huh Dad?" asked Terran.

Word spread from protester to protester that I was standing at the fence. Me. I heard whispered mentions of my name, "There's Estelle Wells," and, "I see her–there she is." People reached out toward me, grasping at my fingers as they danced by. At first I rollicked and danced and cheered, but as more marchers pushed toward me to say hello, or touch my hands, I felt hushed and introspective. Would any of these protesters disappear tonight? Would this protest change anything? They were acting like I was special, but I wasn't. I was just a girl. They were out there in the streets, and I was in here, behind a fence. Safe. As I stood there watching these citizens dance toward an uncertain fate, I felt sadness wash over me. It seems like nothing ever changes, as hard as we might try.

The last of the protesters passed us by and Terran said, "We're going back to the fire pit, coming Estelle?"

"No, I want to stay for a minute." I remained alone watching the backs of the protesters as they moved away through the still grey night. "I'm just a girl," I said, to no one at all.

a lot to talk about

Our fire pit was in the far east corner, surrounded on two sides by the two structures—the hammock room and the bathroom. The third side was sheltered with the majority of the materials we intended to recycle into a shelter. We were constantly trying to find refuge from the watchful eyes of the ever curious. When we fell asleep in the murky grey light, we were alone, but at dawn most mornings I would wake up and look out to see a handful of people watching from the perimeter, sometimes, lately, a lot more. Whenever we put a pot of water on to boil, as we dug and carried and sweated, and made mistakes, and whenever we ducked into the bathroom, people continuously watched us.

We understood the novelty of what we were doing. In theory, we knew the more people watched, the more contagious our disobedience would be, and that would be a good thing. Contagious disobedience was a part of our goal after all. More people deciding to live differently would provide more opportunities for *everyone* to live differently, which would be wonderful. We all agreed on this point, but being watched was annoying, inconvenient, and embarrassing. So we were completely unprepared the day the tour group showed up.

I was tilling near the west wall. Terran and William were

surveying for a small wooded area and arguing good-naturedly about whether it should be oblong or circular. Frederick was planning the pond. We all came to a halt when a large tour bus came rolling down the street and pulled up right in front of our land.

Passengers stepped out and jostled together at the edge of the chain link fence. A uniformed woman stepped in front of the group and said, loudly, "Here you have the *Old Time Farm*, part of the New City Museum System. Notice the antiquated tools they're using. You can take photos. Feel free to walk around, and if you have any questions, I'll be happy to answer them when we meet back here in thirty minutes. Here are a few things to look for, you might spot Estelle Wells, the celebrity creator of the Old Town Farm. If you look closely, you'll be able to see the dirt. Aren't you glad there's a fence and wall separating you?" She chuckled at her joke. "Lastly, there's a kitten–a young domesticated cat–being kept as a pet, an authentic part of the Old Town Farm experience." The group jostled a bit more and splintered off into subsets, roaming awkwardly, as if they had no idea what to do with this unexpected free time.

I dropped my hoe and marched over to Terran and said, "Did you just hear that?" Frederick glanced confusedly around. It felt surreal. Were we dreaming? If we were then our dream was being interpreted incorrectly. We were purposefully doing one thing, and the observers were completely getting it wrong, totally wrong. We weren't a museum. Who said we were a museum? How did we become a travel destination?

We stood in a circle mulling it over. I must admit this was probably unfair for the tourists, because they certainly had paid someone, and they probably had worked all year for this vacation. They wanted to see some people acting out a historic scene, doing old fashioned things, like tilling and surveying. They just wanted to see us, historical actors, with our toes in the dirt. It probably wasn't fair to stand there talking, while they stood there staring, but we stood there talking anyway because we were totally confused about how to handle the situation.

We had an outraged conversation, which began and ended with "This is outrageous!"

William sighed resolutely and said, "Well, it's like we've decided to write a new story, different from any they've ever heard before. By the size of this tour group, it looks like . people want to hear our story, so we better start telling it."

"Yeah, okay," we all agreed. We'd have a lot to talk about tonight. We went back to work just as the tour group drove away.

That night we talked about our goals. William said, "I need to ask you, and I guess I really need to ask myself; is this just a project, or is this a whole new way of life? Will this continue, or are we going to change our minds? Will we eventually miss our luxuries, our medications, warm showers, and television? Will we just quit and rejoin civilization?"

"Not me," I said. "I believe too much in what we're doing. We're setting out on a completely different course, one that respects hard work and living purposefully, but also embraces fun. Like the other day, I laughed until I couldn't breathe when Terran tripped and pretended to keep tripping, and then went face down in the mud."

"Hey, I honestly tripped!" said Terran.

"For twenty feet? *Really?*"

"It was totally worth all the washing I had to do to see the looks on your faces."

I said, "I love moments like that. Just one trivial moment

in a day became something I'll remember forever."

"I'll remember it forever too," said Terran, gesturing to the front of his shirt. "Because this stain is never coming out."

"I feel as if I have been on a roller coaster of emotion since we started. I've been enraged, inspired, overwhelmed, exhausted, and exhilarated, sometimes all in the same day. Who am I kidding, the same *hour*. Each one of these is a *new* feeling. Until now I hadn't lived a full life. How could I go back to that?" I asked.

William nodded in agreement and I continued, "Every morning when I wake up, gently swaying in my hammock, and look around at this seemingly endless pile of dirt, I think, 'What new thing will happen today?' It's all so real and frightening, but now I can't imagine living any other way, can you?"

"That's what I needed to know," said William, he looked at me intently. "That's all I needed to know."

We stared into the fire, quietly thinking, enjoying the heat and the dancing flame. After a time, when it seemed the thread of the conversation had been lost, William said, "What we need is someone willing to spend some time telling our story, and if no one else minds, or is willing, or um...I'd like to do it."

He acted as if this was a big deal, but we agreed easily. If he wanted the job, he could have it.

From then on, William spent a small bit of every day writing, sketching, and planning. On the fifth day after this discussion, on the ninety-third day of our new life, he left for three hours and returned looking like he was so excited he would burst from containing it. William had a secret.

"What are you up to?" asked my Dad.

"I can't say. Just make sure we have a shelter, about five feet by nine. Over there." William pointed.

"When do we need it?" I asked.

"In three days."

So that was it, we built the shelter.

let us rejoice

Another delivery truck drove up to our Old Time Farm and Museum three days later. Four men dropped off the load, and our humble little lot of dirt gained a working printing press.

"We're going to publish books," William said matter-of-factly. He nodded and was so positive and sure of himself that I nodded along. His excitement was contagious. Of course we were publishing books. This was how the whole plan had started. The farm was just a part of it, right? I could see now the press was integral.

"Books? Maybe this is a bit more than we can handle right now," my father said. "It's not part of the original plan."

"Okay, pamphlets then," said William, watching as Terran pushed and prodded the machine's mysterious levers and buttons.

I touched its cold metal frame and with the other hand searched through a box of letters and symbols looking for the one I wanted. I knew it would be there. It was a star. "I have an idea for a name." I paused for dramatic affect and said, "Star Farm." It was decided.

I went through my case of clothes and found the origami crane. It seemed like a relic from the past, though it had once been such an important part of the me that existed before my land. I hung it over the press, "For good luck."

I was a former New City girl, only seventeen years old, used to thinking about fashion and shopping, and now I had become a celebrity farmer and a pamphlet publisher. I was the Owner of Star Farm and Press.

Later that week a messenger brought Frederick a sealed letter from Sylvia that stated:

Dear Frederick, Estelle and Terran Wells,
 You have been granted a water easement to fill ponds and irrigate for six months daily. At that time, you will have to reapply to the water board, a licensed regulatory member of the Water and Utility Conglomerates.

Sincerely,
Sylvia Wells

The letter was cold and impersonal, but we had water–all the water we could need. Terran ran into the bathroom and tested the toilet. It flushed! He ran back out and threw his arms open to the sky. "Let us rejoice. From this day forward the inhabitants of Star Farm will flush their toilets after every, ahem, visit, in accordance with the common rules of the civilized and unstinky!"

"Hear, hear!" agreed William, and we all laughed merrily.

"We can also take showers to cut back on the stink, right Terran?" I teased.

"Oh, let's not get crazy. I think the once a week shower is suiting me just fine," and then he chased me with his arm up, threatening to touch me with his armpit.

I screamed and ran in mock desperation. "Help! Help! Get that thing away from me!"

Terran chased me until he passed a laughing William who

said, "That pit is toxic Terran, seriously, you need a bath!" Terran turned course and chased him, instead. William ran behind me and attempted to hide behind my back.

"No fair! You're hiding behind my sister!"

"She's strong enough, or at least her smell is!"

"Hey! I'm not protecting someone who insults me!" I said through my laughter.

Terran threw his arms up and said, "All right, All right, I agree. I'll bathe."

"Good," I said and relaxed a bit. The chase was over.

Terran turned away and William released the handfuls of my shirt he had been clutching and stuck his head up from behind me. "Safe?"

"Yes, safe," I said as Terran lunged. He grabbed us both into a bear hug that somehow managed to get each of our faces into each of his armpits.

Terran gleefully yelled, "I'm King of the Stink!" Then he released us to the fresh air.

We affectionately named that game *armpit tag*, and it became a perennial favorite around the farm, even though Terran was almost always declared the king.

a simple question

The first series of pamphlets we wrote were essays about living life in a simple manner. The three of us who shared the Wells name discussed our ideas ahead of time and edited for each other during the process. Terran wrote about farming in a sensible, direct way–tips, instructions, descriptions of what to expect. Dad's essay was about a new idea he had to recreate the archaic use of solar power. His was technical and wonky. I wrote about a metaphorical sense of place, the loveliness of dirt that you turn and rest your head upon, the glory of the sky above, and the nuances of light as it falls across my land. William waited until his was finished and read it for us while we gathered around the fire one evening. His was the wild card essay, the one we had no idea what to expect.

Terran sat between Frederick and William. I sat to William's right, close enough to almost touch. He was a friend and I was comfortable with him, but still it felt like there was an electrical charge in the space right between us. I was hyper aware of his every movement.

William's essay talked about nonviolent resistance to the marketplace culture, a treatise against the new and improved. He was our radical. He began, "I find in these small acres a promise. A promise of a future in which nothing is new, but instead forever good and just right. A promise of a seed which feeds a world unimproved, and the promise of an idea which improves a world with its food."

I was gripped by his intensity. He denounced life on the outside of our fence as an anti-life and called on every man, woman, and child to drop what they were doing, to forget about their things—their purchases, their fashions—and to live, breathe, and laugh with us. He said, "You, out there, are the children and grandchildren and great-grandchildren of people who looked at the stars in the cool night sky, who communed with bugs and worms and beasts in the humidity of an overgrown forest. You are descendants of people who touched the Earth. It's time for you to embrace your legacy and rejoin the family of life which once teemed over this land, to again steward the Earth through direct representation. It's time for you to touch the earth. Join us."

It was so beautiful and unexpected. William, the angry delinquent, declaring his love of my land, *our* land. All of us were thrilled and awestruck by his quiet demeanor and forceful words.

"That was really great, William," I said, as I felt the first raindrop plop onto my face.

While the first few drops hit the ground in a scatter around us, we stared confusedly around at each other. More fell, and more. The fire sizzled and smoked. We all jumped up, energized by our urgent need to find a place to get out of the downpour. The rain came down, fast and loud, a sudden rainstorm on a piece of land that had almost no shelter, at all.

Everyone talked at once. "The bathroom?" asked Frederick. He had to almost yell to be heard.

"No roof!" yelled Terran, and he and William turned

together and ran toward the shelter over the printing press. We all rushed in and packed ourselves into the small space between the press and the only end wall. We had to lean over the machine to fit under the roof. Terran and Frederick were on the outside edges, so their backs were exposed as the rain poured down.

"So, Dad, why is it raining?" I asked, only half joking.

"Because it's the rainy season, I suppose." He put his hand out to test if it really was raining. Water poured down his arm into his sleeve. "Let me guess, you don't have a contingency plan for rain?"

"Does this look like a contingency plan?" Our faces were all within inches of each other as we huddled under the only shelter on the land.

Terran said, "It suddenly seems like a gigantic oversight to forget to build a roof."

"Roofs? Who needs roofs?" I asked, and we stood shivering and listening to the rain come down all around us. A sopping wet Walden rubbed against my ankles. "How long will it rain? Any guesses?"

"I'd guess at least all night, and then who knows?" Frederick answered. "If we had access to a weather report, we might be able to make an educated guess."

We stood for a long moment. The storm was almost deafening.

"I forgot how peaceful rain could be," I said sarcastically, "and how wet."

Frederick said, "We can go home. We can check the weather report, and if it's going to do this for longer than just tonight, we can grab some tarps and tents and come back. We could also gather some dry bedding. I'd like to point out that you kids left your blankets and pillows out to get soggy. This is why *I* put my things *away*."

Terran said, "Okay, Dad, thanks for pointing that out." He grinned all around. "I'm going with Dad."

"I'm not," I said. "I don't want to leave the farm. It's a good idea for you to go, though. I'll just make a pallet here on the floor with Dad's dry blankets."

"Really? A shower, dry clothes?" asked Frederick. I shook my head. "What about you William? Want to come home with us?"

"No, I think I'll stay too. I can keep Estelle company while we wait for you to get back. I don't want to leave the farm either, or the press."

"Okay," said Terran, "ready to run for it Dad?" and they raced out across the wet and muddy fields. After a few feet they disappeared in the storm, but we could hear them splashing and laughing as they went.

William said, "Wait here, I'll go grab Frederick's blankets and pillows." He turned and raced away, past our hammocks covered in wet bedding, to Frederick's storage box.

"Keep them dry!" I yelled as he ran into the rain. I knew dry would be impossible. Walden jumped up on the press and rubbed his cheek on my chin.

When William returned, we arranged the slightly damp pillow up against the supporting wall. We had dripped all over the floor of the shelter, but it was dry compared to outside. If we sat right in the middle and extended our legs under the printing press, there was just enough room for us both to sit. We might even be able to stay almost dry. After a few minutes of adjusting and pulling the covers up over our legs, we settled back.

This was awkward. I was right beside William, touching him down the length of one side. I couldn't move away, or I'd be sopping wet. If I stayed in this position, I'd be dry, but uneasy, agitated, and hopelessly self-conscious. My whole left side vibrated where we touched. Could he feel it too? Maybe I could move an inch away, but if I moved away, he'd know it. What would he think, that I didn't want to touch him? I didn't, did I?

I could just fling myself off the cement floor into the rain. It was pouring, but it would definitely be more comfortable than sitting right beside William under this shelter.

Just as I had almost convinced myself to jump, he asked, "Are you comfortable?"

"Yes," I lied. Well, I couldn't jump now, I'd look ridiculous. We both leaned our heads back again. Now what?

"What do you think your mother's going to say when she sees Frederick and Terran dripping wet?" he asked.

"Oh, Sylvia is going to completely freak out." All I could hear was my own breathing. Why was it so loud, and shouldn't it be slower? I couldn't remember what pace it was supposed to be, or come up with a reasonable rhythm. I would faint from lack of oxygen, because I had forgotten how to breathe, proving conclusively that I wasn't capable of sitting beside a handsome boy.

"So, Estelle, name something you miss about living out there, in civilization." William turned and smiled at me, waiting.

"I miss my warm dry bed."

"I thought you loved your hammock?"

"Oh, I do, I just miss the bed *today*."

"I mean, is there anything you miss a lot, all the time?"

I thought for a few seconds. Thinking made me more comfortable. Anything was better than attempting to remember how to breathe. "I miss my window seat. I know it sounds weird because I can just look up at the sky from my hammock, now, but I would sit in that window and stare out and dream about all the things I was going to do. I'm living those dreams now, but I sort of miss the longing."

William's right hand slid carefully under my own, until our hands were palm to palm, and his fingers entwined around my own. William was holding my hand. Maybe he didn't mean to. Maybe it was an accident.

He turned ever so slightly and softly placed his other hand over mine. This was no accident. My breathing stopped for a second. Would he revive me if it came to that? And wouldn't it be awful if he had to?

I felt panicked and couldn't think straight. I knew I didn't want him to take his hands away though, so I adjusted my fingers so they wrapped around his. I saw him smile slightly from the corner of my eye.

"What would you dream about in your window seat?" he asked in a perfectly calm voice. Could I possibly sound as calm, or would my answer squeak out of me, or catch in my throat? I shook my head trying to clear it.

"I would dream about navigating by the stars. How it would be so exciting to look up into an endless high-reaching sky, and from that depth, find my location in the city, or perhaps one day navigate away from New City and travel somewhere else. I imagined them, tiny, with twinkling brilliance, bright, but such a long way off. I desperately wanted to stare into a deep, deep sky and know it went on forever. I'd love there was such distance from here."

William traced the back of my hand with his finger. We sat for a few minutes in silence until I shivered involuntarily.

William turned to me and, speaking in a whisper, asked, "Are you cold?" He pulled me forward and brought his arm and coat around my shoulders and pulled me close to his chest.

For a minute, my body went completely tense. I could smell him, a boy, up close. It was a foreign smell–body and sweat, but it was also a familiar scent–of our dirt and the work and my farm. My entire body shivered now, uncontrollably, but heat emanated off of him. I breathed in deeply and could feel his warmth entering my lungs. I exhaled and relaxed completely into his chest. I placed my hand over his heart. He was solid, I was liquid, flowing on and around. His face nuzzled into my hair. His hand held mine on top of his chest.

We sat like that for so long I thought he might be asleep, but every so often I could feel the hand he rested on my shoulder twirl through my hair. Right at the edge of drifting off, he asked, "Can I read you something? I have to get it though, and if I leave, you have to promise to come right back to this position. Promise?"

I nodded and sat up to let him move. He stood up near the press and went through a book I recognized. He had been writing in it for the last couple of weeks. He laid down in his former place and held his arm out for me to curl back under. "I've been writing this, and it's not finished," he warned me, "at all," and then he read,

"The stars above shine in your faraway eyes,

Twinkling sparks, alight, the desire of deep Wells,

I share your wait, beside and under these grey night skies,

Until we wander into those fields where happiness dwells..."

He wrote a poem for me. I couldn't even wait for him to read another line. I pulled my head up from his chest and moved up toward his face. He let the book drop to his side. With one movement he used his arm that I leaned on to pull me toward him. His other hand steadied my cheek, and with his fingers twined through my hair, we kissed. I could feel his breath catch in his chest. We kissed longer still. It felt like being underwater. I felt sure I would have to come up for air. I had to keep stopping to rest, and while waiting for me, he would kiss my cheeks, my forehead, my neck. Overcome, I moved down and away and curled back under his arm and over his chest. He, all sharp angles and lines, me, all soft curves, softening his edges. His lips hovered just above my hairline, simultaneously kissing me and breathing me in. I swore right then there would be no navigating. I would stay right here beside him forever.

The rain continued to pour down, and the sound eventually lulled us both to sleep. I awoke hours later in the same position, stiff, but happier than I'd ever been. I sat up and wrapped my arms around my knees and looked around at the printing press looming over us and the sheets of rain creating our walls. Could last night have been a cement-floor induced dream? Did I really kiss and kiss and kiss William? Did he really write a poem, for me? I turned onto my knees and sat right beside him, looking down at his sleeping face. I leaned in and tried to memorize him, just in case it was a dream, and I'd never ever get this proximity again. He looked so peaceful, despite the hard slab of cement that had been his bed all night.

His eyes opened and he looked at me with a start. Yes, I was twelve inches from his sleeping face, that was probably a little disturbing. He remained lying there and took a quick look around, as if reminding himself what had transpired, and gave me a sheepish and sleepy smile. His arms stretched up in a yawn, wrapped around my shoulders, and pulled me down into a big bear hug.

My face was nestled into his neck. I kissed his pulse just to be sure he was there and not something I had imagined. He quietly asked, into my hair, "Me and you, huh? Really?"

"Yes," I answered. "Truly."

Through the rain, we could hear laughing and splashing headed our way. William and I sat up quickly, and I yelled, "Dad, Terran?"

Terran's voice answered, "We brought tents!" He and Dad appeared at the edge of the shelter, each carrying a large bundle over their shoulders. "Sylvia had them. It says in the directions it should take about three minutes to assemble."

William and I scrambled up to help them raise the tents. With trial and error, a massive amount of grumbling, and the rain pouring down all around, we got both of the shelters up, installed them over the four hammocks, and sealed the walls closed. It took almost half an hour. I couldn't believe anyone could be this wet.

Frederick said, "Sylvia is waiting in the car with the dry bedding and some tarps to lay over the wet hammocks. We'll be right back," and he and Terran dashed away with a singular purpose, leaving William and I standing together under the new shelters. William reached for my hand and pulled it up to his lips, kissing the back of my fingers. We stood like that, enjoying the solitude until we could hear Terran and Dad racing back through the rain. They loudly chattered with all the commotion and excitement, and we stood silent, relaxed.

They had two big waterproof boxes full of bedding, towels, and some treats and food and soaps and lotions, all from Sylvia. Frederick said, "Sylvia told me to tell you hello, she misses you, and you're crazy for not coming home."

He held open one of the boxes, when he noticed William and I were holding hands. He stopped still in his tracks, "Um," he said and paused, unclear what to say. He shoved the lid closed, uneasy. I understood the reason. I was betrothed to Jack. Hand-holding with another boy was unacceptable. Everyone knew that.

Terran lightened the mood by asking with a smirk, "So, anything new happen while we were away?"

"Very funny, Terran," I said, and then to Frederick I asked, "Do you disapprove, Dad?"

He rested with his hands on the box for a second, and turned toward me, "No, I wouldn't want William to think I disapprove of him. How could I? He's a part of all of this, of the *family*, but what about Jack, Estelle, where's he in all this?"

"I don't know where he..." My voice trailed off.

Frederick continued, "You're legally bound to Jack, Estelle. There are contracts, laws. Do you want to complicate absolutely *everything* in your life? This is complicated, really complicated."

"I know, I just..." I couldn't decide what to say, I hadn't thought past kissing William. I hadn't thought it through at all. William peered at my face, and seeing me falter, gently let my hand drop.

"What do you think, William? Speak up. What do you think about the difficult position Estelle finds herself in?"

"Estelle can speak for herself." William looked down at the ground. "I understand it's complicated. I'd never want to cause her grief or harm."

"Dad, I..."

Frederick looked me right in the eyes, and seeing my dismay, realized an explanation for my feelings was too difficult for me to give right now. "Okay, Estelle. I understand. I do, I really do."

He asked, "So this is all good?" He pretended to mean the

box full of stuff, but he mostly meant me and William. It was a simple question, but it meant a lot more.

"All good," I replied.

"Okay, like every day with you kids, this one is full of surprises," and with that, Frederick smiled at me and then William. I reached back out for William's hand.

ready for more

Every morning we placed our printed pamphlets in little stacks by the gate with a small can and a label that read, *Donations for Star Farm and Press*. We loved watching our spectators pick the pamphlets up and look them over and decide whether they were enticed enough to take it or put it back on the pile. Some became regular readers and seemed delighted when a new one was printed. Instead of waiting to get a glimpse of me, now they were there for the latest reading material. I figured this was a huge improvement. It had to be.

William's was the final pamphlet printed of the group of introductory pamphlets, and we knew it was the most compelling. When we placed them out in stacks, his disappeared into the crowd. The money they brought in helped to pay for paper and ink. Over time it helped with other things we needed to buy.

Soon there was a group of about ten teenagers who gathered daily and intently watched us work. On one particularly boring day, Dad worked on the pump for the pond, I weeded the vegetable garden, and William placed type on the press, those teens watched us like we were the most interesting show in the world. Later, one of them engaged Terran in conversation and shook hands with him through the gate.

Over dinner, Terran told us the group had started a club to discuss the ideas in our pamphlets. They planned to gather here every few days to learn what they could about our plans. They hoped to eventually have their own farm, or something, but they didn't even know what to do first. Terran told them he would be happy to meet with them once a week at the fence to discuss our project and answer any questions.

Direct instruction was a new thing for us. It had been easy to acclimate to being watched because we were odd and different. It was not so easy to get used to being watched for words of wisdom and enlightenment. This was a ton of pressure. When the teens arrived on lesson days, I would duck behind *anything* that would block their view of me and pretend to be busy. I hated being a spectacle while I was so filthy and unfashionable, but, admittedly, our farm was amazingly successful as a teaching tool. The numbers of interested spectators grew and grew, and the pamphlets kept selling out.

On the land, the first shoots of trees and vegetables sprouted, and the eye beheld a layer of green spreading out over the land. Green—what a glorious color juxtaposed with the dark brown of the dirt. I was in rapture at the sight of them both.

William and I sought each other out constantly. At moments of rest, we sat beside each other, his arm around me, my head on his shoulder. I kissed him hello and goodbye just to walk alone across the fields, even when I was due to return within minutes. We looked for every chance to work beside each other, so we could talk and laugh. We held hands all through the evenings and made excuses to stay by the fire when Terran and Frederick left for bed. We kissed then, a lot. We'd lean back and I'd curl up beside him like the first night, and even though we had talked all day, we still found things to talk about, in between all our kisses. I found myself in turns eager to be near him and comforted by his presence. Terran joked that William was good to have around because he was an acknowledgement this 'farm thing' was not a delusion that ran only in my family. For me it was so much more. I loved him, I truly did.

The tour groups kept coming. The police cars circled around the farm more than ever. We were relentlessly watched, so we decided to build a permanent shelter. We didn't want to find ourselves without a roof during a storm again, but we were also desperate for some privacy. We built a three-sided building, with decking that extended beyond the roof. The bathroom was incorporated inside, so people couldn't watch us walk in and speculate about what we were doing there. Thankfully, that part of our spectacle was finished. After we finished the building though, I couldn't bring myself to sleep inside. Terran agreed, so he, William, and I kept our hammocks outside under the sky.

We used far less of our materials than we thought we would, but kept what was left for future projects. We broke from New City tradition and *saved*. We kept extra wood to burn in the nightly fire. It would be some years before we were wood sufficient, and that had become a big topic: how to be self-sufficient. To get to that point we needed more forest, crops, prairies, and ponds. We discussed how to acquire extra land.

When William had decided to come help on the farm, he knew his parents wouldn't care, and he was right. They promptly disowned him. He hadn't planned to ever talk to them again, but we urged him to ask for the leases on their old houses.

"Seriously, Estelle, you don't know them," he said, but reluctantly agreed to ask. I had learned William was a true, loyal, constant soul, but he could be angry and sullen if unfairly judged. He believed his parents would never relent.

"I feel like a huge ass even going there," he said, as he kissed me and left. I watched him go on the errand with a tug at my heart. I desperately missed him when he wasn't there.

It was late when William returned. The crowds had dispersed and the streets were empty. It was the best time for a troublemaker like him to travel. We stayed awake, waiting, and when he came across the field I yelled, "Hello!"

"Hello, Friends!"

He kissed me, sat down, and put his arm around my shoulder. Terran asked, "How'd it go?"

There was a long pause while he gathered strength, "John wouldn't speak to me, and Marie barely said a word. Our dinner was completely quiet, except for August, my sister, who asked question after question, while John and Marie shot me angry glances. To say it was strained would be an understatement. I left, errand unfulfilled, but Marie followed me outside."

"That's good, right?" I asked and hoped it was.

"She asked me if I was keeping clean and shot a nervous glance at the dirt under my fingernails. I told her I was fine. She leaned forward and whispered in my ear, 'Your great-grandfather would be proud of you,' and placed some papers in my hand. I stood there downright flabbergasted while she went back up the steps. It was the first *nice* thing she'd said to me in years. It wasn't until I walked away and looked down, that I realized I held the leases to six houses. SIX, an entire city block. Two blocks away, and only separated from Star Farm by the Old Stadium and the parking lot!"

"Seriously?" asked Terran, "*Seriously?*"

"When do we start?" I laughed joyously.

We were thrilled jubilantly talked about the new farm until it dawned on me that our group would now need to work on *two* farms. How would we manage that? "Wait, this means we have to split our group doesn't it? We need someone to stay here, and someone to go work there, don't we?" I asked.

"Well, the good news is, we don't have to do it alone," said Terran.

"Yeah, I mean, that's true...but there's only four of us, that's not much consola..."

"No, I meant the teens. The teens with the *book club*," said Terran with a subtle smile spreading across his face. My brother, who had leapt with me when I needed someone to take a big leap, needed companions, friends, and a social life. He was ready for more people to join our farm, and who could blame him? We definitely needed the manpower. William reached out and took my hand in his. Everyone quieted and reflected on our impending changes.

That night, when everyone started to fall asleep in their hammocks, I spent a long time listening to the crackling of the fire as it slowly died away. The smells that had grown so familiar over time were with me–smoke, dirt, sweaty men. I looked over at William, who had moved his hammock closer to mine. I reached out and put my hand over his and whispered, "Good night, William, I love you." He stirred, half awake for a moment, and then drifted back into sleep.

covering things up

Where was Jack? I hadn't heard from him in weeks. My feelings were all in a jumble. I was relieved he stopped coming to see me. His absence saved me from having to make a decision, and, possibly, a messy confrontation. I knew in my heart I chose William, but I'd never been allowed to *choose* before. Would I be allowed to now? What would happen to Jack if I chose to spend my life with someone else? Would he be reassigned? I couldn't wrap my head around it, or imagine it would be as easy as that. Breaking a legal contract with the Maranville family would be difficult, extremely difficult.

I was also confused about William–did he want me to break the contract? We had never talked about the future before, so what were our plans? Were we allowed to make plans without a contract? How would that even work? And Jack was picked to be my husband, *twice*. He would make a great husband, rich and powerful, but also considerate and understanding of my, ahem, eccentricities. Maybe I was crazy to pick William over Jack. The Office was never wrong, right?

I was scared. Choosing William meant I was leaving behind all security and safety for something that was less sure. I left New City for a farm in Old Town, but I was still right here, on the edge. I was close enough to change my mind.

Deciding to break the betrothal contract with Jack was very final, terrifyingly so.

Ultimately though, I didn't believe Jack and I were right for each other. He didn't plan to ever live on my farm. I never planned to live off of it. For that reason alone, we couldn't be married. The system chose him for me, and if there was one thing I had learned in my time working on this land, it was that the system was not always right. In fact, I was coming to realize it was rarely right. I now knew my questions were valid and completely necessary.

Ultimately, my entire way of thinking had shifted. I questioned everything now—the way babies were born and cared for, the way school and medicines were a form of control, and how our partners and work were chosen for us. I questioned why everything in our life was owned and operated by the big conglomerates, and why the government's whole purpose was to keep us under control. So wasn't my relationship with Jack just another offshoot of a system I didn't want anything to do with anymore?

I was relieved he hadn't come by. That made things easy, but it did occur to me everything had been *too* easy. Why hadn't I been given papers of Betrothal Dissolution yet? I no longer cared about being deemed unmatchable, or what the Office of Future Affairs thought about my prospects. Therefore, my future happiness no longer depended on their opinion. Right? Unless it did. Sigh. Better to not worry and enjoy the quiet.

Then, one day, Jack stepped out of his car, walked up to the gate, and waved as if he'd just been there yesterday. I took a deep breath, walked over, and said, "Hi, want to come in?"

"Yeah, it's bustling out here." Indeed it was. The crowd around the fence was two deep in some places. We were certainly popular these days.

He stepped through the gate and followed me to the fire pit. "I came to see if you would please come for a walk. I know we've never come to a conclusion about us, about what we plan to do. Well, I've been thinking a lot. I talked to my parents and now I need you to hear what I have to say."

"Um, Okay, I guess,"

I told Terran and Frederick that I was going with Jack for a while. They tried to argue, but I told them it was important. "There are loose ends I have to discuss and tie-up. Really, Dad, I'll be fine."

I could see William at the far end of the land, leaning on a shovel and watching me, and Jack. I knew he wondered what I was doing. I waved good-bye, and he walked toward us, *fast*. I didn't want to explain it to him, so I quickly led Jack to the gate and into the throng outside.

"So, what do you need to talk about?" I asked, wanting to get the discussion over.

"Estelle, are you back on your medication, like we discussed?" His voice was impersonal, cold, and businesslike. He had his arm on my back as he steered me through the crowd and out into the street. We walked a short distance, headed toward New City.

"No, I mean, I never agreed to do that."

"I see. I also see now you're publishing pamphlets." He looked at anything but me. "Everyone's talking about it–the Conglomerates, the Governmental Oversee, and my parents. They're all furious. I thought I should warn you."

"Warn me of what? What's going to happen, Jack?"

"Look, here's the thing, if this is a project, an Old Town Farm Museum, that's *great*. If you want to live there and act it all out, no one will stop you. You're famous. You've inspired fashion and music. It's all new and exciting. There's an entire industry based on you, thanks to the work of my family. Don't forget the Maranvilles *created* your career. Of course, we're doing very well, so there's no need to thank us." Jack sounded just like his father, like he read from a prepared script, "but when you publish those pamphlets, you're criticizing everyone in power, the whole system, and our entire way of life. You can't continue doing that. The people on top are *not* going to let you."

I stared at him, flabbergasted. The color drained from my face. I felt a bit sick. Actually, I felt a *lot* sick. I couldn't fully decide if what I felt was fear or anger, but both wanted me to shove him hard in the chest and run back to the farm as fast as I could. I wanted to cry too, and that would totally suck. I would cry and seem weak, and worse, *unrestrained*.

I struggled to keep my eyes dry. "What do they plan to do?" There was a squeak to my voice.

"I don't know, Estelle. I'm just here to tell you to stop–to urge you to stop, or *else*." His eyes were fixed on a light pole at the edge of New City.

"Just for the sake of argument, what happens if I do quit printing the pamphlets?"

"If you quit printing the pamphlets, then everything is good, Estelle. Your farm exists. You're where you want to be. My family continues to help. Look, Estelle, I know this is all hard to hear. I'm your friend, hell, I'm your future-husband. I know you, and what you want to do. You want to ask your questions and make people think. Your farm does that. My family helps keep you in the news, and your message gets out into the world. If you farm, you've succeeded in what you set out to do. Isn't that worth it in the end? Isn't that enough?"

I looked at him long and hard, a jumble of thoughts running through my mind. Was that enough? If starting a farm on the edge of New City, in absolute defiance of everything our system stood for was a great idea, then didn't it stand on its own? Were the pamphlets really necessary? If they lost us our friends, and left us vulnerable to arrest, or even worse?

"I need some time to mull it over," I said.

"Of course."

"I can walk back by myself."

"Don't be silly, it's almost *night*."

When I arrived back at the farm, I could see the guys at the fire pit, probably talking over the day's work and planning the work of tomorrow. I walked slowly towards them across the fields. Everything was in jeopardy–my farm, my family, William–all in danger. We would be arrested. The police circling the block were just waiting for their orders. How had I become so complacent? I played at love when I had a legal contract with someone else–someone who was protecting me from arrest. I knew from the moment this all started that there was risk involved, and I had to keep the risk to a minimum. Instead we published pamphlets. How could I have been so stupid? What would I do if I had to watch everyone get arrested? What if the people I loved were *disappeared*?

Terran and Frederick talked animatedly, while William sat quietly staring into his hands. He must be so worried about me. I approached the circle and they stopped short at the look on my face. William jumped to his feet.

"What's going on Estelle?" asked Frederick.

"Jack and I just talked about the future." I didn't look at William, so I could discuss it without my voice cracking and betraying my feelings. "He mentioned that, maybe, the *publishing* part of the farm detracted from the *message* of the farm."

I just wanted to find out what they thought. I hadn't decided anything, and only wanted their opinion. On a scale of one to ten, how important was the printing press, anyway? That was what I wanted to ask. The last thing I wanted to do was tell them Jack had threatened me with arrest if we didn't stop. Instead, I hoped we could come to an agreement. We could move the printing press back out, and everything could go back to the way it was–without an argument. Because maybe it would be best if we *did* stop publishing. We were a farm, right? We could just be a farm. Jack could stay my friend, and his family would help us. William would hold my hand, and it all could be just like before Jack showed up this evening– just without the pamphlets. Wouldn't that be a win-win? I hoped I could just convince them of that.

William sat back down. He leaned forward and looked like he was about to say something, but clamped his mouth shut, shook his head, and looked down again. I plowed on, "Perhaps we've said what we need to say. Let's just go about finishing our farm and starting William's. More people will follow if we just keep doing what we're doing."

Terran looked like he was trying to discern what I was leaving out. "What did Jack *really* say, Estelle?"

This was not going how I wanted it to go. I said, "He *suggested* we might want to change some things..."

Frederick interrupted, "I think the book publishing is integral at this point. Even I had trouble with it at first, but it wasn't until the press showed up that people understood what you were doing. Those teens are meeting here weekly, *precisely* because of the pamphlets. We're changing lives."

"If we didn't publish, it might be less complicated. You like uncomplicated," I said.

William said, "Without the pamphlets, Estelle, we're just

drop outs on a farm, and a farm *museum* at that. Sure, you're a celebrity, but that's just a creation of Mr. Maranville and his handling of you in the press. He's telling them about you and what you're doing. Do you want *him* telling your story?"

I was incapable of answering, even if I could have thought of something worthwhile to say. There was nothing to say, but William didn't understand my silence at all.

He looked furious, "You know, frankly, I don't even want an answer. You've got Jack advising you on how your life should go. You sound like you've made up your mind. You want to farm and not publish anymore, right?"

"It would be easier, I think, to persuade more people to follow us if we weren't so far outside of the law. I guess, you know..." My voice trailed off. I wasn't convinced. How could I convince them?

What I could do was look around the circle and think about our life on this land. I could remind myself how important this all was to me. In the face of all this, how could I continue to be insolent and risk arrest? What would jail be like after sleeping outside? I had to think about these men. Terran loved working in the fields—how could he live inside a jail cell? Until he recants, or worse? He wouldn't change his mind about wanting to work the land.

What about Frederick, he'd given up his job, his marriage, *everything* to be here? He didn't even like the press when it arrived. How could I let him go to jail for publishing pamphlets? He'd lose all he had left.

Then there was William. He wanted to keep going because the press was his idea, but he was a troublemaker and they would certainly love to get their hands on him. He would be disappeared for sure, just for being the kind of guy who pissed them off. I had to consider all of this, even if it meant arguing against all the men of my life. I had to be safe and keep them from harm. I couldn't be awesome, inspiring Estelle, the kind of girl who starts a farm in the middle of the city—not anymore. I had to be the cautious girl, who keeps her head down and does what she's told.

I looked down at the ground, not meeting anyone's eyes, and said simply, "I just want to farm. I don't want to publish."

William stood up, pissed, but trying to remain calm. "I wish I knew what Jack said to you," he searched my face for a clue, but I found it impossible to meet his eyes. "I suppose I'll just have to follow your wishes. Good night everyone." He stalked off to his hammock.

Frederick looked at me as if he understood. "It's complicated, huh Estelle? Your friends need you to be a farmer, not a publisher? They asked you to stop?"

A sob escaped my chest. "Yes, they need me to stop publishing, but they're okay with the farming. So, you know, it's not that big a deal." The tears were sliding down my face unchecked now.

Frederick moved toward me around the circle, held my hand, and looked me in the face. "You've done an amazingly brave thing with this farm. From the day you gave up your meds, to this day when you negotiated for it, you've kept your friends and the land in mind. You need to do what you need to do. You know your own heart best." He patted my hand and stood up to go to the hammocks too.

Terran looked confused by the whole thing, and I really couldn't blame him. "Estelle, I've been with you in this plan since the first day you shared it with me, but you're not acting like I'm a partner. I know you aren't telling me the whole story. If you told me what was going on, I might be able to help."

"There's not much to tell." I tried to shrug it off, though I still couldn't look at him.

"No, I think there's a lot to tell. I think Jack told you to quit publishing the pamphlets, because it made the big Congloms uneasy to have you question the way of life they're selling. I think he's getting pressure from his father to do something about you. Jack is the only link to New City you have, so they sent him to talk to you. Am I right, Estelle?"

"Yes," I said through my tears. Apparently I wasn't very good at covering things up. It had taken them both something like twenty minutes to figure me out. "Terran, I just want us to have what we had yesterday, a farm and friends and a fire to sit around. If we just farm, we can have all of that."

"You know, Estelle, I hope for your sake it can be as easy as that." For a second, we sat in silence. "On a completely unrelated note, when William begins work on his land, I'll need to go with him—at least during the day—to help with the cement. It won't take that long. The teens have offered to come help. We'll have about six extra hands now."

"That's great, Terran. I guess I'll stay here and watch over this place."

"Yeah, I think that makes sense, and it will only be for a little while—a few weeks, at the most." He got up and headed for bed.

I sat and stared at the fire for an hour or so. I cried mostly, but I also thought about what had just happened. How had everything gone from so perfect to so completely screwed up? And was there anything I could do to take it back?

When I went to bed, William's back was turned toward me. "William?" I said it quietly, not wanting to wake Terran, and not knowing what I would say if he answered. I had hoped he would turn and tell me it was all going to be okay, but he didn't. I passed a fitful night.

The next morning William was packing up his belongings. I went to the bathroom to splash water on my face and had to hold onto the side of the sink to keep from crumpling in a pile on the floor. I didn't want to hear what he would probably say. I felt ashamed–like I had done something terribly wrong, and there wasn't any way to fix it. Maybe I could just stay here in the bathroom, indefinitely, but I knew I had to go out and talk to William–now, before he left.

I forced myself to open the door. William started talking, like we had been talking all night, and this was just a continuation.

"I'm not really so mad." He stuffed his bedding into a bag. "Just surprised, and you know, I needed to go to my own land, anyway, and tear down the houses. You know that has to happen, so now is a good time I think." His voice was curt and angry. "I'll leave the press here until the cement part is done. I've covered it. It can sit idle. Then I'll move it to my land, and we'll discuss what we, or rather I, should do with it. Okay?"

He stood up and put his bag over his shoulder to leave. He looked right into my eyes, but his were cold, and betrayed no emotion. "Terran told me. He said you were warned by Jack that you're risking arrest by continuing to publish, but just because you made a deal, doesn't mean we all have to follow it. I don't have to follow it."

"Yeah," I wasn't sure how any of us would ever be free from the fear of arrest.

William walked out through the fields to the middle of the land. He was a formidable figure, tall and striking. He wore his long sweeping coat that flapped around his ankles and made his angry stride even more dramatic. I followed about ten yards behind, searching my thoughts for anything I could say to keep him from going out the gate. I felt sure that if he left now, he would never come back.

He stopped, put down his bag, and turned to me. "What I don't get is this, Estelle. You're so smart about some things, but about this—your land, your Big Plan. You're *obtuse*. You don't comprehend what's going on. You think you've made a bargain, either freedom or arrest. You think you're free here on your farm, but look around Estelle, you aren't free. You're surrounded on all sides by a chain-link fence. You come whenever they call. You perform for the tours. You're a captive, Estelle, still totally controlled."

My jaw dropped. I wanted to respond, but couldn't think of anything I could say to convince him he was wrong—because he wasn't.

"Oh, they gave you a choice; stay a captive or suffer arrest, and the trouble is, you think they're your friends. Hell, you're choosing Jack over me. Don't deny it. You know it's true." With that he picked up his bag and stalked to the gate.

As he pushed it open, he said, "What are you people looking at? I'm sick of you staring all the time!" His voice was almost a growl.

The crowd parted as he waded through. He was headed to the Old Stadium, and then past, toward his own houses. He was going to crunch cement again, creating new land somewhere else. Someplace that wasn't here with me.

a place I'd never seen

Tears rolled down my face and obscured my sight so I couldn't see the point where he disappeared. Walden rubbed my calves. "You're small comfort, little guy." I picked him up.

Terran and Frederick were packing to leave, too, and why not–William needed the help. My land was in grow mode. Sure, there were abundant chores, but I could handle them myself for a week or two, easy. This all made sense, but still my heart was broken. How could he leave me? How could I be all alone? Sure the farm was the Big Plan, but love had become the most important part.

By midmorning, Terran and Frederick were ready to go. They thought they'd be back that night, but just in case, they took their hammocks along. They would be sad to miss the nightly fire, but the first part–destroying the houses–was so backbreaking, they'd probably just fall into bed when the work was done for the day. We all remembered what it was like. They might as well sleep there.

I tried to be stoic as I said good bye at the gate. Frederick reminded me to keep my chin up. Terran promised he'd get William to cool down. "I'll try to get him to see that giving up the publishing is a smart move. I'm just not completely convinced, Stelley, but I'll talk to him about it."

I turned back to the land and gave Walden a rub. "Well, it's just you and me now." I smiled, though I didn't feel like smiling at all.

I spent the rest of the morning weeding our vegetable garden and watering seeds around the land. It was hard not to feel hopeful with all the green shoots coming up everywhere. This was good, right? Even alone?

Then, just after lunch I heard a familiar call from the fence and turned to see Mj standing there. She waved. "Hi Estelle, remember me?" I was already racing to the gate to let her in.

Mj was just the same as she had been a few months before, but Beatrice was cooing and smiling from the sling. She hid her face inside her mother's shirt when I embraced them both in a big hug. "What are you doing back so soon? Oh *man*, am I ever so happy to see you!"

Mj laughed and scanned the land with her eyes. "Where is everyone?"

I told her the condensed version. That William, Terran and Frederick had left that morning to go collapse the buildings on William's land.

"That's awesome, Estelle, your movement is growing!"

I tried to act upbeat. "Yeah," I agreed, "there are even more people to help now. Terran has *fans*." I grinned.

"Well, it was only a matter of time." She joyfully laughed. "I'm here for a week. I know I said I'd be gone a long time, but there was a break in the work at home, and I couldn't wait to see how it was going. I kept talking about you and wondering about you, and my husband said," she mimicked a low booming male voice, "'You really should just go and see for yourself.'

"It looks great, Estelle, really great." Her eyes took in the expanse of the land. "Are those the trees? Oh man, I can't wait to walk around it all and talk it all over and hear how it is."

"First, I brought presents that want out *desperately*." She busily unbundled the load on the small wagon and brought forth a wicker container that she held up to my eye level. Inside were a dozen young chickens.

To keep the chicks out of the new plant shoots in the gardens, we spent the afternoon building a small coop. While we worked, we caught up on the news from the last few months. Mj told me about the new calves that were born on her farm. One was a soft brown, the other was white with black spots. "Their nuzzles are so soft!" she said, to my astonishment. I might be a vanguard, but I couldn't get past the idea of touching a cow. At my discomfort, Mj teasingly launched into a whole diatribe on how to milk a cow. Enjoying herself immensely, she told me about the marvels of milk coming out of her *own* body to feed little Beatrice.

I listened in amazement, content to have my friend back. I had forgotten how fun it was to listen to her outlandish stories. She talked about her mother's knitted sweaters. The newest one, still vibrantly colored, had an apple tree design that looked kind of like a stalk of broccoli, with the measles.

"Who was the lucky winner of that sweater?" I asked.

"My brother! He looks ridiculous!"

She told me her Dad, her husband, two sisters, and brother had a band, called the Growing Embers. Mj played tambourine and sang, whenever she was asked. Then she told me a long story about a recent gathering. "Everyone came after working their land and stayed until the wee hours of the morning, playing music and dancing." As she detailed this wonderful and mysterious story, I put down my hammer and let the two nails that dangled from my mouth drop to the ground. I was breathless at the thought of crossing the fields to go to a gathering of musicians.

Mj continued, "Even babies, like Beatrice, joined in, until they fell asleep to the rhythmic drumming. Later everyone walked home, hushed, but still laughing in the dark."

"The dark! Really, really dark? Do you see stars?" I had a million questions I never thought to ask before.

"Seriously, Estelle?" She looked at me as if she intended to say, you silly civvie, but decided against it. "Yes, it gets really dark at home. I forget you don't know what that's like. It's beautiful, Estelle. You should come see it sometime."

"I should, I really should." I shook my head to clear my disappointment. My friend Mj could look up into a starry night sky whenever she wanted. Why did something so simple have to be so difficult for me to acquire? "I wonder why I never wanted to go to The Beyonds before? Why haven't I ever heard about the farms and the families and the music and the dark?"

Mj squinted her eyes at me, as if wondering if she should be blunt. "I don't know."

"Well, what's your guess?"

She kept her eyes on the chickens, clucking around in their new digs. "I think it's because you, the civvies, have a way of life that's really difficult. You live independent, fearful, lonely lives. Your sole purpose seems to be buying things from the Conglomerates–the latest clothes, medicine, and toys. I think to keep it all going, you have to tell yourself a story; that though it's hard, it's the *best* way, and all other ways are terrible. Imagine, if everyone heard stories about other ways of living, they might stop shopping," and then she said, in a mock-scary voice, "and your whole civilization would crumble."

I chuckled because it was true. "You know, a while back William said we needed to tell our story, instead of letting the powerful people in New City tell it for us. That's why he bought the printing press."

"He's a smart guy." I'm sure she could see the sadness in my eyes.

She sighed, loudly, implying I was the silliest person in the world for keeping something from her.

I sighed back, letting her know I found her insufferable. Okay, fine, I would tell her all about Jack's threat, and the decision to stop publishing, and how everyone deserted me— but later, when I built up the courage. Not now.

She sighed again, and batted her eyes imploringly.

I sighed back. "You are so exasperating sometimes!"

"I know. Everyone says so. They also say it's impossible to keep secrets from me. I wear everyone down eventually."

"Fine, I'll tell you." I let the whole story tumble out in a rush, or most of it, anyway. It felt good to have someone to talk to.

At the end she asked, "Okay, now tell me what Jack *really* said." I sighed and added some of the details I had left out. As I explained it all, her face grew increasingly serious.

Ultimately, because I was one big chicken, I made the threat sound more like a *suggestion*. Mj looked piercingly at me, trying to discern what I was still leaving out. "Jack's a friend," I said at last. "He warned me, as a *friend*."

She nodded her head as if she agreed. "Once my brother, three years old at the time, was very sick. The memory of the sound of his terrible cough still haunts my mother. He was in bed for weeks. There were many nights when mom didn't think he'd survive. She still nursed him of course, which helped him, but the local herbalist told us he should stay in bed and continue to rest for a month, or more. This prognosis was difficult because there were six of us at that point."

"Six children?" I asked of no one in particular.

She carried on, but as she talked she leaned over, and allowed Beatrice to slide to the ground from the sling. Beatrice plopped to her bottom and happily clapped her hands, looking longingly at the little chicks. Mj scooped a chick up and placed it in Beatrice's lap, who giggled endearingly. "Everyone in our area pitched in to help. Neighbors made food and delivered it at meal times; they came and worked the fields and fed the animals when my parents could do little else than worry. They pitched in, and it's the only way my family made it through."

"Oh," I said, not entirely understanding what the story meant, but not wanting to seem dense. I looked down at the baby chick I was absentmindedly petting.

"The point is, Estelle, those are real friends. That's what friendship is, helping each other unconditionally. You need to ask yourself if your friend wants you to change who you are, or if he's giving you *conditions*." She patted my shoulder.

"Oh, I see what you mean," and I did, finally. We spent a few moments watching Beatrice try to catch the little chicks that flocked around her, taunting her with their speed. "What's your husband like, Mj?"

"His name is Adam. He's great—a hilarious, strapping, hulk of a guy, like a big teddy bear. His favorite things in the world are writing songs and playing music. He has a wonderful voice. I love to hear him sing, but he prefers to hear me sing, so we have to duet most of the time." She laughed to herself. "He adores Beatrice."

"I hope I get to meet him someday. Do you think he'd ever come here to visit?"

"It would be too risky. He's a runaway from New City. The civvies might arrest him, or worse, if he came back. Nope, he's content to be in The Beyonds, and I wouldn't want him to risk it. Losing him would be the worst thing I can imagine." I looked at her and thought through all the myriad of things she had said that I didn't understand. Here I was trying to get some answers, and all I seemed to get were more questions, but I saw that stories were crucial for explaining, well, everything.

That night we—Mj, Beatrice, and I—sat on our own around the fire. We were exhausted from our ceaseless talking, the catching up, the dreams we created, and the new projects we discussed and planned. Beatrice nursed contentedly. I could hear the timing of her suckling grow slower and slower as she fell asleep.

I cleared my throat, and without even planning to, asked, "Mj, would you be willing to write a story about life in The Beyonds? Something simple. Maybe like the story you told me today, about the music and walking across the fields in the dark?" There was a long pause while the fire crackled and danced. I wondered if she had even heard me.

"For publishing?" she asked quietly.

"Yeah, I've helped William set up and run the press. I know I can figure it out."

"You know what you're doing?"

"Yes, I do." I knew full well we weren't talking about working the press anymore.

"Good. That's really good." She clapped on her knees and looked at the fire. She stood, came to my side of the fire pit, and sat down right beside me. "In The Beyonds we have a way of taking leave of a good friend. We put our left hand on the back of each other's heads and put our foreheads together, like this." She leaned forward, and I awkwardly followed suit. From up close her face was blurry and doubled. She said, "Close your eyes, Estelle." I did, and we paused there, head to head, for some time. It changed from too-awkwardly-close, to okay-close, to, at last, comfortably close. She pulled her head back, smiled softly, and patted my knee. "Good night, see you in the morning." She left with Beatrice for their hammock.

The next morning she wrote while I walked the land with Beatrice, humming and talking to her about what was growing. I asked her questions about life on her farm. She couldn't talk yet, so they were questions she couldn't answer, but it mattered little. Stories were part of our lives and our lands, whether you were old or a baby. I knew that, now, and wanted everyone to know it.

By lunch Mj had written a story. It was four pages and told of the gathering where she first met her husband. It described the band that played, the dancing, the music, and about how Mj and Adam had walked home hand in hand and kissed at the end. Her story was about being young and falling in love, and about how she knew right away she would have a family with this man of her choosing. It was a beautiful tale, perfect for publishing. I only wondered if romance would be something the citizens of New City would be interested in.

I typeset that afternoon, while Mj did the chores. Just after dinner we were pleasantly surprised by a small contingent of workers returned from William's land. My heart raced as they came across the field. I scanned their faces, Terran was there, Frederick, and others, but no William. Oh. I scanned the faces again, and he really wasn't there. He had stayed behind on his land. I gulped back tears and tried to regain my composure.

Terran hugged me, and hugged Mj and Beatrice, with a hearty and happy, 'hello.' He introduced me to his Crew—Angel, Jake, Cameron, Kenneth and Paige, all wearing New City clothes covered in dust and sweat. They had weary smiles, but spoke with exhilaration, even though they were oh, so tired. It was a look I remembered wearing myself, just a few months ago.

"So how's it going over there?" I led them to the fire pit.

Terran answered, "Good, with all these extra hands, we're going fast. We'll be done with the cement in just a few weeks. That reminds me." He turned to Mj. "Maybe you could go with Angel and Cameron to the Museum, to place an order while you're here?"

"Definitely," agreed Mj. "Oh, check these out!" She ran to the pen, scooped up some chicks, brought them to Terran, and deposited them in his lap. Mj and I laughed as his face lit up, so similar to the joy that had been on Beatrice's face yesterday. Everyone passed chicks around and exclaimed and gasped in wonder.

Once we were all comfortable and happy, Terran said with a cheeky smile, "I brought all these guys because they wanted to meet you."

"Me? Why?"

"Because you're the famous Estelle Wells, the one who did all of this," said the red-haired girl named Paige.

"Well, Terran helped." Heat rushed up my neck to my face. "It was nothing really."

"Are you kidding? It's huge! You defied all the Conglomerates and the Governmental Oversee for a farm on the edge of the city. It's the bravest thing I've seen in my lifetime!" said the lanky kid, Cameron. He was obviously prone to hyperbole.

"I just wanted to have a farm. I don't think I really..." My voice trailed off uncomfortably, and I glanced at Terran who was enjoying my discomfort.

He broke in to change the subject, "Angel's father is a

pharmacist for the biggest Medicine and Health Conglom. She told me she's figured out what many of the common meds are, their size, shape, colors, and dosages. She's come up with a method for getting off them, an order that helps with withdrawals."

"Terran told me you were hospitalized when you quit?" Angel asked.

"Yeah, I was on quite a few."

"Sure, I heard. You were probably on the mind and behavior controllers, as well as the sleep, and probably the love and birth controls. Because of your history, you probably had quite a cocktail." She smiled at me, empathetically. "We all got off our meds in just a few weeks, easily enough."

"Don't forget, my sister is a Drama Queen," teased Terran. "William and I were thinking we could publish a how-to manual about quitting." He remembered to add to me, "After we have our conversation, of course, about whether William will keep going with the publishing..." It was Terran's turn to uncomfortably babble.

"I'm printing a story that Mj wrote," I said. "I typeset half a page today. I hope to have it all done by the end of the week. After Mj heads back home, I plan to publish it."

Terran said, "Okay then." He turned to Mj and smiled childishly. "Is it about chickens?" He rubbed the soft fluff of a chick on his cheek.

"Nope, it's about love, about how my husband and I met." Mj leaned down and kissed Beatrice's brow.

Terran faked a grimace and said, "Bah, who wants to read about love? *Chickens*, now that's a story! I think I may have fallen in love with this chicken!" We all laughed merrily as Terran kissed the little bird.

After another hour or so, everybody stood up to leave,

each hugging me as they passed out of the circle. Dad decided to stay the next day to help Mj with the chores, so I could typeset more of the story. As I hugged Terran goodnight, I tentatively said, "Tell William I said hi, okay?"

"I will, Estelle, no worries. You know he talks about you and the farm all the time. He really misses you. Do you want me to tell him you're publishing Mj's story?"

"No, I think we should keep it quiet. Let me see if it causes trouble first. If it does, it would be better for him not to be involved. He's too much of a trouble magnet. If nothing happens we can tell him the publishing empire is a go again, and I can ask his forgiveness for being a jerk."

"Yeah, I think so too. Besides, I definitely don't want to be the one to tell him that while he's breaking cement, you're over here living the easy life and typesetting on his machine. That's his baby!"

They left me to walk across the fields to the gate, laughing and singing a song Mj had taught them about bean sprouts and fairies. I felt hollow inside, like my heart followed them and hovered near William, on his land across a giant parking lot, in a place I'd never even seen.

just a story

For days I typeset the story. I placed type while my father worked, while Mj went to place the order at the Museum, and while the little chicks clucked and jostled each other for food. I enjoyed the work of transforming a written story into a printed page. Placing type in the press was methodical, a shift from the physical labor of the farm. Using my brain and my hands at something intricate was a welcome change.

I went back and forth in my thoughts:

First, doing something this enjoyable couldn't be wrong.

Second, some people, especially the Conglomerates and the Governmental Oversee, would think this was really, really wrong.

Third, it was just the story of how a couple met, a romance, what could be wrong with that?

Fourth, love wasn't an emotion that New City would embrace. No one would want to read the story, so why bother?

Fifth, it was about The Beyonds–practically a foreign country. No one would identify with it.

Sixth, there was a reason why The Beyonds weren't talked about, so people in New City didn't get antsy to go there, to experience another way of life.

Seventh, if it was just a story, it wouldn't get me into trouble, right?

Eighth, Oh, I was totally going to get in trouble. I better get ready.

On and on my brain went, while my fingers placed type into sentences that told a story about a young girl falling in love with a young boy on a farm. Seriously, what harm could come of that?

The week came to a close, and Mj took her leave of me and the farm. Terran had said good-bye the night before. Frederick was back at William's. William had seen Mj the day she went over to help him create his order for supplies and seeds. She had a gift, that girl, for starting a farm. What, I wondered, would I have done without her?

We put our foreheads together and held them there for a very long pause. Just before she pulled away, Mj softly said, "I'll see you soon, Estelle. It's all going to be okay." She slowly turned, grabbed the handle of the wagon, and headed for the gate. I stood watching her go, the continuous back and forth conversation in my head silenced for a moment by her calm demeanor. I would be okay. It all would be. Fine.

I printed Mj's story that evening, twenty copies in total, to leave by the gate in the morning. It was titled, *A Night in The Beyonds*. I was proud of the way it had turned out. The Star Farm and Press insignia was on the back.

That night, I was alone by the fire with Walden on my lap. I enjoyed it, bright as it was–the fire, the warmth, the quiet of being alone. "It's all good," I said to no one in particular because it seemed like everything was, on my farm.

The next morning I placed the small stack of pamphlets by the gate and watched them quickly disperse into the crowd. As I turned to walk back, a woman asked me, "Why are you alone now, Estelle?"

Surprised to be addressed, I stepped back to the gate and said, "The others are working on William's land right now. Most of them, or maybe just some of them, will be back when that's done."

"Oh, good. There are a few of us who were worried about you." She smiled maternally and seemed to wait for a reply.

"Thank you, that's comforting to know." How strange it was to have people watching and worrying about me, people I had never even met.

"After I get finished reading this, I'll pass it along."

"I hope so. Share it with everyone." I walked back to the pond. There was a clogged filter that needed to be fixed, work to be done.

That day, those twenty booklets were read by the first people who grabbed them up, passed to the next people, and on to the next. By midday, they had passed through a large number of hands. Some school kids had a copy and asked about The Beyonds in class. Employees of the Governmental Oversee discussed the pamphlet over lunch. They were worried about controlling the story and keeping it from being read by too many people. By the end of the day, a reporter at one of the biggest Magazines had heard about the pamphlet, and wanting to be the first on the story, reported about it the next morning.

On my farm, I had worried no one would want to read a romance, but came to find out, in New City, everyone wanted to read about love. The crowd around the farm ballooned in size as people clamored for more copies. The original readers solemnly passed their copies from person to person. Trouble was, now that the story was being read, everyone wanted to know why they had never heard anything like it before.

I tried to work the next day, but kept being interrupted. "Estelle, can I ask you about the story?" They would call to me from the fence with questions, so many questions. I stood there and answered as best I could.

"Yes, the story came from someone in The Beyonds."

"Yes, it's true."

"Yes, they do play music, and fall in love, and walk in the dark holding hands."

"No, I've never seen it, though I'd love to."

As I answered questions, I could see my answers being passed from person to person through the crowd, and then more people asked questions that were passed forward to me.

Many of the questions about The Beyonds were easier to answer than the ones about New City. Issues here were more complicated, or the answers too confusing, and seriously, wasn't I the one who asks the questions? How would I know what the answers are? Things were confusing, and complicated, and painful in our world. Who *would* know?

"I don't know why we never hear full stories, only the excerpts. I suppose the people in charge fear the written word. They think we'll learn things that will make us challenge their power."

"I don't understand why it's safe to walk in the dark in The Beyonds and not here, but I think maybe it's safe to walk here too. We're just scared. Maybe we should try to not be so fearful all the time."

"I don't know why we don't fall in love and choose a

husband that way. It would be wonderful though, wouldn't it?

"Your confusion is probably the medications. Certainly the meds have something to do with it."

"No, I don't know what to do about any of this. I just wanted to farm and look up at the stars at night."

I answered questions all afternoon. The crowd kept growing in size, as if word of mouth had brought them all here to listen to me speak. The questions would be called forward loudly from the crowd, and everyone would hush for my reply. I opened the gate and stood on the outside of the fence, talking to them for the first time. I almost forgot the fence usually stood between us. My back was to the farm, but I gained strength from it. My feet still on my land.

There was jostling from the back. It grew more pronounced as a figure came closer with his hands raised. It was Mr. Maranville, furiously trying to get the crowd to part and let him through. "Estelle, is this your pamphlet?"

"Yes, Mr. Maranville. How are you today?" I hoped my politeness might diffuse his anger.

"I thought we had an agreement. You weren't going to publish this kind of incendiary writing anymore." Nope, he was still angry.

"We didn't have an agreement. Jack asked me to stop publishing. I considered it and decided to publish this story anyway. Why in the world would *this* story be a bother? It's just a love story."

"Can we go inside, to talk about this?"

"No, I have work to do." Mr. Maranville looked at me flabbergasted.

"After all my family has done for you. This is how you repay me?"

"Mr. Maranville, I appreciate everything you've done for

me, but I think you've been repaid handsomely by our association, in money and prestige. If I honestly owe you, then I apologize for being unable to live up to my end of the bargain, but see, I never went willingly into an agreement with you. Our relationship is one based on government contracted betrothal with your son, and I no longer agree to submit myself to that contract. I'm now a free person, see, and I can do what I want, and what I wanted to do was publish my friend's love story." I was hot, red, and panting from exertion. I stared into his glowering face.

He spoke in a measured tone that was even more unsettling. "I have kept you safe, Estelle. The Congloms wanted to arrest you on day one. With your history, questioning everything, they would have sentenced you to life in jail, easily. I even heard that because of your defiance, *some* people in power thought you should get the death penalty. They wanted rid of you, Estelle. *I* kept them from dealing with you harshly. I showed them you could be useful. That a farm museum could even be a moneymaker..."

"I'm not a farm museum," I interrupted. "This is my own free land. The separate country of Star Farm. Thank you for all you've done for me, but I don't need help anymore." I turned and walked through the gate.

My hands were shaking so hard that it took forever to get it locked behind me. I had said everything I wanted to say. I was so proud of myself, but now I fumbled with this stupid lock, while Mr. Maranville gaped. Lock, lock, lock! It clicked into place, finally.

The crowd was strangely, eerily hushed. I was done though, my dreaded confrontation with Mr. Maranville was over. That was the worst of it, I hoped. I walked to the far side of the land and busied myself near the sheltered corner. I could barely see the jostling near the gate as Mr. Maranville made his way through the crowd and back to New City.

After Mr. Maranville left, I went back to the fence and found the maternal woman who had spoken to me that morning. "Do you think you could take a note to my brother, on the other side of the Old Stadium?" I asked.

"Sure, it won't be dark for a few hours yet." She was ever true to her civvie nature. I wrote a note for Terran:

Dear Terran,

Stay put tonight. I've been at it pretty hard today, and plan to go to sleep early. I'll see you tomorrow night.

Love,

Estelle

I was gone

I made a small fire at dusk, just to keep up my spirits. I sat in my usual spot, and held warm Walden on my lap. I ate what I could of my favorite dinner bar covered in an excessive amount of extra pink sweetener. I twirled my hair absentmindedly and watched the gate as the evening sky turned a redder, murkier grey. Night was here. The crowd gathered around the fence hadn't dispersed like before. That was odd, but I guess they understood what was coming and wanted to bear witness.

I was thinking maybe it wouldn't happen. Maybe everything would just blow over, even with my outburst at Mr. Maranville. Maybe no one would come and confront me. I even felt a modicum of relief, but it was short lived.

Two cars and a large van came around the corner from the direction of New City, and pulled up as close as they could to the gate. Six fully armed men got out. They pulled and tugged at their belts, preparing to swagger toward the fence. One man reached into the back of a car and grabbed a tool that looked like a large pair of scissors. They walked up to the gate and used it to effortlessly clip my lock in half. Argh, that stupid lock. You gave me such trouble before, and now you opened easily for these guys?

Well, ready or not, they were coming now. I stood up, put sleeping Walden gently down on my warm chair, and went to meet them half way across the field.

The men looked menacing before they even opened their mouths, but when the one in front spoke, it was even worse. "Are you Estelle Wells, Owner of lots 741-752 in Old Town?" he asked.

"Um, yes, I own this land." I tried to sound sure of myself. I gulped to keep the tears from coming. I did *not* want to look weak in front of these guys. From the left side, the butt of his gun swung at my jaw and made a loud THWONK noise. My head jerked so violently I couldn't see for a second. I could taste what must be blood, then pain, unimaginable pain. It washed over me. Were they allowed to hit me? I was engulfed and fell to the ground. I was totally weak.

"Let me ask you this again. Are you Estelle Wells, owner of lots 741-752 in Old Town?"

"Yes," I answered from the ground as a boot kicked me in the stomach. Hey, I answered, hadn't I? Surely it had been loud enough? Another boot pushed me onto my stomach, held my head on the ground, and ground my face into the dirt of my land.

My arms were roughly pulled behind me until they met, and a tight restraint was wrapped around my wrists. Jerkingly, I was grabbed by one elbow, pulled to my feet, and pushed ahead of the group of men toward the gate. I could feel wetness flowing down from my cheek and my lip was swollen.

"What's going on? Where are you taking me?" I was shoved forward onto my face, *again*. I could feel tears coming, but I tried to stay mad. I knew anger was my only chance for looking as dignified as I wanted to be in front of the ever-present crowd.

"Estelle Wells, you are under arrest for violating the code of Old Town properties, for construction without a permit, for obstructing the existing properties, for creating a public nuisance, and for acting in defiance of the laws and codes of New City," and then he kicked me in the face, probably breaking my nose. The rest of my walk to the van was just a blur of blood and incredible pain. As we walked out the gate, I could see the crowd jostling to get a look at me, though they were still quiet and subdued. Quiet and subdued even when I was bleeding right in front of them. That was my *blood* people– *wake up*. Now would be a great time to do something, *anything*. The men pushed me into the van.

I caught the eye of the closest face, a complete stranger, looking over the police officer's arm trying see the famous Estelle Wells. "Make sure my farm is okay," I said, as they shoved me into the back and sped off toward the New City Jail.

I woke up in a jail cell. My left eye was swollen shut. My right eye had just a sliver of space to see through. My bottom lip felt like a balloon. I looked around. The tiny room was beige, with a sink, a toilet and a small hard bed. There was one tiny horizontal slice of a window high up on the wall, too high to see through, and just a light bulb in the middle of the ceiling to see by. I had never ever been in any room so bleak before, so lonely. I almost wondered if they had made it just for me, the exact opposite of a farm. The antithesis of the life I wanted.

I stumbled to the wall and tried in vain to reach my head to the window. I tried to stand on tiptoes, to jump and grab the sill, and to stand on the toilet and grab it from the side. None of it worked, but I became increasingly certain that from the window I would be able to see my farm, and seeing my farm would make being alone in this room, forever, okay. After struggling frantically for some time, I had to give up. I stood with my face to the wall, my right arm raised, and my fingers curved over the bottom window sill. I felt if my fingers were in the window, that it was like they were outside the window, out in the air, the same air that touched my farm. The very same air. To my beleaguered mind that meant as long as my fingers were curled on the window sill, it was like *touching* my farm, almost, maybe.

I couldn't leave that window. I couldn't bear to. I would stand facing that wall forever if I had to. I leaned my forehead to the brick and pretended like I was in a good-bye embrace with Mj. I missed Mj. A tear slid down my face. When my right arm grew tired, I switched to my left, and then switched again, back and forth. It seemed endless. I stood at that wall until I grew too tired to stand. Then I slept on the hard slab of a bed to gather my strength, and stood at the wall some more.

I thought I could hear voices, crowds, from far away down below, but it was night, and I knew that was impossible. I decided it must be the whole of the city, every single solitary voice, floating out in the street and mingling, drifted together from separate homes. After what seemed like hours, a dinner bar was passed through a hole in the door. I caught a glimpse of a glove, but no voice, no human interaction. I dreamed of sweetener.

A song kept playing through my head. It was a lullaby Mj had taught me, that went something like this:

Tell me why the stars do shine;
Tell me why the ivy twine.
Tell me why the sky is blue,
And I will tell you just why I love you.

I didn't know it all, just that part, and though it was lovely, it broke my heart. I laid down for a while, crying. I missed my hammock, my wondrous hammock, so much that I felt like my heart would break for an inanimate object. Wasn't I past that? Did I really love my things so much that I would sit here crying over sweetener and hammocks?

I tried to think of the people, William, Terran, Dad and Mj. Tears poured down my face and I sobbed into the hard slab of a bed. It was far better to cry over things than people. It wasn't that I valued them more, not anymore. It was just that thinking of things was more bearable.

I stood back up. I didn't want to be sleeping when my captors showed themselves. I stood at the wall, fingers in the window. Was this it, *everything* from now on?

The voices almost sounded like a chant. It was so faint I couldn't make out what it said, but there was a rhythm that made me sleepy. I slept a pain-filled, heartbroken, fitful sleep. When I awoke, I felt my face, and it seemed a tiny bit less swollen. My side's bruise was a spectacular blue and red. How long had I been here? I couldn't tell. I pressed my fingers further into the window. I thought if I could stretch far enough, I would feel my home.

I dreamt of Walden, and William, one soft and one strong, both loving and ever present. Ever present? No, William had left me, and now I would never see him again. I woke up crying. *Don't leave!* I cried and cried until I slept again. Then I stood at the wall, right hand in the window, and twirled my hair with my left. I thought I heard the song again, that lullaby I only knew a part of. I thought I could hear it through the wall, faint, but beautiful. I sang it to myself and, this time, remembered more of the words.

I thought about Mj and imagined The Beyonds. I went over every detail she had ever told me and imagined some of my own. I traced, with my finger, the words to a poem I had heard when I was young. I stood there, right hand up. I stood there, left hand up. Rarely did I eat. I just waited, stood, slept, and cried.

I tried to imagine a parallel universe—one where I stayed in school and married Jack. I never farmed and never sat in a prison cell. I tried to imagine it was all fine, but I cried because it wasn't. I slept again, only to wake, to stand again at the wall, arm in the window and forehead to the brick.

I was afraid this was it for me, because one thing was certain, people don't come back from jail, not in New City. I was disappeared. I cried some more. I wished I could have some medication to numb this pain and control my mind. Maybe they could give me a forgetting medication. Someday, if anyone ever spoke to me again, I would ask for it.

I stood some more. I imagined my fingers had two little eyes at the end of them, and that from the window, they had a clear view of the farm. Walden circled the legs of Mj while she spread feed for the chicks and cooed to baby Beatrice in the sling. Terran and Dad were shoveling cement chunks into wheelbarrows and had paused to laugh over something that was only hilarious because they were so honestly tired. They mopped their brows and leaned on their shovels, completely at ease. I could see William, setting type and rubbing his inky hands on a towel. He smiled when he looked up, as if he could see me, too. In my imagination, I could see them all at work on the farm, happily continuing the story for me, though I was gone.

Stories were important—the ones we heard and the ones we

shared. You should pick your stories wisely, and if a story was to be told about you, better tell it yourself. These things I knew now.

I had believed the stories told in New City were firm and unyielding, set in a layer of cement meant to hold down the truths of the earth, but I had torn apart that cement and released stories that were new, and vastly improved. Stories could change. That was the truth. Change also came from stories. That was also true.

I found comfort in the truth that stories went on without us, but I never could have imagined the new story that was being told. It went something like this…

the story about the girl

Once upon a time there was a beautiful farm girl who was held captive in a tower. She sat in a magical window seat and looked out over the whole wide world. She could see her farm and the neighboring land belonging to William, the boy she loved. She was despondent. She feared she'd never ever live there or see him again. When the men had come to take her into captivity, they had treated her brutally. She was in despair. No one knew where she was and she was all alone. There was no way to rescue her. Her hope was gone. However she could see a man running through the night, carrying the news of her capture to her beloved William on his land.

She saw the people she loved, William and her father and her brother, as they heard she had been beaten up and taken away, and no one knew where she was. They worried they would never see the girl again. They decided to go to the girl's farm. Her brother drove the Scorpion, her father drove the truck, and William ran all the way, beating everyone else there.

He asked the assembled crowd, "Where did they take her?"

They answered, "The Tower, probably," and everyone agreed. William, the beloved, was inconsolable. He had been angry with the girl at the time she was taken and had almost stopped believing she was brave and true. Now he heard the girl had been brave and had published a love story. He also now understood she had been, and was still, true, but it was too late.

"Why didn't you tell me?" he kept repeating to the girl's brother, who knew of her bravery before her arrest. "You should have told me." He was frantic with worry, the story goes.

The girl's father turned to the crowd and said, "It doesn't sound good. They have her at the jail by now. There's not much that can be done."

"I'm going," said William, "I'm going to go and sit on the steps until they let me see her." He tested the weight of the shovel and looked ready to leave. He couldn't think of anything else but getting closer to where she was.

"All right," said her father, "I'm coming with you."

"I'm going too, definitely," said her brother from the seat of the Scorpion. He waved at the crowd to give him room, and drove the Scorpion out onto the main road. William climbed onto the side and held on. Her father followed in the truck.

The girl saw them lead the crowd out of Old Town, up the middle of the road, through New City, to the front steps of The Tower. Once there, the girl's beloved, William, climbed the steps and stood at the top, with his back to the crowd, facing the doors. He didn't intend to leave until he saw the girl again. He knew he had to see her, to say he was sorry, and to tell her he had been wrong.

The girl's father sat on the steps. Her brother remained in the Scorpion on the street in front of the jail. All around them the crowd from the farm gathered. It was night, so the noise they made attracted the attention of others. Lights flicked on and doors opened. More young people came. They were't afraid to be outside at night, as long as everyone else was, too. The story spread from one person to another, of how the girl had been arrested and beaten and was in the jail now, alone.

Morning came. The people who had remained on the steps were exhilarated at having spent the night outside. The crowd had grown bigger as the news spread. The girl's estranged mother, Sylvia, heard and came to join the vigil. Students met in front of the school, discussed what they knew of the events, and milled in the streets all the way to The Tower. Filled with compassion for William standing quietly at the doors of the tower, everyone chanted, "Is the girl okay?" Over and over again. The chant grew louder and more unified, until it became almost a song.

Everyone in New City talked about the crowds in the street:

"The farm girl is in jail."

"She was beaten for publishing the love story."

"No one's seen her since."

From her magical window seat, she could see Jack, her once future-husband, at his breakfast table when he heard the news. "The girl has been arrested. It serves her right for ignoring our advice." He was distraught that his family had been involved in her arrest, but felt powerless to defy his father. He ran out and joined the crowds in the street and watched William watch the door. What could he do to help, though? He was her once future-husband, but still only a boy.

Then he overheard a student beside him say, "She was beaten for publishing a love story," and knew what he needed to do. Searching, he found a copy of the love story and hurried it to the offices of a celebrity news magazine. There he gave his permission, as the girl's public relations agent, to publish the story in its entirety.

A message was dispatched to the girl's best friend, Mj, in The Beyonds. Mj and a large contingent of her family, including her husband, and many of their friends, rode back to New City. Mj and her baby, Beatrice, stayed on the girl's farm to take care of the land. The rest of their party walked to the prison where they pushed to the front and surrounded the Scorpion, lending their strength in numbers to the girl's cause.

Mj knew the young people on the steps of the Tower were afraid to be out at night and needed hope and comfort in order to stay. So at night, she would go to the tower steps and sing with her family. She sang lullabies, and her husband sang farming songs, about the seasons and starlight and flowers. The crowds in the street remained all night and all through the days. Their numbers grew and grew.

The beautiful girl had published a love story, and because it was in a magazine, everybody in the street had read it. The people who chanted for the girl's return were sure she shouldn't have been arrested and beaten for a love story. One student in the crowd said the realization, "Was like waking up for the first time." She, like many others, had never noticed before how unfair, even brutal, their way of life could be. They knew it now.

Because the occupation began at night, the government employees who worked at The Tower couldn't pass through the crowd to get to work the next morning. Employees that were working within couldn't leave to go home. Over the next few days, it was as if the building was under siege. The presence of the assembled masses made it impossible, in most of the city, to do anything the usual way. Students quit attending classes. Teenagers gathered everywhere in the streets.

The chanting continued, as the students went from asking where the girl was, to demanding that they see her.

The wait for her release went from one night to two, and then on, without an end in sight. From her magical window seat in The Tower, the girl could see that William would only occasionally sit, or sleep. He didn't sing. He barely ate. His entire focus was on trying to will them to let her go.

At night, when Mj sang on the steps, she'd put an arm around him to comfort. She hoped the girl could hear the song, too, from her window in the tower. Perhaps the lullaby would drift up above the heads of the crowd, catch on a breeze, fly up to the window, and faintly whisper into the girl's ear. Mj hoped this was true.

Mj taught William how to place his forehead to hers, wrapping their hands around the back of each other's head. Forehead to forehead, they drew strength and peace from each other. From then on William would stand at the front of the courthouse, between the locked doors and press his forehead to the brick, trying to give the girl strength, somehow, through the walls.

The girl saw the crowd grow in size, and over the next few days, become agitated and ornery. They demanded the girl's release, and talked amongst themselves about full-blown insurrection. Anger pulsed through the crowd. It was impossible to see how the confrontation could end without violence of some kind. The men in charge cowered and discussed and planned, but with huge crowds of students demanding to see the girl, they panicked and did what most brutal regimes do, lost their minds.

The occupation filled the streets, so the police used tear gas to get them to disperse. This just drew more outrage, and there were open skirmishes. The young people in the street threw rocks, and the police fought back with batons. There were injured, bloodied students, and anger, and talk of retaliation, *everywhere*.

The authorities gave permission for the police to fire into the crowd. Three men fired, seven bullets in all. Three people wounded, one dead. There was no going back from there, everyone in the city was outraged and enraged. Rage, all was rage. The girl in the tower despaired.

you're the messenger

The door to my cell opened, and I was brusquely grabbed by two men. "Where are you taking me?" I demanded, but they didn't speak. I tried to slow them down by struggling to get away, but their grip only tightened. "I won't go until you tell me where you're taking me," I threatened, but it was an empty threat, and they knew it. I was already being led down the hall. I stumbled down stairs, and then was pushed through a door.

My eyes adjusted to the unfamiliar surroundings to realize that William sat a small table in the middle of the room. William! How was he here? I had never been so happy to see anyone in my life. The men shoved me down into a chair across from him and turned and left. I was sitting at a table with William. I wondered if the joy I felt at seeing him might make my heart explode.

I stood to run around the table and grab hold and never let him go but he quickly said, "No, Estelle," so firmly that I stopped in my tracks. My heavy heart fell into my feet. Why was he here if it wasn't to take me home? William pointed discreetly at the cameras in two corners. Oh. We were being watched, of course. He didn't want me to hug him in front of the cameras. I nodded and wiped the tear that rolled down my cheek.

He was in a suit that looked too short, but was clean and stylish. I hadn't seen him dressed like that in a long time. Wasn't he farming anymore? His hair wasn't unkempt, like usual, but slicked back away from his face. There was a smile plastered on his face, as if he had only just seen me yesterday, but it was fake—to cover his dismay.

I must have looked terrible—beaten, bloodied, and hopeless. This was a fine way to see him again. Hi William, remember me? I wiped another tear off my cheek and caught a look at the back of my hand. Dirt, blood, and snot were smeared across it. I laid my hands in my lap and ducked my head. I almost wished I really would disappear.

"Hello, Estelle, I'm *Tom Maranville*, here as a representative of Maranville Public Relations. You hired us to handle your situation. Jack Maranville, your usual representative, sends his regards." He said it firmly, as if to say, "There is no argument."

"Okay?" He leaned across the table and tried to look into my face, but I couldn't bear to look him in the eyes. None of this sounded like I was going home.

I nodded and took a deep breath. "Yes, thank you for coming." I have to look up, if this is the last time I ever see William, then I better at least look at him. I pulled my face up to meet his and saw that he was worried, almost panicked.

"Estelle, are you all right? Are they treating you okay?" I didn't know how to answer. I was not all right, and I hadn't seen or talked to anyone until today. How long had it been?

I shook my head no.

"I see." He looked like he was struggling to keep his temper under control. He quietly took out a pen and fiddled with it for a few minutes, like he was choosing his words, carefully. "I'm here because there's a situation in the streets. An uprising of sorts, in reaction to your arrest."

"What? Where? I don't understand." I tried to read his face. I understood William had come in to see me under false pretenses, so I couldn't tell if what he said was true, or not. It was all in a code, and I only had a small bit of the information I needed to figure it out. I felt lost, completely confused.

"The streets are full of people, Estelle. Everyone is there—your family, your friends, even friends from farther away." He cut his eyes in the direction of the camera to show me he couldn't say who, but I knew. I knew now that Mj was there, outside. "Friends, working on your behalf, with connections to the magazine industry, have released the story that got you arrested. It was printed on the front page a few days ago. Since then there have been even more people protesting your arrest. Masses, Estelle."

He paused and looked down at the bag that was beside him on the table. His hands were shaking as they held the pen. I saw dirt under his nails, beloved dirt, from my farm, our farm. He continued, "The trouble is, there's been some violence. Um, the *protesters* are being unruly and have been openly fighting the police." He looked over at the cameras again and continued on, trying to tell me everything, but apparently only allowed to tell me bits and pieces. "The police fired on the protesters yesterday. There are three people wounded, and one person dead. The situation is incredibly dire."

I squealed and my hands clapped to my mouth. "For me? My fault?"

William shook his head. "No, not," he said quietly and continued louder, "the authorities asked if someone could come talk to you, and I stepped forward as the head of your Public Relations team. I'm to ask if you would make a statement asking the people to stop protesting and somehow *end* this. I've been told to tell you that if you get the protests to stop, in exchange, they will deal with you more favorably in your upcoming trial. I've been told that, of course, there are no promises."

"Oh," is all I could think to say. I looked at William. My William. All I wanted to do was hold him, but here we were stuck within feet of each other, on opposite sides of the table. He sighed and looked at the doors and the walls. I guessed he was trying to think of a way that we could rush out past the guards and all the way back to the farm.

"What do they want me to say, exactly? I'm not sure how I could word it so anyone would listen."

"Just to stop protesting. That's what they'd like you to say. They don't know how to handle the crowds, and the violence is escalating." He paused, and looked at me meaningfully. "I have an idea, though. Maybe, you could imagine how your favorite writer, what was his name, *Henry*? How he would say it."

He was reminding me of Henry David Thoreau, but what did he want me to do? To say? My brain was a jumble of thoughts and worries. It was difficult to think straight. Henry, huh? I bet he was reminding me of, *Civil Disobedience.* "Oh yeah, the *essay.*"

"Yeah. I thought you could find some inspiration in his writing, and that might give you an idea." He looked at me for a long moment. His face was expressionless, but his eyes were concerned. "Estelle..." He started to say something, but stopped.

He looked at my clothes. My eyes followed his to the blood on my shirt and the back of my hand. It was probably on my face. "I look like crap, huh? I washed in the sink, but there was no mirror, and I hadn't expected company." It was a poor attempt at a joke, but true. I hadn't thought I'd see anyone ever again, and not William, certainly not him.

His expression was irritated. "No one has told you any of this?" He shot an angry glance at the cameras. "Because of the crowds in the streets outside, the staff of the prison has been stuck in here with you. They can't leave, and no one else can get in. I'm sure that's why your clothes haven't been replaced with prison garb. Are you being fed enough?"

"Yes, enough, and I'm not hungry anyway." I put my right hand out on the table toward him, and he moved his left hand, ever so slightly, closer, so they barely touched, pinky to thumb. I wanted to hold him so badly, but knew I had to keep him safe. I couldn't let whoever was watching know how much he meant to me, or that he was a fellow farmer. This little bit of contact, though, helped to steady me while I thought. "When do you need my statement?"

"Right now, Estelle. The situation is extremely tense. We need you to say something to cool things off." He smiled a sad smile. "No pressure, but we're all counting on you."

"Okay, give me a second." I hung my head forward, closed my eyes, and in my mind unfolded the origami bird again. I creased and unfolded and marveled over what a huge, unwieldy problem this was. People I loved were in the streets, getting hurt, and possibly even killed, all because I published a pamphlet, but *why* should anyone get murdered because of a love story, a printing press, and a farm? That's ridiculous and brutal and immoral.

What *would* Henry do? He went to jail rather than pay taxes to an immoral regime. He refused to participate then. I believed he would refuse now. I stopped participating the day I moved onto my farm, but I wasn't thorough enough, or *Thoreau* enough. I chuckled to myself. Seriously, I had to concentrate. Had the solitary confinement made me completely unhinged?

The problem was, I didn't stop participating completely. I let ties remain, thinking they kept me safe, but they didn't, and here I was, *in jail*. If I ever got out of jail and back to my farm, I wouldn't want to live there in fear of arrest. I wouldn't live enclosed in a fence with everyone telling me what to do, not again. That wasn't really living. It was better to not participate, and to disappear, than that. Participation was the problem. The origami paper in my thoughts folded back up into a beautiful bird: I would tell everyone to stop. I would tell them to stop participating. Yes, okay, fine.

"Are you going to video tape me?" I asked, raising my head to see William brush a tear out of the corner of his eye.

"No, they think the way you look right now might worry your supporters." William remembered we had an audience, and sat up straighter in his seat. "You can write your statement, and then we'll print it in New City Magazine with a photo. We have one that will fit the story, I think."

He handed me a pen and paper. "Okay, here goes," I wrote:

Hello everyone, this is me, Estelle. Thank you for your worry and support. I'm the owner of Star Farm and Press. I was arrested...

"How long has it been?"
"Seven days."
"Oh. Oh, wow."
I wrote again:

I was arrested seven days ago for publishing a pamphlet, a love story, written by a friend of mine that lives in The Beyonds. I was told, a few weeks ago, that my farm and my liberty were at stake, that I would be arrested, or worse, if I continued to publish pamphlets. I decided to continue to publish.

In the time since I started the farm, I have made friends, read books, and learned about things I think many of you would like to hear about. I've published pamphlets about love, about farming, about what freedom means. I call the transformation I've been undergoing an Awakening. It's like I was under a spell before, I was controlled, made to do things, be things, regardless of how I wanted to be. I'm not under anyone's control anymore. Even in jail, I'm freer than I've ever been because I'm not participating in everything that's wrong.

We like to think we're an enlightened people, that we're learned and fair, that we are free, but I'm telling you we aren't. The people running things are afraid of what we might do if we know what medicines we're taking, if we read books, if we stop being afraid of the dark, if we ask questions. You see now they're dangerous when they're afraid, they're violent.

William read upside down, and when I looked up from the paper, his eyes darted nervously to the cameras. "It's okay, really," I continued:

I'm not afraid anymore. I hope you'll stop being afraid.

The world is a wonderful place. In The Beyonds, people fall in love. People dance in the dark and stare up at the stars. Right at the edge of New City, people farm. Some things in life are unexpected and surprising, maybe even scary, but it's that they're different that makes them so wonderful. It's time to embrace the joy of love and work and laughter. It's time to have some fun and be spontaneous. It's time to embrace each other.

We need to have an awakening, but first, friends, we have to stop participating with the organizations that want to control us. They want to keep us afraid, so they can tell us what to do.

They came to me today and told me to ask you to stop. I am. Stop participating. Don't fuel the violence, please. Don't stoop to their level. I'm asking you to stop being a part of a culture that would put a person in jail for publishing a love story. Don't participate in a system where the powerful can make people disappear without a trial. Don't participate with a power that's willing to shoot into a crowd.

If every one of us stops, today, we will make the Congloms and the Governmental Oversee incapable of continuing to control us in these ways. You can help me if you stop participating in the system, now.

"Is that good enough, do you think? I asked them to stop. It might be a different version of stopping than the authorities expected, but still, I asked." I smiled at him, trying to cover my unease and lessen his worries.

"Yes, I think it will..." his voice caught and trailed off. It was clear he was sad–really, really sad. Through his sad expression, he attempted to return my smile. It made me even more depressed. He looked at the door again and whispered, "I can't leave you like this, here. I can't walk out of here without you. I can't."

"You have to. You do. You're the messenger."

He gave me a nod of agreement and acquiescence and filed my writing into his bag. "I have to go. They gave me a time limit. So, um, thank you, Estelle." His voice shook, "It's been great seeing you." He stood, and without meeting my eyes, nodded at the camera, letting them know he was finished.

"Is there any message you'd like me to pass to your family and friends?" I could see his eyes were closed, his hands trembling, as he faced the door.

"Yes, tell them this is right where I'm supposed to be. That I'm okay." I looked down into my hands and waited for the men to come and march me back to my room.

the story continued

The farm girl was still held captive in The Tower. She had passed a message, through her beloved William, to the people outside who waited for her to be released. The message didn't contain instructions for getting her out of her prison, but was more a treatise about how to carry on with their lives. She couldn't imagine that she, herself, would ever be allowed to carry on. Seeing William had failed to give her hope, only resolve. She knew being captive in The Tower was necessary to change the world, but she was also sure she would never get to witness the changes. The girl had to be content to watch from her window seat as the rest of the story unfolded.

Through her magical window, she saw her William walk out of The Tower carrying the message in his bag. No one stopped him to look it over. Perhaps they were more worried about when they would get to go home, but it was a tremendous lapse in protocol. The girl watched him walk on by the guards, with a fake smile on his face and an uneasy confidence in his stride. He was free.

William read her statement on the steps of the prison, to a hushed crowd. What could be remembered was passed from person to person all through the assembly.

That evening, her message was the cover story in a special

edition of New City Magazine. There was a cover photo of the girl with her hand on her farm's fence. A close up of her smiling face, with the gritty realism of the photograph accentuating the glint in her eye. She looked feisty, interesting– and most said very beautiful, even in all of that dirt. The preface to her statement was written by William. He told of their meeting in The Tower. He said the girl's needs weren't being tended to. He told everyone he was dismayed at how the girl had seemed broken and alone. He said at the end of their conversation, it struck him he would never see her again. That the girl from the farm might be gone forever.

He privately huddled with Sylvia, Frederick, Terran, and Mj, passing them her assurance that she was, "Okay." He was attempting to calm their fears, but it didn't work. They could see in William's eyes that the girl wasn't okay, and their worst fears were confirmed.

The crowd that occupied the steps of The Tower was made up, mostly, of young students. They had become radicalized through their concern about her treatment, then outraged as they were made aware of the everyday injustices happening all around them, then enraged by the brutality of the police. Once the girl's message was published, the radicalized, outraged, enraged students became more introspective. How were their actions complicit in the captivity and disappearance of the girl? They knew one thing–they did not like being associated with a regime that would incarcerate a young girl for publishing a story. How could they separate themselves from those actions? The girl wanted them to stop participating. They passed her message from young person to young person throughout the city. "Stop being a part of the problem. No violence, just don't go along anymore."

The girl saw the students on the steps stop. They sat down.

They laid down. In doing so, they continued to block the entrance to the Tower, the main road in front of the tower, and the side streets leading away from it, as well as other buildings throughout the city. They didn't shop for toys, or even for food. They just sat and talked. They discussed the Conglom's abuse of power and the Governmental Oversee's control over their lives.

The police tried to break their will. They clubbed and pushed and stomped around. They tried to get the crowd to react, but the young people just sat together, locked their arms, and refused to be moved. They were nonviolent, and they resisted.

The girl saw this, and the citizens of New City saw it too. Young people asked questions of their teachers and parents. As their elders struggled to answer, they questioned things themselves, "Why *did* someone get arrested for publishing a love story?" Why are the police being so brutal to our young people?" More men and women and children, who had not been involved, decided to leave work and school and home to go outside and discuss it with others in the streets. Many people wanted to understand what this was all about. The crowd swelled in numbers. The occupation grew.

The Maranville family had done such a great job of turning the girl into a celebrity, that she was almost universally adored. Many people were willing to do just about anything for her cause. For those who weren't so committed, to not participate was easy enough. It took many forms—slowing down at work, being absent from school, not shopping, and milling about in the streets. The crowd kept growing. The commitment of the students slowed down the machine of civilization. The participation of their elders caused almost total disruption.

The authorities, having tried a violent squashing of the rebellion, and having tried to instigate the protesters to more violence, realized a nonviolent adversary was a formidable foe. They threatened the crowd with arrest. In response, the students organized a polite queue of young people waiting to be charged that stretched as far as the eye could see. One at a time, the police bound their wrists and roughly pushed them to the side where they waited to move into the tower. The police became overwhelmed with the process. There was no administrator available to process all the arrests. The justice system crumbled under the strain of so many willing criminals. The citizens of New City were outraged at the treatment of their young. The exhausted bureaucrats just wanted to go home, and get back to their routine. After a day of arrests, creating a huge backlog of paperwork, everyone's wrist cuffs were cut, and they were released with no charges. No one knew what the hell to do with all the people who had stopped doing anything.

The girl in the Tower saw all of this from her window. She was still despondent about her own chances of a future, but felt confident the citizens of New City had a fair chance at a different kind of story.

back to the reality

My days stretched endlessly in front of me, each one more of a torture to get through than the last. I stood at the wall or slept on the hard bed, and occasionally ate an unsweetened bar, but that was it. I knew that now. I had seen William and released a statement. Now I was done, thrown away, disappeared.

The lightbulb in the middle of the ceiling never turned off. I couldn't find a light switch, though I looked everywhere. I just wanted a pretense of dark, even if it was the murky grey of ambient light–anything to help me mark the passage of time. I watched for an occasional strobe-light from the nightly projections shining through the window, glimmers of red, blue, or green. I would try to guess which pattern was being projected and which night of the week it was. I might have missed some. My best guess was it had been four or five days.

The bruise was fading, slowly to brown. I could touch the skin without feeling a sharp pain. Time passed while I stood and slept and cried. Some days, when I stood with my fingers curled over the window sill, I heard what I thought might still be faint chanting. It couldn't be, though. Not for me, not anymore. William said there had been protests for me after my arrest, but there was no way they could still be continuing. I knew the limitations of the world I lived in. Shots had been fired. That had been the end.

When William told me the protests had become violent, I secretly wondered if violence would lead to my release. It was probably my only chance at going home, and I wanted to go home more than anything, but what was the tradeoff? One person was dead. How could I live with more? Was my family unharmed? Was William? It was better I stay here, and the violence stop.

I had sent a message asking everyone to stop participating. I wanted them to be nonviolent, and I hoped they might even rise to civil disobedience, but I knew their limitations. I did indeed. These were the citizens of New City. They were afraid of the dark, so they projected patterns on their grey night sky. They were afraid of emotions, so they allowed themselves to be unnecessarily medicated. They were afraid of love, so they let the system choose their mates. These were not the kind of people who would find courage in the end, not now. Not over me, and definitely not because of a farm and a love story.

I was standing at the wall, under the window when they burst into my room. They bound my wrists in front of me, and pushed me down the hall. I didn't struggle this time. I was numb, and at least grateful that I wasn't alone anymore. I didn't want to be alone. We went down the stairs and through a wide corridor. Then I was shoved through the doors into a finely appointed courtroom.

I was introduced to a man who I was told was my lawyer and asked to sit down.

The Judge asked, "Estelle Wells, do you understand why you're here?"

"You mean in a courtroom? Because I deserve a trial. If you mean in jail, then I have to answer that I don't understand at all." The courtroom filled with the sound of murmured discussion. I felt so dazed by the attention on me that I couldn't hold my head up without feeling ill. I stared down at my hands. My hair was loose. My clothes were filthy. There was no way I would inspire sympathy, distaste maybe, but not sympathy.

The judge gave me a stern look and asked, "Was it your intent to flout the common and important laws of the New City Governmental Oversee and the Federation of Conglomerates?"

"No, my intention was to create a farm and to live on it. Oh, and I wanted to publish books that were entertaining and informative and helpful to the citizens of New City." The murmuring increased. It had taken a while for my mind to adjust to the fact that I was in public. I glanced around at the large contingent of well dressed, perfectly coiffed, powerful people. Was being here good news or bad news? No one was mentioning my statement, so it must be bad news.

"Is it your opinion that the Governmental Oversee and the Federation of Conglomerates are in need of your criticism? Are not your pamphlets inherently critical?"

"Yes, they're critical. There's much in New City that deserves criticism." I didn't want to falter, or waver. I didn't want my voice to crack, and I definitely didn't want to cry. I met his eyes with what I hoped looked like steady defiance, though I sort of felt like fainting into a heap on the floor. Smelling salts for the lady, anyone? This might be the last time I spoke to anyone before they...what? This might be the last time I *spoke* to *anyone*.

"If you were released from jail, would you live within the boundaries of New City?"

If I were released? Was that a possibility? If I said yes,

would he let me go? If yes would lead to my release, then yes, absolutely, yes! But how could I not live on my farm? I took a deep breath. "No, I would live on my farm." The murmuring reached a crescendo. I could only imagine what they said, but I'm sure it involved my questionable sanity.

"You would continue to farm? Would you continue to publish these pamphlets?" He pulled one up by the corner and held it up for the room to see. I recognized that one, it was one of Terran's instructional manuals. That question was easy to answer.

"Yes, I would continue to publish those pamphlets." Thank you Terran. What a relief that he didn't hold up William's pamphlet on overthrowing the system. I would still have said the same thing, but it would have required more bravery than I could possibly have mustered. All the courage I possessed was being used to stand here and answer questions while disappearance and possibly even death loomed over my life. On the table was the shadow of my lawyer. I looked at his face. It was impassive. I couldn't believe he hadn't said a word, not one word.

My wrists ached. The restraints were too tight, and my skin felt like it was being ripped off. Why was I in restraints anyway, so I didn't throttle my lawyer? That had to be the reason, totally.

The judge and the men that stood behind his chair conferred for a moment. He said, "One more question. Estelle Wells, do you plan for your farm and pamphlets to be models for other citizens of New City? Are you attempting to persuade others to follow your lead?"

"Yes, I am. In the words of my favorite writer, 'Let your life be a counter-friction to stop the machine.'" There was total silence. My lawyer closed his briefcase with a loud echoing click. Well, there it was, the end of the story for sure.

The murmuring reached epic volumes. It seemed like everyone was in conference with someone else. It hurt my ears after the complete silence of my last few days. I didn't know what was coming next. I felt like throwing myself at the judge's feet and begging for mercy, but the pain in my wrists kept bringing me back to the reality of the situation. These people were not my friends. These bureaucrats were not here to help me. There was no help for me. All I had to do was look at my lawyer to see that.

The murmuring persisted as the judge and a group of lawyers and a few government officials all conferred. They were trying to decide how to let me go while still maintaining their authority, and to somehow gain a modicum of order in the streets below. Of course, I knew none of this, only that I was at a table beside a stranger, and I wanted to go home to my farm. In lieu of that, I wanted to go back to my window. At least there I somehow felt connected to the farm. Here, at this table, beside this stranger, I felt like I was on the verge of tears.

Without any explanation, two men grabbed me by my bound arms and dragged me away from the table. "I'll walk. Let me walk." There had been enough indignity, thank you very much. They let me stand, but still pulled my arms so hard I nearly stumbled anyway. So much for looking dignified. They briskly walked me back to my cell, cut my arm restraints, and shoved me in through the door. It closed with a loud bang. I went and stood back at my wall, relieved to be alone.

the story came to an end

The beautiful girl held captive in the tower watched as the Federation of Conglomerations called an emergency meeting. Only three of the seven Congloms were represented because the rest of the officers couldn't move through the city to get to the meeting place. Those four voted by proxy. The powerful came to one conclusion: regardless of how the girl had answered the questions during her trial, they must let her go.

There were more meetings the next day. The Conglomerates met with brand marketing personnel, the government met with public relation experts, then everyone met with each other and it was decided. They would expand the farm museum system within the Old Town proper and make the girl the figurehead. The Congloms had figured out a way to profit, so they had no further objection. No one imagined anyone would object.

The following day it was in the paper first thing in the morning:

Estelle Wells Cleared of Charges, Permitted to Continue to Farm

The happy ending for the beautiful girl happened, and she didn't even know because she didn't really have a magical window in her cell in the tower. Instead, she had a tiny sliver of a window that she couldn't see out of, and a fading memory of what it was like to have hope.

I wasn't alone

I hated my cell. I was returned there from my trial, and didn't know if they had made any decisions. I had answered their questions, truthfully answered them. Would I get credit for that? What would happen to me now? Would anyone ever speak to me? I tried to stand with my fingers in the window, but my arm ached after just a minute or two. I stood with my forehead to the brick wall, but it felt stone cold. I couldn't feel the attachment anymore. Where did the air that floated to me from my farm go?

With my fingernail, I picked at the wall. I closed my eyes and tried to imagine I was there. Mj would be feeding the chicks, and Terran would be digging a hole, but I was far away, floating above, not there at all anymore. My mental image of it was blurry and unformed. However I tried, I couldn't become a part of it again. I cried. My farm was gone. No, that wasn't the trouble. I was gone. I had become *disappeared*.

I laid down on the bed, and that was where I remained for three more days.

The authorities had hoped the occupying crowds would disperse with the announcement about my release, but they remained, determined to see me again.

I was lying on the bed, curled around my knees, when the door banged open. Great, the dragging would start again. Perfect. The brusque hands grabbed me into a standing position, but when I looked up Sylvia was with them.

"Let her go," she said, and they dropped my arms and stepped away to the wall.

Sylvia grabbed me up in a hug. "We've been so worried about you. You're going home, Estelle. They're letting you go."

I pulled back to see her face. "Really? Going home?" My brain felt muddled, as if I'd forgotten the meaning of ordinary words. Home? Me? Going?

"I'm to bring you to the steps of the Governmental Oversee building, where they're going to make an official announcement about the conditions of your release. Isn't this wonderful?" I could only nod, speechless. She looked me over and clucked disapprovingly. "I didn't bring new clothes, but maybe I can do something with your hair."

She fussed with the dirty tangles when one of the guards said, "It's time to walk her over."

Sylvia huffed irritatedly. The door was pushed open and we were led out of my cell. Would I really never be here again? Was I truly free? I couldn't believe it was true. One of the men had a firm hand on my back and pushed me up the stairs. I still felt an awful lot like a captive. Sylvia walked behind, and whenever she had a clear shot, would try to brush dust off my shoulders. It would take a lot more than that to make me presentable.

We entered a glass skyway that connected the top floor of the prison to the top floor of the Governmental Oversee building. It gleamed and glinted so spectacularly I was momentarily blinded and stumbled when the hand on my back continued to push me forward. Once my eyes adjusted to the light, I looked down. "Sylvia, what's going on down there?" I ignored the firm hand on my back, stepped to the side, pressed my forehead to the glass, and looked down. I couldn't make out individual faces, but from my bird's eye view, I could see a massive crowd that filled the street between the two buildings.

"That's for you," she said.

"Me?"

"It's why they let you go."

"Oh," I said, and imagined I could see the simple syllable slip through the window, catch flight on a light breeze, and float down towards the masses below. "Oh." Hands and faces turned toward me in the sky. The news that I was in the skyway spread, and I could barely see they were waving up. I waved back towards them from my perch in the air. "Oh," I said again.

"Move along," said a guard in his gruffest voice. We made our way down the elevator of the Governmental Oversee building. They pushed me through the lobby, and then they pushed me right out the front door. It seemed like the lights and sounds were going to set me spinning dangerously off the earth. Dizzily, my eyes searched for something recognizable to rest on. It was an exuberant, chaotic welcome. I couldn't believe the size of the crowd. My breath was stolen away, and I felt myself gasping for oxygen to replace it.

I was on a stage that had been built on the top step of the building, standing behind a row of microphones. I was grateful for the barrier between me and the pressing crowd, but the microphones also made me feel frantic. Would I have to speak? So far this morning, I hadn't managed more than a syllable at a time, and those had been unintelligible even to my own ears. There was no way I could speak in full sentences. There was a group of well dressed men and women at the other end of the stage conferring with each other and giving me furtive looks. They were talking about me.

To my left were three presentation easels. The first had a map of Old Town with a big gold star situated above my farm's location. The second had a poster that proclaimed: The (insert sponsor name) Farm Museum. The third was a photo of a stack of books that had the seal of Conglom approval emblazoned on their spines. What were these images, and what did they mean to me? My fingers were furiously spinning in my hair.

A pinched-faced man stepped up to a microphone and said, "I'd like to introduce, though she needs no introduction, Estelle Wells, the owner of the Farm Museum." He gestured me toward the other grouping of microphones. I stepped up. I was almost to the edge of the steps and the front row of the pressing crowd. My mind reeled. I inhaled with a gasp and couldn't remember how to release the air again. I was going to suffocate right here, moments after being let out of my cage. That would be a fine display of my awesomeness. Remember that Estelle girl, the one who forgot how to breathe in front of the whole wide world?

The man spoke again. "We have an agreement. Estelle has been released from prison. She will be allowed to farm. We are selling the naming rights to the farm museum that she will run, and..."

I stopped listening because I couldn't understand what his words meant. I looked at the microphone to steady my thoughts and my nerves. It was so close to my face that my eyes almost crossed. I had every face in the enormous crowd directed toward me, and I was acting like an idiot—filthy, cross-eyed, gasping for breath. I wanted to look out at the crowd, but could I bear the vertigo? One, two, three, I looked out and there was William.

William! In my misery and confusion I had forgotten there could ever be such a familiar, friendly sight. He was in the front row, three people down, intently waiting for me to notice him.

William mouthed the word, "Hi," and then smiled and put his hand over his heart. I didn't have the strength to return the smile, or the salutation, but both of my hands went up to my heart as I stared into his eyes. He pantomimed breathing deeply in through his nose, and opened his mouth and slowly reminded me how to exhale. I followed along, breathing in and out to his instruction. After the third deep breath, I could feel my strength coming back to me. William smiled.

With a subtle gesture, he pointed up. My eyes followed his up through the buildings to the sky. I was out under the sky. I breathed in and let air fill my lungs. I closed my eyes and exhaled. When I looked at William again, I was able to return his smile.

Now that I was steady, I noticed Terran was right beside him, grinning merrily. His grin was infectious and I returned it with a happy smile that was right on the edge of a laugh. Many in the front of the crowd applauded when my expression changed. I was returned to the world of the living. I could focus on people now, but could I understand their words?

I turned my attention to the man who was speaking just as he said, "...she will be proprietor and consultant of the all new Conglom Publishing Company. Estelle Wells!"

Wait, what? I looked quizzically toward Terran and William, who looked just as confused as I felt. My father stood just behind them. He met my eyes and shrugged his shoulders. I sensed something important had just been announced, but I had been too untethered from reality to hear it. I was back now, but I'd missed the crucial information–information I feared my life depended on.

The man raised his eyebrows at me, expecting me to say something. I looked over my shoulder at the easels. I grasped their meaning now–the first, the map, stated that my farm was the Congloms' Farm Museum. The second offered sponsorships and naming rights to the highest bidder. The third was about publishing with the Conglom's approval. I had stepped out of prison into a world I thought had changed, and here it was the same old story.

The man impatiently leaned into the microphone. "Do you have anything to say, Estelle?"

I looked at William and Terran and gave them a halfhearted smile and a sigh. We had tried. They had tried. Look at how we had all tried, yet the Congloms still owned us. We couldn't seem to escape this truth.

I leaned into the microphones and said, "No."

"No? You don't have anything to say to all of these people? People who have been outside for *you* for days and days?" He looked incredulous. He was chastising me like I was a young child. Jerk.

"I have plenty I want to say to them, starting with, thank you." A loud cheer went up from the crowd. I smiled at them. Their cheers gave me strength. I waited for them to quiet down enough so I could continue. "I'm not saying no to them. I'm saying no to you."

"About what exactly?"

The crowd completely hushed waiting for what I would say. "About it all. The farm is *my* farm. I own it. I built it. I named it Star Farm and Press. It's not your museum, or even *a* museum. I will run it the way I want to run it. I will publish what I want to publish." My thoughts came out in a jumble, but they got my point. The men and women at the other end of the stage huddled and conferred with each other again. There was an excited buzz that rose up over the crowd as, neighbor to neighbor, they all discussed my defiance.

I looked over at Terran and William desperately hoping for some sign of support and found none. They both stared straight ahead, their facial expressions frozen and stoic. I could imagine what they were thinking. Here goes Estelle again. Whatever we do to keep her from making trouble, she still finds a way.

"You realize your release is *contingent* on your working to help the Congloms operate a farm museum and create a publishing house? You're to work for them. It's a negotiated deal." Oh yeah? Who negotiated it? Not me. Not my friends. I didn't like this guy, which made it easy to gather myself into an imperious stature.

"I can't imagine *who* would agree to this deal in my name. I still say no. I won't. I refuse to work for the Congloms."

"Even if it means going back to jail?" The audience almost simultaneously gasped. The man wore a mean-spirited smile.

"Yes, even if it means going back to jail." I wasn't afraid, because I wasn't alone. I didn't know what would happen to me, but I did know living as a farm employee for the Congloms wasn't a part of my plan. I had had a good year. I had farmed. I made friends. I fell in love. Maybe, probably, that was good enough.

I looked at William. He looked at me with his jaw set. No easy smile now, no charming gestures. He was rigid and furious. He nodded almost imperceptibly. I knew it wasn't a nod of agreement, but of acquiescence. He knew me. He knew this was what I had to do.

The man at the other side of the stage said into his

microphone, "Okay, you heard her. She *wants* to go back to jail." He was practically gleeful. He motioned to the guards. They stepped forward, grabbed my arms, pulled them behind my back, and roughly bound my wrists. The audience erupted into a cacophony of noise. I couldn't tell if it was outrage or agreement. I hung my head to hide the tears that filled my eyes. I was so disappointed that all of this had been for nothing. He turned to the audience. "You heard how ungrateful she was. We offered her a deal for her life—a good deal, and she wouldn't take it."

I looked out of the corner of my eye and Terran and William and Frederick were talking animatedly in a huddle. They had to know there was nothing they could do. There wasn't a solution. I wouldn't back down. The Congloms definitely wouldn't. I felt so ashamed because the jerk-man was right. Sylvia was right. I couldn't do anything the easy way. I had squandered everyone's good will.

The man attempted to rile up the crowd. "You've been out in the streets for days, all for her, and how does she repay you? Well, you see how..."

Terran stepped forward and shouted, "My name is Terran Wells. I'm Estelle Wells' brother and farming partner." My head jerked up in time to watch him stride up to the microphones. The man and his government cohorts stopped short, surprised by the interruption. The gathering became instantly subdued as everyone watched him step up and lean on the podium. "I heard you say the Conglomerations and the Governmental Oversee want someone to operate a farm and create a publishing empire."

Terran smiled out at the crowd and turned to the government officials. "Just between you and me, Estelle's really not at all suited for that kind of work. She thinks she is, but you know, delusions of grandeur." He dragged the word delusions out and the crowd laughed.

He looked over his shoulder at me and blew me an air kiss. "I love you Sis, but it's true. If the Congloms want the job done well, I'm their guy."

"You would run her farm museum instead of Estelle?" The man looked confused.

Terran turned to the easel that contained the map. "No, not her farm. It's way to small for what I have in mind. What about here?" He pointed at a former shopping mall. "Me and my crew will raze the buildings, dig up the cement, and create a mega farm. I'll organize, plan, and implement the whole thing as your employee. We'll have gift shops, product tie-ins, full sponsorship deals." He turned to the audience and asked, "How does that sound, everybody? A farm museum with classes and gatherings and a market?" The crowd showed their appreciation of his plan by exuberantly stamping their feet, cheering, and applauding.

Another one of the government officials stepped forward to the microphone and asked, "What about the publishing?"

Terran was putting on quite a show at this point. This wasn't just an ordinary jig, his usual dance of joy. He performed for his life, or rather *my* life. I could see he was nervous, but he covered it well.

He chuckled into the mic, "Oh, I can start a publishing scheme. I have much better taste in books than Estelle. First, we'll publish a classic tale about a wizard school and then one about magical dragons." He swept his arm out as he said magical. People laughed uproariously now, enjoying Terran's easy confidence. He was teasing the Congloms, by not taking their threats seriously. "In exchange for my being the best Farm Museum Creator you've ever hired, you will permit

Estelle Wells, and any other Old Town landowners, to farm and publish, with *no* fear of arrest."

The officials huddled and conversed, using many more gestures this time. Terran smirked at them. "We're all waiting for an answer." Everyone grew quiet in suspense. Tears poured down my face unchecked. My brother, the uncomplicated guy who liked to dig in the dirt and dance a jig, was bargaining for me. He was saving my life. They had to agree to it, had to. Didn't they? I closed my eyes, too afraid to watch what would happen.

The man walked back to the microphones. "You have a deal. We will renegotiate in two years. Estelle Wells will be released by the end of the day." Did I hear him correctly? I was pulled by the arms backward through the doors of the government building, as the cheering reached its final jubilant climax.

space and time

I sat in a hard chair against a wall in a long hallway. I had a clear view through a window into the conference room where Terran, Frederick, Sylvia, and a large assortment of officials planned, deliberated, and negotiated an agreement for Terran's future career. I wasn't at the meeting because I had been deemed uncooperative. Uncooperative people like me sit on hard chairs with their arms bound. It made perfect sense.

I watched Terran as he talked to those officials. He exuded confidence, but he was still just a boy. What, eighteen? Older than I was, yet I still worried about him. Did he know what he was getting into? Just then he turned to look at me through the window and grinned conspiratorially. He had signed away two years of his life and fixed everything for me, and he still took a second to make me laugh.

The door swung open and Terran rushed out into the hallway, jumped in front of me, and did a happy jig for my enjoyment. He grabbed me up out of my chair into a rib crushing hug. "Wait, why are your wrists still bound?"

"I'm forgotten in the hallway while you're busy being the center of attention." I smiled at my dear courageous brother. Was there anyone in this whole wide world who would have done what he just did for me? A guard came over and cut my cuffs. I threw my arms around Terran's neck and sobbed into his hair. "I can't believe you did that for me. I can't believe it. I don't know how I'll ever thank you enough."

He returned my hug. "It's okay, Stelley. It's really okay." He held me at arm's length, peered into my eyes and said, "Think about all you've given me–farming, joy, friends. Everything I value most in this world I have because of you and your bright idea." I sobbed again, overwhelmed by his generosity.

I wiped the tears and snot and dirt that covered my face with my sleeve. "Two years, though. You have to work for them for two years. It's such a long time," I said with a snivel.

"It's nothing compared to you disappearing forever. I would have worked for them my whole life in exchange. I'm frankly glad I forgot to offer it. Two years is nothing, and think about it, Estelle, I love the work. I get to create another farm, a big farm. I can hire all of my friends. I can sit around the fire pit with you every night. I get to publish some of the first complete books the citizens of New City have ever seen. I can't think of a single down side. Well, my bosses suck, but that's merely a trifle." I chuckled a little, his easy attitude slowly lifted my spirits. "I do have one big problem, though."

"What's that?"

"Do you think Mj will come and tell me how to do it all?" His smile broadened, and I couldn't help but laugh.

Frederick stepped forward and hugged me. I laughed again, this time with relief. It felt like it came from deep down in my heart. "I'm so glad to see you, Dad."

Then, before I could even comprehend what happened, Sylvia scooped me up in a hug. Her mouth to my ear, she said, "I didn't know. I didn't understand."

Was she talking about me, or my farm, or the actions of the government, or my popularity? I wasn't sure, but I knew she was comforting me, and her hug made me feel so much better that I answered, "I know." Because, of course, she was talking about it all—everything that had happened from the first day I began, to this day when I was allowed to continue going on. "I could write a book," I said, "with all the things I don't know and don't understand."

Sylvia released me from the hug and attempted to discreetly wipe her eyes. "We should leave before someone here changes their mind." I laughed for the third time in as many minutes. I felt better than I had in ages, and I hadn't even left the building yet.

We headed down the hallway and passed the office of the pinch-faced man from the stage. I stopped dead in my tracks. I had just formed a *plan*. "Just a minute, I have something I want to do," I said.

Terran said, "Don't screw anything up, Estelle. I can't keep freeing you from jail indefinitely."

"Who me?" I feigned surprise.

I stepped up to the doorway of the man's office and knocked politely.

"Yes?" As he looked up from his work he had a look of distaste on his face. He didn't like me. Fine, I didn't like him either.

"Hello sir, I'm leaving now," I said, just to be courteous.

"Sure. Keep yourself out of trouble."

"Funny thing, when Terran told you what he wanted in exchange for working for you, he forgot something I really, really want."

"What you want? Give you something? I wouldn't give you anything you wanted, except maybe the opposite of what you want. I think we've been far too agreeable. I think you deserve more punishment. Count yourself lucky you get to walk out the doors." He was full of spite. I hoped this would work.

"Oh, well, I just wanted to tell you that I'm terrified of the dark, and I hope you'll keep the lights on in Old Town. I knew it was only a matter of time before you realized that turning the lights off would keep the citizens away and would help you control their movements. So, before you came to that conclusion, I wanted to ask you to please keep them all on, especially the ones around my farm and the Old Stadium. I see I was wrong to ask, though, my apologies." I bowed awkwardly and walked back to Terran.

I hated that guy, but if he did what I hoped he would do, he would be my favorite pinch-faced man in the government offices.

Terran and I pushed open the doors and stepped out onto the steps of the government building. The awaiting crowd was smaller than before, but still daunting. I needed to remember to breathe, just breathe. Terran waved at everyone and did one of his happy jigs at the top of the stairs. The crowd roared with delight. He bowed to me in mock deference, and I curtsied and blew kisses at the crowd. The applause rose to a deafening roar.

"Where's William and Mj?" I asked. It was hard to see with such a big crowd before me, but I knew they ought to be there. Where were they?

Terran said, "They're probably at the farm, Stelley. No one knew what time they would let you out, so I bet they went back to get things ready for you."

With Terran's arm protectively around my shoulders, we pushed slowly through the crowds. Unfamiliar faces surrounded us. Strange hands reached out to grasp mine. Everyone seemed to want to touch me or speak with me and know I was okay. I tried to accommodate them. I laughed and smiled and waved, until Terran and Frederick bundled me onto a seat in the Scorpion. Terran started the machine, and we were headed home at last. Except, the crowd barely parted to let us pass, so we crept along slowly—so slowly I wanted to scream, *Move out of the way people!* I stood up and tried to wave them aside, but it still took forever to drive forward a few feet.

I couldn't wait to see the farm and my friends. My anticipation grew until it felt like my whole heart would burst open. I pleaded, please not here, heart, not moments before arriving home. That would be terrible, atrocious timing. We turned down the wide avenue into Old Town, and, from my high seat in the Scorpion, I saw the farm.

There was bustling activity, a large group at the perimeter collapsing the fence that encompassed my land and stacking the dismantled pieces in the road. I scanned the crowd for William and found him right in the middle, directing the work. After days and days in solitary confinement, William was seeing to it that I wasn't a captive anymore. When the Scorpion came into view of the farm, I leaned my body off the side and waved and yelled as loud as I could, "Hello!"

Everyone dropped their tools and waved back. I watched as the people I loved, and even people I didn't know, hugged each other and cried. I put one foot out of the Scorpion, right at the spot where the gate to my farm used to be, and stepped onto my land. My land. I felt such joy that I froze in time. Tears welled up in my eyes. I looked around at all of these people who were now part of the farm's story too. They were tearing down the fence. How had my life gone from bleak to perfect in such a short time? William stood in the middle of everything, watching me take it all in.

Walden rubbed William's legs and brought him out of his

trance. He walked toward me across the land. His long firm strides caused my breath to catch in my chest. All I could manage to say was, "Oh," as his strong arms folded around me. He lifted me almost off the ground. His face was pressed against mine, his breath in my ear.

"Estelle, oh man, I can't believe you're home." His voice caught on the word home. "I'm so sorry." He held me tighter still. "I was so sure you were gone. It was all gone. Everything."

"I know. Me too." Tears ran down my face. His arms held me so tightly I was sure he would never let go. That was good. All the anger and fear and longing of the last few weeks poured out of our hearts. The others worked quietly, tearing down the perimeter fence, giving us the space and time we needed.

Our last remnants of sorrow subsided, and his hug picked me off the ground as he arched back and yelled to the whole wide farm, "Estelle's home!"

I threw my arms out and gleefully yelled, "I'm home!" People all around us made hooting noises in appreciation.

William dropped me to the ground and we kissed. Like a deep breath, the kiss filled me with presence of mind, and I could feel my body relaxing to the tips of my fingers and toes. I *was* home, really truly home. After the agitation of the last weeks, here was peace and comfort and joy. I knew it was here. I may have begun to forget, but now the memory came flooding back. It felt like we could stand there and kiss forever, but life intervened, or rather smell. I giggled finally, and said, "I *really* need to bathe."

Without breaking the embrace, William said in a sappy romantic voice, "Oh, Estelle, you absolutely, seriously do." We both laughed. Laughing with William? Now *that* I could do forever.

whole entire world

I took a shower, thankfully, and put on some clean clothes. It wasn't until I pulled the shirt over my head that I realized it had been designed in my honor. It was moss green with a brown question mark and my face silk-screened on the front. I stepped out of the bathroom, and another cheer went up from everyone. "Very funny, do you *really* expect me to wear my own face on my shirt?"

Terran said, "We're not cheering because of the shirt. We're cheering because you bathed." At that, everyone roared with laughter, including me. I wore the shirt because it was clean, and it made us happy.

"I'm famished," I said, and William handed me my favorite dinner bar. I sat in a chair and ate bar after bar, covering them in luxuriously sweet profoundly pink sprinkles. Now that the gate was gone, well-wishers streamed in over the low cement-stone wall. They filled in all the paths to the fire-pit area and through and around the fields. When they noticed me in my chair, they stopped to stare, mouths agape. "That's Estelle Wells," they whispered to each other, and, "There she is." They filed past my chair, in a greeting line of sorts, not seeming to mind that I was constantly chewing. They said, "Hi," and, "I hope you're okay," and "I'm so glad you're out." I shook hands with them, one after another, most of the afternoon. Then they'd wander away to gather in groups, throughout the streets of Old Town and into New City.

I needed to get up and walk around after my fourth helping of food or I would just keep right on eating. William and I went for a wander through the fields and saw Jack coming toward us down one of the paths. He stopped dead in his tracks and stared at me for a long awkward moment.

I broke the silence and said, "Hi Jack."

He grabbed me up in a hug. "I knew you were home, but seeing you still surprised me. I'm so glad it's over."

"I know what you mean."

Jack held his hand out to William, and they shook heartily. William said, "I'm going to check in with Mj," and walked away. When in the world had they arrived at a gentleman's truce?

Terran said, "You know, I was the one who published your story in the papers. No need to thank me."

"I'm waiting for my check," I said with my hands on my hips. "And I'm waiting for an explanation. How did William end up being the one who came into the jail to see me?"

He chuckled. "I still can't believe he passed as an employee of Maranville Marketing and Public Relations. It looks like we *really* need to work on our brand." He smiled at me and took my right hand up and held it in both of his. "So, I hear you're going to try *love* for a while. You do know that's an archaic feeling? Civilized people gave love up long ago."

Not sure what he meant, I laughed. "Who's talking about love?"

Jack squinted his eyes as he attempted to read my face. "William. William's talking about love."

"Oh." My eyes widened as I grasped what he said. I wasn't sure how to respond, but I did know I wanted to run to the fire pit and throw myself into William's arms.

Jack pulled me toward him and wrapped his other arm around me. "I'll see you later, *former* future-wife. Be good, but you know, *your* way."

He looked at me with his head tilted to one side. "I'm glad you're okay and that, somehow, I could help. It's important what you've done." Then he let himself be swept along with the celebrating crowds.

I rushed back to the fire pit where everyone was eating their dinner. "Oh good, I'm famished," I joked and fell into the seat beside William. I looked at him expectantly.

"What?" he asked.

"You know what." I waited for an answer, but none was forthcoming. He either *didn't* know, or else he was being secretive. Probably the latter. "What happened between you and Jack? How in the world did *you* end up coming into the jail pretending to be a part of Maranville Public Relations?"

Terran jumped up. "I want to tell it. Me! Me!"

William pretended to be hopelessly embarrassed and said, "Okay, okay. Fine, tell it. *Sigh.*" He took my hand in his.

Terran sat back down and using his arms widely and gesturally, began. "We were gathered on the steps of the prison, confused and upset by the fighting in the streets. I, of course, wanted to go join the fighting because, you know, I'm *brave.*"

William asked, "Is that why you spent most of the week sitting in the Scorpion?"

Terran said, "Hey, I needed to have a good view of the surrounding area, and, anyway, this isn't about me. It's about you and *Jack.*" He continued, "William believed we needed to stop the violence. He thought the police were just going to get more brutal, that everything would escalate, and we'd never get you out. He had a point, but we had no idea how to get you out either way. No idea at *all.* Our only plan was to stay on the steps of the prison, indefinitely, just staring at the doors. Not a plan, more like a queue. At this point, the fighting was way down the street, but only because the police couldn't get through the crowds, yet. We were talking about the options that were open to us, endlessly discussing, when the people on the steps parted to let someone through. As the person got closer, we realized it was Jack.

"Imagine it, Estelle. Jack was freshly clean and dressed in his stylishly perfect way. Almost everybody else there had spent a few nights outside, and, of course, William, Dad, and I had been outside forever, it seemed. Let's just say he presented a striking contrast."

William said, "Frederick, I don't know about you, but I'm feeling insulted." Frederick laughed in agreement.

Terran said, "Did you smell him? He smelled marvelous!" He continued, "Jack strode forcefully up the steps and swept right up to all of us–all business, like he does.

"He said, 'I just intercepted a message from the Congloms to the Maranville Public Relations Firm. They want someone to go in and see Estelle and persuade her to tell her 'followers' to stop being violent and go home.'

"William, who as you know was never a fan of Jack, got testy. He said, 'It's not the *followers* that are being violent. You do know the police started it, right?' I thought for a second William was just going to shove him right down the steps." Terran smiled proudly at William.

William said, "I considered it but couldn't be bothered to put down the shovel I was holding."

Terran continued, "Jack turned, with that regally condescending way he has, and looked William up and down and said, 'Yeah, I *know*. I'm just telling you what the message said. *The Congloms* want Estelle to tell her people to stop. So I'm going to go in and see her, as a representative of my father's firm. I'm going to help in some way.' Then he pretended like William and I weren't even there and turned to Sylvia, 'Is there a message you'd like me to give her?'

"The crowd all around the steps was understandably curious about all of this. Everyone had been watching and rooting for William, because of how despondent he was over your disappearance. Now Jack was on the steps too, and his attire and mannerisms were attracting attention. So everyone was hushed, listening, when William said, 'I want to go in with you.' He said it simply and quietly, as if there was no argument. He was a little menacing too because he still carried that shovel."

William laughed. "Me, menacing? I didn't feel menacing. I felt totally insignificant, like Jack could just brush past me and knock me to the ground with his wake."

"Well, maybe not *you* so much, but the shovel, the shovel was menacing." Terran went on with the story, "Jack said, 'I don't think you need to. *I've* got this under control,' exuding confidence the way he does. He said, '*Besides*, you're one of the farmers. There's a high chance they would just arrest you and keep you.'

"So William countered with, 'You don't understand. I need to see her. I have to.' His voice shook with anger, but he, quite impressively I might add, kept his composure and finished, 'I *have* to see her.' It was a sight to behold, *William* with his anger under control." Terran pretended to wipe tears from his eyes.

I turned to William. "You controlled yourself, with *Jack*?"

He shrugged his shoulders. "That's me, totally cool-headed."

Terran rolled his eyes and said, "Jack stared at William for a very intense few minutes. Neither one would look away, and I thought we might have a skirmish break out right there on the steps. Jack said, 'Don't be silly. You *know* I'm her future-husband, right? We have a betrothal contract. In the eyes of the government, we might as well be married, and they're *never* wrong. *I* should go in and see her.'

"William looked incredulous and cocky. I thought, 'Uh oh, Jack's done it now.'

"William pulled himself up to his full height and said, 'Jack, look around.' William's arm swept over the crowd that filled the steps and the streets, and he said, 'What about *any* of *this* makes you still believe The Congloms and the Oversee are right, about *anything*? If you think your contract with Estelle still matters after all of this, then you're the one being silly.'"

I said, "Whoa."

Terran said, "I know, Estelle, I know. It looked like the wind was knocked out of Jack's sails. He sort of lost his height. He was, I *swear,* a whole foot shorter. His confidence was gone. It was impossible for him to argue with William, because William was right."

Mj and her husband, Adam, walked up, and she said, "Oh, are you telling the story about Jack and William on the steps of the jail? I've heard it already from witnesses, but I could listen to it again and again. It's good, isn't it, Estelle?"

Before I could reply Terran said, "And this is the best part. Jack asked, 'Give me one good reason why you should see her, instead of me?'

"And then..." Terran beamed at me. "William said, 'Because I love her, and I have to see her. I can't *not* see her.'"

I looked at William, speechless. He nodded at me. Love. William loved me, and had said in front of everybody in the whole entire world. His thumb softly rubbed the back of my hand.

Terran continued, "Jack just stared, but you could see he had softened toward William's plight. 'Does she feel the same way about you?' he asked, looking out past the crowd.

"'Yes,' William said, so quietly I had to lean in to hear it.

"'True?' Jack asked Dad, who nodded.

"Then we just stood there awkwardly, while Jack kept staring into the distance. It took forever for him to figure out what he was doing. I guess he was thinking it all through, coming to terms with it.

"Jack said, 'I guess if Estelle only gets to see one person, if that's it, then it should be you.'"

Terran turned to William. "And what did you say?"

"I said, 'thank you,'" said William. "It's all I could think of to say. I was ready to run for the jail, but somehow I managed to stand there calmly while Jack organized his thoughts again for even *longer* this time. I swear I wanted to shake him and say, 'Come on man, let's do this thing.'"

Terran finished, "Jack said, 'Okay, I'm hiring you as a representative of Maranville Public Relations and Marketing.' He looked William over and said, 'I'll trade clothes with you, and you can go in my stead. You need Estelle to write a statement asking the people in the streets to stop. That's why you're there. Don't screw this up, okay? We've only got one chance to fix this, if we can.'

"They went to the side and exchanged clothes. William looked hilarious in his too short jacket and pants, and Sylvia had to spit clean his face. We got him looking acceptable enough, huh, Estelle?"

"He was the most beautiful sight *ever*," I said, as I cuddled in under William's arm.

Sylvia said, "I love that story too, but I've got to go home. Night's coming on." She hugged me good-bye. "I've got work to do starting tomorrow first thing. Can you believe two police cars drove by this afternoon? Someone has to be in New City keeping them out of your hair.

"I was thinking, Estelle, now that permission to farm has been granted, maybe you could farm and live at home, maybe part of the time. Our new house is almost ready. We could all move into it together?"

"No, Sylvia, I mean, you've seen my hammock, right? I could *never* give it up." I wasn't joking, not really. "You could come live here. We're going to build a house out of recycled dinner bar wrappers." Everyone, including Sylvia, laughed at my offer.

"I don't think sleeping in a hammock is my thing. Where would I put my decorative pillows? Anyway, I've been thinking about changing my order from the New and Improved Three Bedroom House, to a smaller and even better New Condo Unit. It has new improvements. You'd like it, or maybe you wouldn't. I forget who I'm talking to these days." She sighed loudly. "You're just like Frederick."

"I prefer my houses with a breeze blowing through them." She made a disgusted face and shuddered.

Frederick said, "I've decided to go back in the morning. It's time for me to get back to my job. I think I'll invent some new farming machinery. Something new and improved." He gave me a sly smile.

Terran asked, "Dad, are you saying you'd give up the backbreaking work of cement removal for being an inventor or something? Are you crazy?"

"Well, you are as old as the hills. I can't believe you made it this long," I teased. "But seriously, Dad, how will you give up sleeping in a hammock outside?"

I'm hoping I can have the best of both worlds. Now that there's no chance of arrest, I can work and live there *and* here. Just leave me a place to hang my hammock, and I'll come back. I promise. I've got to say that, so far, it's been an incredible journey. I'm so glad I came along with you."

The crowd dwindled as the day turned to late afternoon. We started a fire earlier than usual and gathered for dinner. Mj found new shoots, young carrots and spinach, and made a salad to complement the meal of New City's best dinner bars. "Your first harvest," she said. "I'm so glad I get to share it with you."

I took a tentative bite while everyone watched. The leaves crunched and tasted a little bit like how my farm smelled.

Noticing my hesitation Mj said, "You aren't ready for plain leaves, Estelle. Put some dressing on the next bite." The dressing was sweet and a little sour and greatly improved the taste. I took a third bite and enjoyed the different textures, the crunch and the crisp with liquid and tiny seeds. I drank a big gulp of water to wash it down, smiled around at the group, and declared it "Delicious!" I did love it. I truly did, but I ate the last bite quickly so I could move on to dessert.

and then more

That whole afternoon, I kept my conversation with the pinch-faced man a secret. I didn't want to build up excitement in case my plan hadn't worked, but my own excitement was totally built. I was possibly excessively excited, ready to burst from the apprehension and the longing and the waiting. Luckily, I was distracted by all the homecoming merriment.

I tried to remain calm. The blazing, too-bright lights weren't that important anyway. I didn't want to get worked up. If the pinch-faced man didn't come through, I would still have my farm, my family, William, but even with my pep talks, I was antsy, and the evening just meandered along.

When dusk crept in, we were all around the fire—talking, laughing, and singing, except for me. My eyes were fixed on the street lights, waiting expectantly. There were fifteen lights all around my farm and about a hundred and forty-seven lights around the Old Stadium, and they usually powered on as the sun set. I quietly listened for the telltale buzzing. I watched for the tiny gleam of burgeoning light. I watched and listened, but the lights didn't turn on, not even a glimmer. It was the three hundred and fifteenth night since our Bright Idea, and the lights in Old Town didn't brighten the fading day.

As the night darkened, truly darkened, the conversation

paused as everyone turned to the sky.

"Well, I'll be," somebody said. Not wanting to miss the show, the whole group of us, friends–old and new, jumped up and ran over to the grassy field. There we all laid on our backs facing the heavens. It took a moment for my eyes to adjust to the deep, dark, blackness. "I see a star." Then a second and then more.

"Me too," said a voice from farther away in the field. There was nothing else to say. The experience overwhelmed me.

In the West, I could see the glow of New City, brightly lit and humming with electric noise, but here in Old Town, we were in quiet, expectant, darkness. It was hushed and still until we heard voices singing through the darkness. We raised our heads to see Terran's Crew and some others coming from the direction of William's farm.

One of the Crew called, "Hey, where are you guys?"

"Here on the ground!" Terran said and jumped to his feet and waved them over. They all laughed and ran to the field where we were laying. "Grab a spot here in the dirt," said Terran graciously, and the Crew plopped down around us– stretching out, cuddling in, laughing, pointing, and making a friendly, joyous noise.

One of them asked, "So, who turned out the lights?"

I said, "I did! I turned off the lights!"

"Really? This was your doing?" asked William.

"Yep, It was me! Terran, remember when I went to talk to that jerk in the government building this morning?"

"Yeah. What did you say to him to get him to help you?"

"Well, it was clear he hated me, so I told him I was afraid of the dark and asked him to, pretty please, keep all the lights on." Everyone laughed uproariously.

"That was brilliant, Estelle, really brilliant," said William through his laughter.

"I know. I did it! I'm looking at the stars!"

Mj and Adam sang a lovely song about starlight and wishes, and it reminded me of the lullaby. "Mj? When I was in jail, I thought I heard that lullaby, the one you sang to Beatrice. Was that you?"

Mj was laying a few feet away and answered, "Yeah, I was with Beatrice here on the farm, and decided I wanted to sing you to sleep. I walked into New City to the steps of the jail and sang the song as loud as I could. You heard it?"

"Yeah, I heard it." She got up from her place on the ground and crawled over to me. She laid down right beside me and held my hand. With her other hand she held Adam's, who had tiny Beatrice asleep on his chest. I smiled at the darkened heavens and Mj sang the lullaby:

Tell me why the stars do shine;
Tell me why the ivy twine.
Tell me why the sky is blue,
And I will tell you just why I love you.

After the song, she rolled over, hugged me, and kissed me on the cheek. Tears poured down my face and pooled in my ears. To be safe and loved, at home and under the stars, was more than I could bear. I held her tight. She said, "Welcome home, brave Estelle. I'm so proud to know you." She rolled over and curled back up with Adam and Beatrice.

Terran said, "I see why you like that song so much, Stelley, it's full of questions."

I nodded, though until he mentioned it, I hadn't realized. Walden padded over, walked in a circle on my chest and curled up there, practically on my neck. He made himself comfortable and purred so loudly he drowned out any other noises. We all giggled. "Way to ruin a moment, Walden," I affectionately said.

I gently nudged Walden off my chest to go sleep somewhere else. I turned to William and gave him a half smile through my tears. He put out one of his arms for me to curl up under and said, "I know, Stelley, I know," and we all looked back up at the sky. There was one more star and then another. Fifty-three stars in all, but I stopped counting after that.

That night we laid there in the dirt, watching the heavens unfold. We pointed at our favorite twinkling points of light. We laughed, full of joy in our hearts. We whispered to each other, hushed by the majestic mysteriousness of the sky. Because it was majestic, and it was mysterious, and I could use those words to describe it. Those words were perfect. I knew that now.

After some time, William sat up on his elbow and looked down at me looking up at the sky, "The stars are reflected in your eyes, Estelle. I always knew it, but now I see." He laid back down, and I curled up around and on him. His body was earth and home. Mine was air and love.

Terran giggled. "Did you really just say that, William?"

"Hey, I'm writing poetry for your sister. Love poems, Terran, they've got the power to change the world."

An embarrassingly loud gurgling noise came from my stomach. William stifled a laugh. "Still hungry, Estelle?"

I hid my face in his chest for a second and rolled away and flung my arms out, open to the sky. "No, that's just digestion. I'm full. I'm satiated. I'm totally content," I said. "This farm is like one big dinner bar."

Mj groaned from nearby in the darkness. "Dinner bar? This farm is salad, chicken, fresh eggs, and sweet warm milk. *That's* what this farm is."

"I know you think that sounds delicious, Mj, but I'm still not sure any of that is edible," said Terran. "I'm with Estelle, this farm is a dinner bar, and my friends and family are the nacho cheese sauce. Especially you, William, especially you." William laughed so hard I could feel his whole body shaking.

"That must mean the stars are the Profoundly Pink sprinkles. They make it all even more perfectly delicious," I said, and we all grew quiet again.

Here was the culmination of all my dreams. I had hoped to see the stars for so long the hope itself had become an integral part of me. This was what I had wanted, my end result, my happiness fulfilled. Right? The stars?

I leaned up on my elbow and looked at the people around me. They were spread out in a chaotic sprawl. These were people that would never have thought to lie in the dirt and look up at the stars, not before my farm. Yet here they were, with me, in the dirt. These people were the culmination, the end result, my hopes and dreams fulfilled.

"I was in jail this morning," I said to them all, "I didn't think I would ever leave, at least not alive." My voice cracked. I was crying again, and it was difficult to get the words out, but I needed to tell them how much they meant to me. "I really believed I was dead. I wanted to be dead. Then, I was on a stage watching Terran bargain for my life." I looked over at him. "I love you, big brother."

"I love you too, Stelley."

"And then I was free and so happy and on my farm surrounded by all of you."

"What a day," said Mj.

"Yeah, what a day." I looked around at them all looking up at the sky. "Now I'm under a night sky—a deep black sky with twinkling stars. *This* is what I've dreamed about. I'm the happiest I've ever been, but come to find out, it's not about the stars. It was never really about revealing the stars. Now I know it was about finding all of you."

"Hear, hear," William, Mj, Terran, Dad, and many others chimed in.

I laid back, and now I could see even more tiny glistening points of light. "The stars are majestic, though. They really truly are."

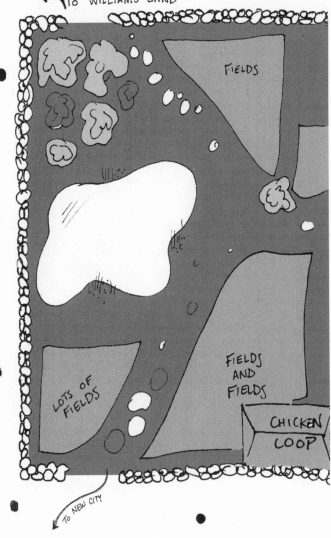

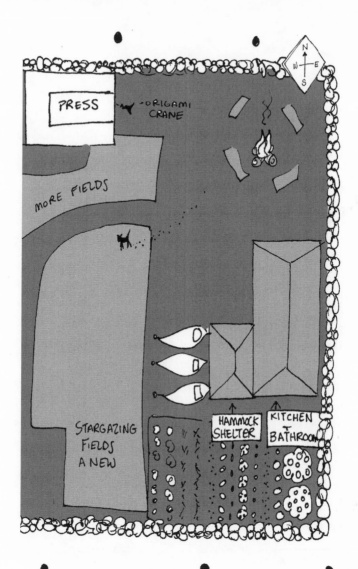

about the author

H.D.Knightley lives in Los Angeles. She's the mother of four children and is married to the surfer boy she fell in love with when she was a teenager. She is not a farmer, has never demolished a home, no longer has compost worms (they came to a bad end while she wrote this book) and most nights she can't see the stars.

She dreams a lot about walking through fields holding hands with her guy under an endlessly magical and mysterious sky. She absolutely agrees with William that sitting around a fire pit with friends is the best thing in the world and she is a true believer in the fine art of wishful thinking. She also unequivocally feels the best heroes are the ones that are completely *in over their head* at least some of the time.

acknowledgements

Many thanks to Denine Dawson for her patience and incredible attention to detail while I wrote, revised, and rewrote. A special thank you to Fiona and Isobel for reading during the early phase, your insight was wonderful. Mara Donahoe, Deborah Marcus, Maggie Baird, and Brenna Johnson for listening to me go on and on about a story I wouldn't even let them read–you get to read it now! April (Maranville) Dowdee for giving a name to one of the main characters. Heather Hawkes for reading and reviewing right when I needed it most. Joanne Ehlinger for the calming yoga. And my Dad for always believing in me, and being the kind of guy who likes to write poetry.

My family: Kevin, Isobel, Fiona, Gwynnie, and Ean for being so wonderful during the endless process, and believing I could accomplish this just because I said I could. I appreciate your patience and love more than you can know.

I especially want to thank my mother, Mary Jane, or Mj to her friends, who taught me to love stories. I miss you.

Ruenn Chiou Hwang
Heather Hawkes
Elisabeth Adwin Edwards
Paala Anderson Secor
Brandie
Dara Young
Janice Peake Reynolds
Kari Aist
Marie-Christine
The Barry Family
IggyJinglesCrafts
Mai Iqbal
Jen Okelberry
Scott & Beth Noelle
Hannah
Caroline D.
Maura Muhl
Lisa and Danica Creahan
D-Rock
Eleta
Emily Stouffer
Jackie Geist
Jenny Kenwright
Arnie & Tracy
Jessica Wigley
James Buckley
The Philbins
The Powell Family
Julie and Alyssa
Suzanne Moore
Mathias and Asher
Michele
Lydia the tattooed lady
Mel Legget
Kathryn Los
Heather Crans-Vargas
Colleen
Karen and Alex Cline
Rommi
The Sevilla Family

Amy Hayes & Chrissy Meyer
Julinda
Ashli
Rebekah, Annika & Carolyn
        Kirwan
MacKenzie Smith
The Donahoes
Bianca K.
Mica Gadhia
Maggie MacMillan Hatfield
Sandy and Dwayne Dawson
Gillian Caan
Kathleen O'Nan
Claudia
The Towler Family
Cheryl O'Donnell
Kena Alonso
Connie Sahlin
Jill D'Agnenica
Kent and Bonnie Wallace
Rachel Singer & Tom Lamb
The Stanton Family
Brenna Johnson and Family
Ben and Mishele Myers
The Baird-O'Connell Family
Jesslyn Chua
Kip Kozlowski
Melissa Scholl
Anne Adams Green
David C. Cushman (Dad)
April Dowdee

Thank you from the bottom of my heart!

7697542R00193

Made in the USA
San Bernardino, CA
15 January 2014